D1808494

USA TODAY BESTSELLING AUTHOR

DALE MAYER

Zapped in the Zinnias

Lovely Lethal Gardens 26

ZAPPED IN THE ZINNIAS: LOVELY LETHAL GARDENS, BOOK 26
Beverly Dale Mayer
Valley Publishing Ltd.

Copyright © 2024 Beverly Dale Mayer

All rights reserved. Except for use in any review, the reproduction or utilization of this work in whole or in part by any electronic, mechanical or other means, now known or hereafter invented, including xerography, photocopying and recording, or in any information storage or retrieval system, is forbidden without the written permission of the publisher.

This is a work of fiction. Names, characters, places, brands, media, and incidents are either the product of the author's imagination or are used fictitiously. Any resemblance to actual events, locales, or persons, living or dead, is entirely coincidental.

ISBN-13: 978-1-778865-13-8
Large Print Hardcover Edition

Books in This Series:

Victim in the Violets, Book 22
Whispers in the Wisteria, Book 23
X'd in the Xeriscape, Book 24
Yowls in the Yarrow, Book 25
Zapped in the Zinnias, Book 26
Merry Mistletoe Madness, Christmas Novella

Boxed Sets and Bundles
https://geni.us/Bundlepage

About This Book

Riches to rags. … When endings happen, … new beginnings start. … Chaos fills the middle!

With Mathew's murder done and dusted, and her future now wide open, Doreen turns to sorting out her financial world, particularly as her antiques are sold. And helping others is moving up her list of things she wants to do. Especially after finding a young woman who wants to get out of the streetwalker world and to move back home.

Of course a decision like that doesn't come without strings, and Doreen and her animals are soon embroiled in pimps and madams. A world she knows nothing about but is quickly learning. Mix that up with Nan getting kidnapped, only to bail her kidnapper out of jail, and Doreen's world is chaos as usual.

Corporal Mack Moreau has a plan, but implementing that plan requires a special moment—the right moment. And trying to figure out when and what that moment looks like is a challenge. Especially as it involves Doreen …

Sign up to be notified of all Dale's releases here!
https://geni.us/DaleNews

Chapter 1

First Part of November …

SEVERAL DAYS LATER, after Doreen had had a chance to really relax, the police had gotten statements from Reggie, and, of course, he would spend the rest of his life behind bars for the murders. She'd gotten copies of the will from the lawyer and a ton of paperwork to deal with, and it would just be the tip of the iceberg.

Thankfully Nick was handling a lot of it for her, and she promised that, this time, she would pay him. He just laughed and noted that, in light of her change in circumstances, he would happily accept payment. Then he looked at her and stated, "Now just tell me that you'll put poor Mack out of his misery."

She looked at him. "You may find this surprising, but people say that to me all the time. Call me slow, but I've never really understood it."

He chuckled. "Something else you need to figure out."

"What now?" she asked, frustrated.

"Did you ever figure out why you don't like the new detective?"

She glared at him. "Not you too?" she snapped.

But Nick just laughed, and, since he was walking out the door anyway, he just kept on walking.

Mack drove over a little bit later and came inside, greeting all the animals and hugging Doreen. He asked, "How's it going?"

"Crazy," she muttered.

His eyebrows shot up. "Crazy in what way?"

"Just all the paperwork the lawyer sent. Thankfully your brother will handle it for me, and this time I'll pay him," she declared, with a grin.

"I'm sure he would like that," Mack said gently.

"I would have figured out how to pay him anyway. I just didn't quite know how to make that happen since I didn't really have any money," she explained.

"Cookies?"

She burst out laughing. "That would re-quire a lot of cookies."

He chuckled at that. "Yeah, but who doesn't like cookies?" Then he looked at her and asked, "Did you ever figure out why you don't like the detective?"

She glared at him. "Not you too. That seems to be a popular topic of conversation today, and even earlier."

"Yeah, it is in some ways."

"I mentioned it to Nan, and she just gave me this mysterious look and said that I would figure it out eventually. I probably will," she admitted. "How about you? Any new cases to tell me about?"

"I don't need any new cases," he declared, glaring at her. "I'm done with cases. So should you be."

"What? Are you retiring and didn't tell me? Shame on you. Besides, one doesn't have to be working to get involved in cases. Plus, just because I have money coming in now, there is still work to be done on the cold case files. Ooh, and Solomon's files when I don't have anything else to work on."

He chuckled, shaking his head. He looked at her and opened his mouth to speak, then frowned and shut up.

"What? Come on. Tell me."

"It's just that you're a very wealthy woman now, and you could do a whole lot better than some country bumpkin cop like me."

She frowned at him, walked over, and pushed him back, so he was sitting on a chair, then plunked herself down in his lap. "Yeah, and who was there for me when I didn't know how to cook or even how to buy the most basic foods and was living off of peanut butter and jelly sandwiches?" Poking him in the chest, she continued. "Who was there when I didn't know how to work an ATM or turn on the oven?" She sighed happily, as she looked up at the strong features of his face and the lovely expression there.

"It doesn't have anything to do with money. True wealth is all about what's inside," she stated, tapping his heart. "So don't you worry about that. I'm perfectly happy with a *country bumpkin* cop, exactly like you." She leaned over, kissed him gently, and said, "But that still doesn't mean we're not getting cases."

"I, for one, would very much like for this town to calm down and to not have anything else happen for quite a while."

"*Quite a while* is fine with me," she replied. "We can go like this for days and days. Hey, even weeks or a few months would be great."

Chapter 2

Days Later …

DAYS LATER DOREEN and Mack were sitting outside, having a barbecue, when his phone rang. He checked the Caller ID, then frowned at her.

"A case?" she asked him.

He got up, glaring at her, and stepped a few feet away, so he could take the call in private. Finally the call ended, and he turned around and shared, "Apparently we've had enough of a break."

"What's up?" she asked excitedly.

"A body was just found in a flower garden."

"Where?" she asked.

"Behind the juice processing plant."

She frowned, as she thought about that. "A garden's back there?"

"Yeah, a community garden," he added.

"They're quite popular in town, aren't

they?"

"They are, although maybe not so much after this."

"Why? Is it not a natural death?"

He shook his head. "No, he was tazed." When she gave him a blank look, he explained, "You know, *zapped with a police zapper thingy*." He laughed when understanding dawned on her face. "Oh my God, you're making me crazy. Now I'm even coming up with your ridiculous descriptions."

"It worked though, and now I understand completely. So, was it the fault of a cop?"

"No, I don't think so," he replied, frowning. "At least I hope not. Seems the guy was found in a special place that contains the flower garden, among those spiky things."

"Spiky things?" she asked, frowning at him. "You mean, *cactus*?"

"No, the flowers, the long spiky …"

"Multipetal zinnias?" she asked.

He raised both hands, stupefied. "Yeah, those. How did you figure that out from what I said?"

She shrugged. "I didn't. I just considered what flowers had spiky blossoms. It's late for them but a greenhouse in the community garden would extend their growing season for a few months."

Mack shrugged. "Don't know for sure until I see the crime scene myself."

Then Doreen's smile on her face grew and grew.

"What?" He stared at her in confusion.

"It's the *Zapped in the Zinnias* case," she declared, with a chuckle.

"Oh no, no," he argued, "we're not going with that name."

"Yes, we are, and you know you like it. You can't stop me."

He glared at her. "If you go with that name, I want something from you first."

"What's that?" she asked.

"I want to know why you don't like the new detective."

She flushed, looked at him, and asked, "Are you leaving right now for the crime scene?"

"Yeah, I am."

"Okay, in that case, I'll tell you."

He slowly raised his eyebrows, clearly surprised. "Okay, so tell me then." He slipped his phone in his pocket, grabbed his jacket, and reached for his keys.

"I don't like her because she's too close to you."

He stared at her for a long moment. "Seriously?"

"Yes," she declared. "I don't want anything to come between us. Particularly a determined, good-looking, sexy cop who is around you all day," she snapped, glaring at him. When his lips twitched, her glare deepened. But when he burst into laughter, she stomped her foot and crossed her arms, still glaring at him, "It's not funny, Mack."

He stopped laughing and smiled. "No, it's not funny," he agreed. "It's absolutely delightful." He picked her up, gave her a huge hug, then a big kiss on the lips, and stated, "You just made my day." After giving her a second big smacking kiss on the lips, he headed for the front door, whistling. Then he called out, "*Zapped in the Zinnias* it is."

"That was easier than I expected," she muttered, following him to the door.

"Hey, I'm always happy to compromise, particularly with somebody like you."

"What do you mean, somebody like me?" she asked.

He flashed her a grin and, stepping out the door, said, "Somebody I love."

And, with that, he was gone, leaving her standing in the doorway, staring after him, her mouth gaping.

Chapter 3

Monday Morning ...

DOREEN WOKE MONDAY morning with a smile on her face, as she remembered Mack's parting comment. It had been hard to go to sleep last night. She'd been completely exhausted and still couldn't believe all that had happened. It was one thing to wonder where their relationship was headed but entirely different to hear his declaration. She had absolutely no doubt in her mind that he meant it. Did she want him to say it again and again? Absolutely.

She pondered what he'd revealed as she dressed and then headed downstairs to put on coffee. She stepped outside to her deck, while the coffee brewed. She'd never heard those words from Mathew. She wasn't sure she'd ever heard them even at the wooing stage. She still pondered the young woman she'd been who had married the man who had made her very wary of trusting her own judgment. After fourteen years of marriage, he wanted her out of the house, since he was seeing Robin at the time. Over these last seven months, living apart from Mathew, she'd grown up a lot. More than grown up, she'd changed as a person. She had seen so much more in life now that she was less concerned about making a poor decision.

Besides, Mack was a very different person from Mathew, as different as two men could possibly be. And, if nothing else, she owed him a *thank you*—Mathew, that is—for being such a greedy, spiteful, conniving, mean person from whom she'd finally managed to separate herself. She was pretty sure it had nothing to do with what he'd wanted out of the relationship, but it had gotten her exactly what she had needed, a chance to regain that part of herself that had become so lost. As a result of all that, she'd found Mack, and that meant her future looked very bright indeed.

Doreen plopped down onto a patio chair, waiting for her coffeepot to finish brewing. Of course she and Mack had a lot of talking to do, plenty of things to sort out, but right now it was all green lights for her. She burst out laughing yet again, knowing that, to anybody else out there, she probably sounded like a crazy lady.

Sure enough, Richard poked his head over the top of the fence and glared at her. "What is your problem this morning?" he asked. "I don't know what you're reading, but all that giggling is darn irritating."

She gave him a beaming smile because not even his bad temper could ruin her day. "Good morning, Richard," she replied in a high singsong tone. His frown deepened. "That's okay. I know you're having a tough day."

"How would you know that?" he scoffed.

"You're grumpy as usual, so I presume it's a tough day. Otherwise how can you be grumpy on a day like today?"

He stared at her. "And what's so special about today? No murder on your hands?"

She shuddered. "I hope not, although I will try to coerce Mack into sharing about one of his cases."

Richard rolled his eyes at that. "Why he wants anything at all to do with you, when you drive him so crazy, I'll never understand."

"Driving him crazy apparently doesn't

bother him," she noted, with a chuckle. "As a matter of fact, I think he rather likes it."

Richard gave her a dry look and shook his head. *"Ya think?"* And, with that, he popped back down on his side of the fence.

She had to admit that she was probably the only one in town who hadn't seen the depths of how Mack felt about her. She'd been constantly pushing him off, blocking anything and everything that could be deemed as progress in terms of their relationship, but why? She wasn't even sure at this point in time. Well, she did understand—waiting for her divorce to be final—but all those obstacles were gone.

Obviously some things needed to be sorted out, but the big one was done. Mathew was gone, she was free, and Mack loved her. She held that secret close to her heart, and, yes, if she finally admitted it to herself, she loved him too. That didn't mean she would give in too easily, mind you. After all, that might change their relationship in some way, and she didn't want that. She was really enjoying what they had right now and valued their friendship as it was.

Of course he would want more, and that was normal, that was life, and she was more than happy to take things a step further, but she didn't want to be pushed. She wanted it to happen naturally. Although what *naturally* meant or looked like, she wasn't quite sure. She frowned as she contemplated that idea.

When her phone rang, she looked down to see it was Nan. She smiled and answered in a bright, happy tone. "Good morning!"

Silence came on the other end. "I don't know what you're drinking," Nan groaned, "but I want some."

Doreen burst out laughing at that. "I'm having coffee, and, if you want some, come on up."

"Or you could come down perhaps. I'm feeling kind of tired today."

Immediately the smile fell from Doreen's face. "Are you all right?"

"Of course I'm all right," she scoffed. "Just a little on the tired side. I didn't have a good night."

"Oh, Nan, I am sorry."

"It's okay. We have days like that. But you, on the other hand, are obviously having a good day."

"I am. A good couple of days. The rest, the time off, has been good for me."

"It's hardly been a rest. You've had what,

three or four days with no chaos now? Still, you have Mathew's estate and everything to get through."

"Yes, but an awful lot of that will be fairly simple, since Nick will deal with the majority of that. Plus some of it was in my name already, and basically everything of Mathew's comes to me. All I really need to do is to give things some time to process, then get ready to start selling stuff."

"Are you taking care of Mathew's remains?"

She winced at that. "Mathew's lawyer told me that he would take care of that. Mathew is being cremated and buried beside his brother, down on the coast."

"Good," Nan stated in a harsh tone. "I'm glad you won't have to deal with that too."

"I did offer to take care of it, but his attorney declared that Mathew had made his wishes pretty clear, and his attorney could do it."

"Good to know, and much more consideration from you than Mathew deserved, after the way he treated you."

"I don't know about all that," Doreen murmured, feeling some of her good humor fall away at the discussion. "All I really know is that I'm free and clear of all that old business, and I have a whole new life ahead of me."

"I'm glad to hear that you've finally got that straightened away in your head," she murmured.

"Nan, you really don't sound as if you're having a good day."

"No, I'm not," she agreed. "I'm just calling to check in and to ensure all is well in your world. I think I'll head back to bed for a bit." And, with that, she ended the call.

Doreen sat here for a long moment, worried because Nan had seemed a bit off. She definitely sounded tired, exhausted really. As Doreen recalled how done in she herself had been for a few days after overdoing it, it made sense in a way.

She got up and had breakfast, wondering how she could squeeze more information out of Mack on his case. When her phone rang again, she thought it was Nan because the call came from Rosemoor, but it wasn't. When she answered, Richie was on the other end. "Is Nan okay?" Doreen asked.

"I think so," he replied cautiously. "She's just … She seems really tired today."

"I know. I spoke to her earlier, and she didn't sound good. I'm not happy about it at all."

"Oh, trust me that she's not very happy about it either," he noted in a joking tone.

Doreen winced. "You're right. She told me how she'd had a bad night and was heading back to bed. Is that why you're calling?"

"I do know that she's pretty worried about you."

"Why is she worried about me now?" Doreen asked in astonishment. "We've just come through that whole mess with Mathew's murder and all that trouble. Things are really coming together now."

"That you have, but I think she's more concerned about the fact that, if and when she goes—no *if* about it, is there?" he corrected himself. "But, when she goes, she wants to ensure that you're taken care of."

"She's done everything anybody could possibly imagine to ensure I'm in a good, safe place, even giving me her home, for heaven's sake. And one stuffed with valuables. And now with the auction money coming soon, finances won't be a problem at all."

"Yet that's not enough for Nan."

Doreen sighed. "This is about Mack, isn't it?"

He chuckled. "I'm just letting you know that she's worried things won't get settled before she passes."

Doreen stared down at the phone. "Please tell me that I have no reason to be worried about that right now."

"No particular reason to be worried," he replied, "but I can't tell you that she'll see another day, any more than I can tell you that about myself. We tend to get fatalistic around this place. We get up one morning and find that somebody didn't make it through the night. You should know that better than anyone, with all these murder cases you work on." He took a deep breath and added, "We've come to the point where we appreciate life on a day-to-day basis, and, while I can tell you that she's having a bad day, it doesn't mean that she won't make it through the night."

Doreen struggled with the shock of something like that. "I'm so not ready to lose her."

"I don't think she's ready to let you go either," he added. "I'm just telling you that she's worrying even more than normal because you're not settled with Mack."

"Maybe I won't ever get settled with Mack," Doreen declared, with a bit of spirit. "So what? Lots of single people live a happy and safe life too."

He hesitated and then murmured, "That is your right, but honestly we would all very much like to get answers about your relationship with Mack."

She stared at the phone. "Please don't tell me that she's got bets on that too."

He chuckled. "She's your nan. What do you think?"

Doreen groaned. "I was really hoping she would stop doing that."

"Maybe when she goes," Richie suggested with spirit. "In the meantime she keeps all of us alive and laughing, and that's worth a lot."

"Oh, I get it," she muttered. "It's just not been the easiest when it comes down on me all the time. Betting on my relationship is crazy."

He laughed. "I'm just saying that maybe you could give your grandmother a break and let her know how you're doing with Mack."

"Right. … Will do."

She sat here a long time after the phone call ended. She understood that Nan and Richie were worried, but what Doreen didn't know was how worried she was supposed to be. Not liking anything about the scenario, yet unsure whether this was just about betting or whether her grandmother really was sick, Doreen decided to take the animals for a walk down to Rosemoor. She had that on her mind now, and, as soon as she was reassured that her grandmother would be back on her feet again, it would be better for Doreen's peace of mind.

She and the animals went down every day or every second day for tea anyway, so this time Doreen would just show up and see how Nan was doing. The last thing she wanted was to lose her grandmother now that Doreen had finally found herself.

She hadn't gotten too far down that mental pathway when her grandmother called back again. "Wow," Doreen replied, hearing her grandmother's voice. "You didn't even get enough time between phone calls to sleep."

"Actually I did," she shared, sounding much more refreshed. "I'm powered up."

"If you can power up at your age, you're still doing pretty well."

"Oh, I'm doing just fine," Nan stated. "Anybody who tells you differently is lying."

Doreen winced at that. "Nobody's telling me any differently, but you scared me a little this morning when you sounded so exhausted."

"I probably shouldn't have called just then, but you were on my mind, so I did," she muttered. "I should have just waited until I woke up the second time."

Doreen privately agreed with that, but it was hardly for her to say, and she was always up for a visit, if Nan wanted to call. "I'm just happy you're doing okay," she replied warmly.

"Will you come down for tea?"

"I was thinking I would," Doreen said. "I was wondering how you were doing by now."

"I'm back up and fine as can be," Nan declared. "I'm putting on the teakettle, so come on down." And, with that, Nan disconnected the call, leaving Doreen with no doubt that Nan was feeling better—at least as normal as could be expected from her right now.

Doreen had just been through quite a few weeks of nonstop excitement, with no small amount of danger. So, if she were honest about it, the stress of all that and Nan's health had worried Doreen. If there was ever a reason to quit doing what she was doing with the cold cases, it would be because of Nan.

Chapter 4

THE ANIMALS WERE more than happy to head down to Nan's but, even more so, to play in the river, to go for a walk, and just to be outside. It had started out as such a lovely day but had dimmed somewhat after talking to Nan initially this morning. Still, Doreen was feeling pretty darn fine on the inside. When she got to Nan's, her grandmother sat on the patio, waiting, completely composed, as if she'd never even made that first phone call today.

Nan looked up at Doreen, smiled, and noted, "Don't you look lovely, dear."

Chuckling, Doreen smirked. "I'm pretty sure I look the same as I always do."

"And that is just lovely," Nan repeated.

Doreen smiled at her. "Back to the cheering squad again?" she teased.

"Not *back to*, my dear," she corrected, with

a smile. "I never left."

"Oh, that's true enough." Doreen sat down in the patio chair across from her grandmother and asked, "Are you happy now? You're doing okay?"

"Yes, of course," she replied, with the brightest smile. "I was really just tired this morning, child."

"I'm sorry you had a bad night."

"Me too. I kept worrying about you," she pointed out in that scolding tone Doreen heard only rarely.

"Ouch. You do know I'll be fine, right?"

Nan stared at her. "I do know that, and I would never want to insult you by making you feel that you couldn't do it on your own. It's just … It's hard when you're my age, and you want to tell everybody exactly what to do, when to do it, and how to do it, knowing they would all be so much better off if only they would listen." She gave her granddaughter a big smirk. "But I also know that you have to learn to do things in your own way and in your own time as well."

Doreen stared at her, not sure where all this was coming from. "Have I messed things up that much?" Doreen asked in astonishment.

"No, not at all," Nan stated. "It's just that sometimes I feel my age, and I can sense the time coming when I won't be here. So honestly it would make me feel a lot better to know that you and Mack had your relationship somewhat together at least."

"We do have it together, Nan." When her grandmother eyed her suspiciously, Doreen had to grin. "We do," she stated, with a bright smile. "Now that Mathew is gone to whichever place he's gone to," she said, with an eye roll, "I'm sure things will move along a little bit faster."

Nan perked up immediately. "Really?" She was almost ecstatic.

Doreen nodded. "Really."

An odd look came over Nan's face. She quickly jotted down something on the small pad of paper before her. Then she nodded and stood. "Let me go grab some snacks for breakfast." She briskly took off for her kitchen.

Doreen wasn't really sure what that was all about and really was not bothered enough to question her grandmother on it. So she waited until Nan returned, a little basket of treats dangling on her arm. "Wow," Doreen muttered. "The center must wonder where everything disappears to."

"Nope, they know exactly where it is. Since Richie fessed up about what he was doing, lots of the other inmates, *oops*," she said, with a chuckle, "*residents*, … a lot of the other residents also admitted to taking treats back to their rooms to save for later."

"Oh, I guess that's probably okay then," Doreen noted, "as long as they're not wasting the food."

"I don't think anybody's wasting anything, and, yes, we get lots to eat here."

Doreen nodded, but it had always been a worrisome side effect of being around her grandmother, wanting to ensure that Rosemoor was looking after Nan as they should. "You know I'll just worry too," Doreen admitted, with a shrug.

"As I worry about you," Nan agreed, with a nod. The two grinned at each other. "So, what makes you say that you and Mack are okay now?"

"A large part of the problem was me and Mathew," she stated with finality. "Our divorce had been pending this whole time, bringing all the other nonsense along with it. Now Mathew is gone."

"Good riddance," Nan declared. When

Doreen glared at her, Nan glared right back. "You can't expect me to even pretend to be upset that he's gone. That man mistreated you and made your life miserable."

"He did, and—if he hadn't made my life miserable and hadn't been the person he was and hadn't had that affair with Robin and hadn't kicked me out of the house—I wouldn't be where I am right now," Doreen pointed out. "And, Nan, where I am right now is somewhere I really want to be, and I never want to go back to being that person I was before."

Nan sat back and beamed at her. "Oh my, I do like the sound of that."

Doreen nodded and took a peek at the basket of treats and smiled. "I don't know how you always manage it, but these look lovely."

Nan just shrugged. They sat down and enjoyed their brunch, and nothing seemed to dim Nan's bright mood. Finally, unable to stand it any longer, Nan pinned down Doreen with a very direct gaze. "You do seem to be in an awfully good mood."

Doreen smiled and nodded.

"Any chance that you and Mack, like, ... you know?" And Nan waggled her eyebrows.

Doreen flushed bright red, then shook her head. "Nan! Not that it's any of your business but, no, not yet. However, we did get a little closer in terms of where we're going."

"I'm glad to hear that," Nan said, with relief. "It's taken you a long time."

"It's taken however long it's taken because I wanted to get someplace safe, with my own judgment intact," she explained. "I didn't want to feel pushed or prodded or forced to go in this direction. I care a lot about Mack, and I certainly don't want to lose him. I'm also very appreciative of the fact that he gave me time."

"He did give you time," Nan noted.

"He understands me, so Mack is a really good guy."

"In which case, you should be grabbing him up and locking him down tight."

"Grabbing him up is one thing," Doreen pointed out, "but locking him down tight won't help."

"Why not?" Nan asked.

"Because trying to tightly lock down some-one doesn't work, and, more to the point, you should release them to do whatever they need to do. If they still come back to you, then that is real."

Nan stared at her, as she chewed away. "That's all fine and dandy, but you could also lose him doing that."

"But then he wasn't mine to begin with," she murmured.

Nan sighed. "Fine, do it your way, but don't lose him."

She chuckled. "Not planning on it."

"So what are you doing to stop going stir-crazy, now that you don't have a case?" When Doreen didn't say anything, Nan's eyes widened, as she brightened up. "Do we have a case?"

As the pronoun changed from *you* to *we*, Doreen smiled. "No, *we* don't have a case. *I* don't have a case either, but Mack does."

"Of course Mack has a case. He always does." The excitement in Nan's tone was too much.

"It is the job he does, after all," Doreen murmured.

"How will you deal with that when you're in a relationship with him?" Nan asked.

"I already *am* in a relationship with him," Doreen stated in a wry tone. "Regardless of what everybody else thinks, we're obviously in a relationship, and I deal with his job just fine."

"Mack couldn't have picked a better person because you *do* understand the nature of his work," Nan noted thoughtfully. "And you're always there for him because, if nothing else, you want information on the cases."

Doreen frowned at her. "That's true, but my curiosity is never over and above making sure he's okay."

"He can take care of himself," Nan stated. "And I'm so glad that he is watching over you too."

"Yes, that's how it started out," Doreen explained. "Mack was just there. He's the one who got me through those first stages of trying to be independent, when I was failing so badly."

"Oh, my dear, you never failed at anything," Nan cried out softly. "You may have taken a couple tries to figure something out, but you didn't fail, and don't you ever think you did."

Nan was always such a cheerleader, but it seemed as if she meant that last comment for real. "I appreciate that vote of confidence," Doreen said, looking at the sun, "because too many times I felt as if I was failing miserably."

"You didn't fail yourself, and you certainly didn't fail this community. You've been there to help out time and time again," Nan reminded Doreen. "And I'm really glad that some people have taken the opportunity to show you that they care."

"Building my deck is certainly one of them," she murmured.

"I'm really happy I gave you that house." Nan smiled broadly. "You've done far more with it than I could ever have imagined."

At that, Doreen stared at her in shock. "You've done so much for me already, and I don't know that I've done much with the house except clean it out."

Nan burst out laughing. "Cleaning it out is good—great really. I filled it, and you had to clean it, and that seemed to be a fair deal to me."

At that, Doreen burst into laughter. "It absolutely was, particularly since I got the benefit of all your hard work."

"If you don't get the benefit, who else should?" Nan asked, with a smile. "Besides, it's good for people to learn to give a little."

"Oh, I hear you there."

"Have you been down to check on Mr. Woo?"

"No, I figured he probably needed more time to heal," she shared.

Nan studied her and nodded. "You're still struggling a bit yourself, aren't you?"

"Not so much struggling, but it was an odd case. And, with Mathew gone now, everything feels different."

"Don't make it too different," Nan warned. "Think of his passing as just another case, then move on with your life, as you are meant to."

"Working on it," Doreen replied, giving her grandmother a wry smile. "Not to worry. I'm not planning on ditching Mack in the meantime."

"Thank heavens for that," Nan muttered. "I was pretty sure I hadn't seen that level of stupidity in you."

At that, Doreen gasped in astonishment.

Nan gave her an impudent grin. "Hey, I'm allowed to say things like that. I'm far too old for beating around the bush."

"I don't know about *old*," Doreen clarified, with a smile at her grandmother. "Yet you're definitely too cagey to want to be bothered."

"Now that is very true," Nan agreed, with a nod. "Life's too short. I keep telling you that."

"I'm working on it," Doreen shared, "and, with these cold cases, I'm certainly finding out how cruel the world can be and how quickly life can change."

"In a heartbeat," Nan agreed gently, "an absolute heartbeat."

Once again, Doreen looked over at her grandmother, her heart clenching with pain at the thought of losing her.

Nan patted her hand gently and stated, "Don't you worry. I'm not going anywhere for a while."

"I hope not," she replied. "That would be devastating."

"Tell me the details about this case. I don't care whose case it is," she added, with a wave of her hand.

"I don't know much," Doreen began. "Something about a body found in a flower garden."

Nan perked up. "A flower garden? Now that case should be one of yours."

"I know, right?" Doreen chuckled, then told her about naming it.

"Oh, I do like that," she murmured, "and you do give as good as you get, when it comes to Mack."

"It's part and parcel of our relationship," Doreen declared, with a smile. When she noticed Nan staring off in the distance, Doreen asked, "What's the matter, Nan?"

"I thought I heard something about that body being found. One of the delivery guys today mentioned it."

"You can hear the delivery guys from your patio?" Doreen pointed to the parking lot behind her.

"I'm right here in the mornings, and shipments are always coming and going. So they talk among themselves, calling out between their trucks. It's not as if they can even see me over here. Sometimes, when the air is clear and everything else is quiet, I can hear them quite clearly."

"What did you hear?"

"Something about it being a sad day, as some poor guy was dead, and these drivers seemed to think he was a local."

"Oh, then it might have been him, but I don't know that it was," Doreen noted. "Mack hasn't even told me the name of the dead man."

"The delivery guys never mentioned a name either, but one did mention something about murder."

"And that didn't get you to stand up and to start peppering them with questions?" she joked.

Nan grinned at her. "No, I was waiting for

my teakettle, so I wasn't really registering what they said."

"Do you know which driver it was?"

"Doesn't matter who it was, does it? Just because someone was murdered doesn't mean these guys did it."

"No, of course not," Doreen agreed, as she thought about it. "And no matter who was murdered, they would surely have had family somewhere."

"We can only hope so," Nan replied. On that note she added, "I didn't see the delivery guys, and they are not always the same ones who come here." Nan sighed. "I should have asked them right then, but I missed my chance." She frowned at Doreen. "Next time I hear something juicy, I'll immediately ask questions and let you know."

"Good enough." With that, Doreen rose, gave her grandmother a gentle hug and a kiss, and said, "If I don't see you later this afternoon for tea, I'll see you tomorrow."

Then she gathered up the animals and headed home.

Chapter 5

Late Monday Afternoon ...

LATER THAT AFTERNOON Doreen heard Mack's truck pull into her driveway. Mugs went crazy, barking and racing to the front door.

"I know, Mugs. You haven't seen him all day," Doreen teased, chuckling. She walked out to the front porch and watched Mack hop out and stride toward her. She opened the screen door and let Mugs out to greet him. Mack bent down and spent a few minutes loving on the dog that was so overjoyed to see him.

"You know," Mack shared, "this is not a hard welcome to get used to."

"No, it's not," she agreed, with a smile, as she studied her dog, who wasn't exactly happy to let go of the greeting just yet, even now as Mack headed toward her. "According to

Mugs, you still haven't given him a sufficient hello yet," Doreen shared.

Mack dropped down to his knee, immediately scooped up the basset hound, and hugged him. At that, Mugs went into an ecstatic mood, then wiggled and wiggled and wiggled, until Mack had to put him down again. "He's quite an armful, isn't he?" he asked, chuckling.

"He is, indeed," she murmured.

Mack came up the stairs, two a time, then picked her up, swung her around, and gave her a passionate kiss.

When he put her down again, she looked up at him. "What was that for?"

He shrugged. "I just felt like it." Then he brushed past her and headed into the kitchen. She smiled, realizing that what she had feared would be an awkward first meeting—after telling her that he loved her last night—was totally normal and so *Mack* that she'd been foolish to worry about it.

Then she had to wonder whether she'd really even been worried about this moment, or was it more a case of anticipation? She was a fool that way. As she headed inside behind him, she found him in the kitchen, putting on coffee. "I gather that means you're staying for a moment or two," she teased, a note of laughter in her tone.

He grinned. "Yeah, at least I'm hoping to."

"So, will you tell me about our *Zapped in the Zinnias* case?"

"Nope, I'm not doing any such thing," he declared and started to whistle happily. She wasn't sure why he was in such a great mood, but, considering that she'd woken up that way herself, she had a pretty good idea.

As soon as he had the coffee on, he opened up the back door and stepped outside, then reached his arms out wide and stretched. "Ah, I do love this view."

"It's all about having the river right there, I think," she added.

He nodded. "You're right. The river, the backyard, nothing on the opposite side. It's really freeing somehow."

"Honestly, if I had moved to Kelowna and hadn't had this place to land, I wouldn't have had a clue what part of town to move into. I think it takes a little time to get to know a place and to figure out something like that."

"Exactly," he agreed. "Did you talk to my brother at all today?"

She frowned at him. "No. Was I supposed to?"

He shrugged. "He told me that he would call you, but maybe he didn't get that far. He's been pretty slammed with work."

"Yeah, and I added to it."

He looked at her. "You say that as if it's a bad thing."

"I did add to his workload, when I asked him for help in trying to figure out where I stood."

"That's pretty normal and would have entailed a phone call."

"Yeah, at three hundred an hour. I'm sure just a phone call still would have cost me," she joked. "I will pay him, now that I can."

Mack grinned. "He does make good money."

"Is he still planning on moving to Kelowna?"

"I think so, although I think you scared him a little bit." She stopped and stared at him. He shrugged. "Enough cases have turned up here that he has to wonder just how safe it is and how much work you'll pile on him." When she gasped in faux outrage, Mack burst out laughing. "I'm just teasing. He does want to move up here, particularly knowing that Mom's remaining years are running away on us. So, he was hoping to get here sooner rather than later."

"I would be so happy for him if he does," she replied. "Your brother is a nice man." Mack looked over at her expectantly, and she added, "Of course you are a nice man too."

He rolled his eyes at that. "I'm not jealous."

"That's good because you have nothing to be jealous of."

"He did ask me how things were going between us though."

"That was nosy of him," she said, staring at him.

Mack snorted. "Come on. Haven't you already been asked that half-a-dozen times already?"

She winced. "Yes, I sure have. Once everybody realized that the case and all the rest of the trouble surrounding Mathew's death was resolved, they all seem to expect me to do something."

"Yep," he agreed, with that bright grin of his. "I'm sure they do."

She sighed. "I'm not exactly sure what I'm supposed to do though."

"Ah, in that case, I'll leave you to figure it out." Then he headed to the river.

"What does that mean?" she asked, rushing to catch up.

He shrugged. "Whenever you're ready, we can talk about it," he replied and kept on walking.

"But what will we talk about?"

"*Us*," he said, looking back at her, "but only if and when you're ready."

She snorted. "Somehow I don't think you'll let me wait all that long."

"I've been pretty patient so far," Mack noted, looking at her with an inviting gaze.

"Yeah, you've been waiting for me to deal with Mathew and the divorce, but now that's off the table, done and dusted."

He nodded. "It is, isn't it?" he stated, a note of intense satisfaction in his tone.

She burst out laughing. "Poor Mathew. I don't think he realized just how much you were waiting for him to get out of my hair."

"Not just me," Mack pointed out, looking over at her. "Weren't you waiting too?"

"Yes, I was. Then I went through these episodes of feeling guilty because I was waiting for him to get out of my life." When Mack rolled his eyes, she glared. "I get it. I'm a fool that way."

"No," he disagreed, touching her gently on the chin. "No more talking down to yourself that way. You're not a fool. You needed to learn a few things, and you did. As a matter of fact, you've come a really long way."

"But not quite far enough, … I don't think," she shared.

At that, he froze. "What does that mean?"

She looked at him. "Nothing about us, just that I'm not quite there yet."

He continued to frown at her, as if looking for clarification.

"I've changed, but I'm still changing. I … haven't completed the change yet."

"It's not as if we ever reach the end of it, right? We are always changing, hopefully improving." He spoke carefully. "I don't think we get to a finish point or something." He paused, as if not sure how to proceed, not without it coming out differently than he intended. "It's an ongoing process, where you keep learning for the rest of your life."

She stared at him. "Actually, I like that idea," she murmured. "There's always so much pressure to be a certain way or to do the best you can. However, when you need more time, I hear in my head, *Too bad, you were supposed to have gotten there already*."

"No, not at all," he corrected her gently. "That's not how this works."

"Are you sure?" she asked, with a smile. "Sometimes it certainly seems that way."

"It's not. Not where we're concerned," he declared. "You take as much time as you need, but there are a few ground rules."

"Oh, I don't know about ground rules, and I really don't know about the *but*." She glared at him.

His lips twitched. "It's hardly much of a *but*, as *buts* go, and it's really quite simple. We don't bring Mathew back into our relationship, and you get to go forward with a fresh perspective, without all that dragging you down."

She pondered that as he wandered down to the water, studying the different water levels, while she stood here studying him. "Nan said you've been more than patient."

He looked at Doreen and nodded. "I think we already established that."

She laughed. "Wow, no ego with you."

"Lots of ego," he admitted, "but the fact is, I have been patient. That doesn't mean I can't be patient a little longer, though I wouldn't want it to be too much longer."

"Just what do you see as the end result of this patience of yours?" she asked curiously.

He turned to face her. "Now that's a very good question. What would you want it to be?"

She frowned at him. "That's deflecting a question with a question."

He burst out laughing. "It absolutely is," he noted. "But, if you're not even ready to talk about a future together, that conversation would be premature."

At that, she wasn't sure what to say. "Aren't we rushing things?" she asked cautiously.

"Not me," he murmured. "I've been ready for a long time."

"Yet I don't want to cheat you by not being whole before I go down that pathway."

He stared at her. "Did anybody ever say you had to be perfect first before going down that pathway? Or that you had to go down that pathway alone?"

Once again, he had surprised her. She stared at him and slowly shook her head. "I guess not. ... That perfection angle was drilled into me by Mathew, so I'm still working on just growing each day. However, it never occurred to me that I wouldn't be alone because it seems as if I always have been."

"That sounds like self-help book stuff, which has a place, it really does," he explained. "But isn't it time for you to just forget about all those things you're *supposed* to do, or what *you think* you're *supposed* to do, and instead just be happy to be the you who you are now and then figure out what else you want?"

She smiled. "Okay, I think I can work on that."

"Good, and, when you figure out what that is, you can let me know. Now let's grab some coffee."

She still wasn't even sure what to do with that, but he was letting her off the hook for the moment, and, for that, she was grateful. "Don't you ever worry that I won't get there?"

"No," he replied, shaking his head. "I don't worry about that at all."

Nonplussed, she stared at him. "How can you be so sure?"

"Because maybe you're already there." He tapped her gently on the nose. "And maybe you just need a little more time."

"Maybe, but I'm not sure for what."

"Then you *do* need a bit more time," he replied, with a chuckle. "And I can give you a little more time."

"What if I need more than a little?" she asked, immediately worried.

"Then I'll give you a little more after that."

She sighed, then looked up at him. "Are you supposed to be this nice?"

He smiled at her. "Sometimes people need a little bit longer to get where they need to go," he stated. "I won't push you into something. I already know exactly where I want to go with this, and, if you tell me that you don't know yet, I won't get angry."

She stared at him. "Please don't get angry. Part of me is insecure and needs some reassurance about where we're going and how it's the right thing."

"We are both consenting adults, and we know there are no guarantees in life," he pointed out.

"No, there sure aren't any guarantees," she repeated, as she stared at him. "This … this has turned into a fairly unsettling conversation."

"That's because we're talking about things you're unsure of."

"But are you sure?"

"I'm very sure of me," he replied. "I'm just waiting for you to be sure of you."

"Oh, *great*," she muttered, "more pressure."

"Nope, no pressure at all—at least not too much." She frowned at that, and he laughed again. "Just relax. Nothing is changing in our world."

And that was all she needed for now and could once again feel a measure of peace. "Okay," she said, with a happy smile. "If you mean that?"

"I do mean it. Obviously I want to move the relationship forward, and I've made that very clear," he stated, with a pointed look in her direction.

She nodded. "I'm just not quite so good at that whole communication thing. What if I make a wrong decision? I've made a pretty major misstep already, a mistake that cost me lots of good years and more."

He stared at her and nodded. "That's a very valid point. You did make a decision back then, one that you came to regret. So ease up. This isn't about me. It's not even about our relationship. It's more about you trusting yourself."

She groaned. "Okay, I get it, but I think I've reached my limit on this topic for now."

"Agreed," he noted, then rubbed his hands together. "What have you got to eat?" He checked her fridge and then started opening up her cupboards. Turning to look at her as if he were lost, he asked, "When did you shop last?"

She shrugged. "It's been a while."

"Have you been eating these last few days?" he asked.

She winced and nodded. "Yeah, I reverted back to peanut butter sandwiches."

He stared at her in stunned silence for a moment. "Why?"

"I don't know," she murmured. "I think it had something to do with Mathew's death."

Mack didn't say anything, but instead he proceeded to pour coffee and handed her a cup. "Are you missing him?"

She looked at him in shock, then immediately shook her head. "Not in the way you would think. There is no need to be jealous of Mathew."

"Not jealous, just wondering if you're over him."

"I'm *so* over him," she declared, "completely over him, in fact. But something about his death and all the surrounding hoopla brought up a lot of memories, insecurities, and feelings of inadequacy. I've spent the last couple days trying to work at getting rid of them."

"Good," he agreed, studying her.

"Now I will admit that what you told me last night helped immensely."

At that, his eyebrows shot up. Then he gave her a slow smile. "See? You're doing just fine."

"Am I though?" she asked, frowning at him. "It all feels like a minefield. I worry that I'll make the wrong decision or say the wrong thing at any time."

"So what? You have all the time in the world to get it right, and no punishment is involved if you get it wrong," he pointed out, with understanding. "This isn't the school of life, where you'll get punished. This isn't that life you had with Mathew because I am certainly *not* Mathew," he declared, his tone hardening. "You won't get slapped around if you say the wrong thing."

She took a deep breath and smiled up at him tremulously. "I know you would never hit me. … I do have to ask for a little bit of patience, if and when these things come up again."

He nodded slowly. "I know that it's possible for certain things to trigger these feelings periodically, but I also know that you're a strong woman. So, each time you address it, you'll probably have less and less of it to deal with."

"What if I have more of it to deal with?" she

asked.

"Then we'll deal with it together."

"You could find somebody easier to get along with. You know that, right?"

His lips twitched, and the corner of his eyes crinkled. "I knew that a long time ago." He brushed his thumb across her cheek. "I lost that fight almost immediately." Then he opened his arms.

She stepped into them, feeling grateful when they closed around her. She burrowed her head tightly against his big, strong chest and wondered at the craziness of what was going on. She was so lucky to have found him. And she was absolutely terrified of messing it up.

For all her confidence when she had been talking to Nan, Doreen wasn't terribly confident about doing the right thing and still honoring the person who she had become. When Mack's phone rang, she stepped back and added, "We still have to talk about the case."

"There is no case," he stated cheerfully.

"You don't have a body?"

"Yeah, a body was found," he replied, "but not a body of any interest to you."

"Anybody who *was* a body," she stated,

rolling her eyes, "is of interest to me." She watched as he answered his phone, hearing little bits and pieces of the conversation.

As his expression thinned out, he nodded. "Yeah, I'm coming." He looked down at her, yet not completely present in the moment. "So, the victim was tased, and that *was* the cause of death. It doesn't happen often, but it can. And unfortunately the Taser was the property of someone who we know."

"Really? Who's that?"

He hesitated. "Arnold."

She stared at him. "Arnold? Arnold, your coworker? Are you saying that the murder weapon was his or that he murdered someone?"

"The Taser had been stolen from him, when his house had been broken into some ten years back. He reported the loss at the time and followed procedure and everything, so no issue there. He was assigned a second Taser on the job, and the first one was never recovered."

"Until now," she noted.

"One of the reasons it was identifiable was the fact that he'd originally had an older model that he refused to upgrade when the rest of us did because he really preferred it. All the others of that vintage and model were taken out of commission."

"So, then it might be his, yet it might not be, right? How can you be sure without a serial number or something?"

"It had an injector that left an auburn pattern when held on too long. As far as forensics can determine, without the actual weapon at hand, it had to be that one."

She nodded. "Which means?"

Just then they heard the sound of another vehicle pulling up. She walked to the front door, and, sure enough, Arnold took the porch steps toward her. "Hey, Arnold. Mack's in here," she said, opening the door.

He stopped at the front step, hitched his belt up over his ample belly, and looked at her, a bit unsure. "I'm not really after him," he muttered.

"What? He just told me about it being your Taser."

He nodded. "But it's not my Taser that I have now," he clarified. "It was the stolen one."

"I'm sorry about that, Arnold. Anything that links you to a death is pretty awful."

He nodded at that. "I know, and it's so frustrating. I can't work a murder case if I'm connected somehow, so I can't work on this one because of my obvious connection to the murder weapon." He stopped, taking a deep breath as he glanced at Mack, who'd walked up behind Doreen. Then Arnold continued. "I'm hoping you can help me find out who broke into my place and stole the Taser."

At that, Mack protested, coming between the two of them, but Arnold shook his head. "I'm off the case because the captain just told me so, and nobody has time to chase that down. Mack, I need this. Back then when it was stolen, we weren't so bothered about it, but obviously we should have been," he shared, "so I'm asking for Doreen's help."

Arnold's gaze went from Mack to Doreen and then back to Mack. "I can help her do that, but I can't help with the rest of the investigation on your current case."

Mack sighed heavily. "Arnold, you have the worst timing ever. I was finally hoping to keep her out of one of our cases."

Arnold shook his head. "Pick another case," he said, his tone harsh. "I'm a cop, and I want to stay that way. And, if for some reason I can't be a cop, I at least want to keep my pension. If any hint of wrongdoing is found on my part, I could lose that too."

Doreen gasped. "That's not fair."

Arnold eyed her hopefully. "So, does that mean you'll help me?"

"Absolutely. Of course I'll help you," she declared, "and so will Mack."

Mack once again sighed behind her. "Of course I'll help him. I'm assigned to the case, remember?"

"Since you don't have enough manpower, will you handle the murder case alone?"

"Can you help out and fill me in?" Arnold asked, looking at Mack, as she faced him too.

"Absolutely he will," she said, almost ecstatic. "I'll be your sidekick again," she exclaimed, looking at Mack in delight. "Besides, if the captain's okay with it, what's the rub?" She turned to ask Arnold to be sure. "Has he okayed it?"

Arnold nodded. "Yes, but we're to keep it on the down low."

"Of course," she replied thoughtfully. "As it turns out, that is what I do best."

Arnold and Mack looked at her, and both of them burst out laughing.

Chapter 6

DOREEN DIDN'T HAVE much in the way of anything to eat, so Mack ordered in pizza. The three of them sat outside, as they discussed the little bit of information that there was on the prior theft of the Taser from Arnold's house. The animals were nearby, enjoying some additional attention.

"I can give you what I know, which is basically all that's in the files. Yet the bottom line is this. I was at work one day and came home to find that somebody had busted into my place and had stolen the Taser."

Doreen frowned. Arnold's account was too short and far too thin to produce any clues. "And, over these ten years, it was never seen again? It never showed up at another crime scene?" she asked him.

He shrugged. "Not that I know of. You can buy these things on the internet now, although I think they're more of a cheap knockoff than the actual police issue. At least I would think so."

Doreen nodded. "Okay, so tell me this. If it did show up in this new case, but you did report it missing at the time and followed proper protocols and were cleared, are you liable for any crimes committed with it later?" she asked both of them.

Arnold paled and frowned at Mack, who immediately shook his head. "No, Arnold didn't wield it. The Taser was stolen, due to a theft. When the loss is promptly reported, and the proper procedures have been followed, I see no liability issue at all."

Arnold took a deep breath and relaxed ever-so-slightly.

"Good," she said.

The pizza arrived just then, and, as Mack brought it to the patio, she heard another voice. She looked up to see Chester ambling behind them. He was a younger cop, who was usually partnered up with Arnold. She smiled. "Hey, Chester."

"Hey, Doreen." He wore a huge grin, as he sat down beside the pizza. "Good time to come and visit, right?"

Doreen smiled, as her animals drew closer

to the food too.

Arnold snorted. "What are you here for?"

"Came to help out," he replied. "I told the captain that I was coming too."

At that, she turned to Mack. "I've got a funny feeling about this." He raised his eyebrows. She looked at the pizza, sighed, and added, "You should probably put in a second order."

"Why is that?" he asked.

Just then they heard another vehicle coming up Doreen's driveway.

He stared at her and grumbled, "*Right*." He quickly grabbed his phone and placed a rush order for two more pizzas.

She smiled. "Good thing one of us has the money."

He snorted and muttered under his breath, "Are you kidding? That will be the end of my paycheck this month."

"I can cover it."

"You sure?"

"I still have some of the reward money. So, yes, I can cover it."

He waved her off.

"I'll cover it," Arnold offered, with a sigh.

With a knock at the door, Mack got up and walked to the front. He returned with two more of the guys she knew from the station. Sure enough, following behind and looking a little bit sheepish, was the captain himself.

She grinned at him. "Hey, Captain. How's life?"

"Not been too bad," he replied, then stopped to admire the backyard. "Darn, we did a good job here, didn't we?"

"You guys sure did," she exclaimed. "I come out here all the time." She looked around, as she smiled.

"That's what backyards are for," he noted, with complete sincerity. "How are you handling this latest problem?"

"If you mean Arnold, we haven't really gotten started yet," she admitted, "or do you mean my ex?"

"The ex," he clarified. "I guess they already told you about the Taser."

She nodded. "Yes, I heard about that. I'm dealing with Mathew's death and the associated trouble very well now, thank you. It was a little too convenient for some people, who seemed to be very uncomfortable around me for a while," she shared, "but hopefully everybody has gotten over that."

"If ever somebody deserved to die," Mack stated, "it was Mathew. And, if ever somebody would *never* commit murder, it is Doreen."

The others all agreed.

She smiled and added, "By the way, we're doing fine. Mack and I are doing great." She patted his hand.

At that pronouncement, grins appeared all around.

"That's good," the captain replied. "Now we can all focus on the current problem." He sat down with a hard *plunk*, reached into the pizza box without asking, and shared, "Vancouver has already called about this one."

"Oh? What about it?" she asked.

"They think the missing Taser might be connected to a couple cases down there."

At that, Arnold groaned and asked to be sure, "My Taser?"

"Yeah, your Taser," the captain confirmed. "About its stupid distinctive pattern."

"Right," Arnold muttered.

"So, Vancouver believes that Arnold's Taser was used in their two cases?" she asked.

The captain nodded. "We don't have a whole lot in the way of a database for that stuff here. It's on the future budget as a needed expense, but we don't have a common database that can connect cases from place to place."

She shook her head. "If I had billions of dollars, that would be one of the first things I would want set up."

"We would be more than happy to have you do that," the captain offered. "It's frustrating to always have our hands tied by something like this. We must constantly reach out and ask each department, 'Hey, do you have any cases like this, or, hey, have you seen anything like that?'"

She nodded. "And, with something like a stolen Taser, I gather it wasn't that important to coordinate at the moment."

"Nope, it wasn't, and, in Vancouver's investigation, they thought the Taser came from somebody local. Therefore, it was information they've had for their cases, but it didn't trigger anything or register on our radar. We had no knowledge that it was one of ours. Now, of course, it's a different story."

"Those cases down there, were they murders?" she asked the captain.

"No, thank God."

At that, Arnold sighed. "At least that's one good thing. I would hate to think my previous Taser had killed anybody else."

Doreen nodded. "It's bad enough that it killed anybody, but that's what we have. Okay, so all we know is that the Taser involved was stolen in a burglary from how many years ago?" she asked, looking at Arnold.

He shrugged. "Must be about ten years now."

She frowned and considered that. "So, for ten years, this thing was around, and nobody's used it?" She turned to the captain. "So, these cases down on the coast, when did they happen?"

Looking at her cautiously, he replied, "In the last six months."

She pondered that.

"You know what it really means," Mack suggested, "is that it only recently came into circulation, even though it's been gone all that time. Either Arnold's stolen Taser came into somebody else's possession recently, or, for whatever reason, this guy's flipped a switch and needed a weapon all of a sudden and just lately remembered he had it lying around."

"I like the idea that it came into somebody else's possession," she stated.

At that, Arnold looked at her in surprise.

"Why?"

"Because, if someone had hung on to that weapon all this time, I can't imagine them suddenly building up the confidence or the bravado to use it after that many years. It's far more likely that they would just keep it packed away or would hand it off to somebody else."

"Or it could have been stolen from him."

She frowned at that. "So, you have no idea who was involved in your B&E?" she asked Arnold.

He shook his head. "Not really."

"Did you have any roommates at the time or anybody who stayed with you even temporarily?"

"Let me clarify my answer. At the time, I did question a buddy of mine, who was living with me and had shown a lot of interest in it. However, he had an alibi *supposedly*," he shared, with an eye roll, "and had absolutely promised me that he had nothing to do with it."

"*Right.* ... How good of a buddy?" she asked.

"He had previously been a good buddy, but we weren't such good buddies after that."

"You still had that bit of suspicion, right?"

He nodded. "Yeah, but I don't really have any reason to suspect him, not to mention any evidence."

"Reasons are evidence and places to start," she muttered, "but I think it's more about instincts at that point."

The captain nodded. "We run by instincts more than we care to admit," he agreed. "And instincts have often saved our butts. Sometimes it's the only thing we have to go on."

Mack spoke up just then. "Doreen and I have discussed that a couple times," he shared, "and I've warned her to never ignore her natural instincts. If it says, *Run*, then you run and don't ask questions, not until you're somewhere safe."

She nodded. "That's very true, though I can't say I've learned how to listen to that *run* message all that well."

"No, you haven't." He glared at her. "You keep getting caught in situations you're not supposed to even be in."

She grinned at him. "You're welcome." He gave her an eye roll. She turned to Arnold. "So, I'll need the address, the date, your friend's name, and anything else you can tell me."

"Check out the police file. Nothing else I

can tell you."

"Sure there is. Where did you keep it?"

"Oh, that's easy enough, in the bedroom."

"In the closet, on the bed, in the night table?"

"In the night table. I was supposed to have it with me that day. I'd come home, put all my gear down on the night table, then had a shower," he shared. "When I got up the next morning, I got dressed and put it all back on again."

"Yet you forgot it that day?"

He nodded. "Yeah, I did. I ended up dumping breakfast cereal down my shirt, so I ran upstairs, took off my belt and everything, then changed shirts and raced to work, not wanting to be late, and I ended up leaving the Taser at home."

"Right, that makes sense."

"It made as much sense back then as it does today," Arnold muttered, "but it still makes me feel like an idiot."

"I understand," she agreed. "How many years until retirement?"

He shrugged. "Six," he replied, with a sideways glance at the captain, who just frowned at him.

"And we need every one of those years

from you. The amount of work we have," the captain noted, turning to glare at Doreen, "is astronomical."

"Yeah, did you ever ask for any extra man-hours to handle all these reports?" she asked. "You've got to be the best department in the country."

He laughed. "We've definitely got com-mendations coming since we closed a lot of cases," he noted, "and I have requested extra man-hours for all these reports, but, so far, no additional money has been allocated."

She didn't like hearing that, but she under-stood. "Of course budget money is something you can never really argue with because they pull that card every time."

The captain groaned, as he nodded. "Eve-rybody does, and economically the country is doing okay. People are not exactly flourish-ing, but everybody is getting by, and it's not everybody who's a problem. It's just that same few."

"It's always just a few people," she agreed sadly, "and they mess it up for everybody else. Now, back to your friend." She turned to Arnold. "What does he do for a living?"

He winced at that. "Back then he didn't *do* anything, and now I'm afraid he'd gotten into an uglier venture back then."

"Drugs?" she asked.

"Not so much, now that weed is legal. Yet he was always out to make a name in that industry." Arnold sighed. "He was always on the verge of disaster and always had big ideas to make some fast money."

"He could work at one of the cannabis dispensaries," she suggested. "It's a big industry and growing now."

"He could do a lot of things if he wanted to," Arnold said, grimacing at her. "But, the bottom line is, he doesn't really want to work."

"Right, so I need whatever contact information you have on him. Then I will sniff around and see what I can find out." She looked over at Mack. "Obviously somebody is *officially* handling this case, so who is that?"

Mack smiled at her. "Yours truly. It's connected to my murder investigation."

"Right," she muttered, pondering that. "I suppose you won't want me to talk to your prime suspect."

"A prime suspect in the murder or in the original theft?" he asked calmly.

Doreen clarified, "The person of interest in terms of the theft."

Mack chuckled. "You see, Captain? I told

you that she would make a great cop."

The captain nodded.

"And I've also told Mack that I don't have the tolerance for all the rules and regulations," she reminded him. Staring around at the people gathered here, she added, "You don't have quite the whole department here. ... Where's Insley?"

"At work," the captain replied, with a laugh. "This isn't her style."

"Maybe it's not her style because she hasn't had a chance to make it her style," Doreen guessed.

At that, Mack stared at her in surprise. "Do you want Insley in on this?"

Doreen shrugged. "I'm not sure what to say to that. Has she got something to offer?" she asked.

"Maybe."

"We don't want any stone unturned on Arnold's case," Doreen pointed out, "but let me wander around and muddle my way through some of this first."

"So, what do you think? Will talking to my buddy from back then give you something?" Arnold asked, eyeing her curiously.

She smiled. "Of course. All kinds of things potentially. People like him won't talk to you because you're a cop, but the things that they say to me are a different story." She frowned, looking around for her animals and found Mugs chewing on a piece of pizza on the ground. She stared at him, then asked Mack, "Did you give that to him?"

He shook his head.

She looked over to Arnold, his face riddled with guilt. "Wow, no wonder Mugs loves seeing you guys coming," she muttered. Just then the doorbell rang. Looking around, she asked, "Can one of you get that? It'll probably be more pizza."

"More?" the captain asked in delight. Then he quickly grabbed one of the last two pieces. Arnold made quick work of the other one.

Moments later, Mack returned with two more large pizzas and placed them on the table. "There you go, guys," he called to the others. "Tank up." Soon everybody had helped themselves to more pizza, including Doreen.

As she sat here munching, Thaddeus hopped onto her shoulder and snuggled up close. "Hey, big guy," she greeted him.

Immediately he started squawking. "Big Guy, Big Guy, Big Guy, Big Guy."

"No, we won't go see Big Guy today," she

replied. "*Shh*."

Thaddeus stared at her and repeated, "*Shh*, Doreen. *Shh*, Doreen."

She groaned. "The talking wouldn't be so bad, but he acts like a two-year-old half the time." Almost immediately, as if on cue, Thaddeus responded.

"I'm a two-year-old. I'm a two-year-old. I'm a two-year-old."

He had slurred the words together, but it was close enough that she understood him. She glared at him. "You're supposed to mind your manners when you have company."

"Mind your manners, mind your manners, mind your manners."

"I can't get him to say anything new for weeks and weeks. Then you guys show up, and all he wants to do is mouth off." She glared at the bird. "You're supposed to be nice."

"Supposed to be nice, *hey, hey, hey, hey.* Supposed to be nice, *hey, hey, hey, hey.*"

With the others in stitches over his antics, she sighed, broke a small chunk of pizza off her slice, and handed it to him. He immediately snagged it up, then dropped it onto her shoulder, making her wince at the concept of him eating pizza off her shirt, and she glared at him. "You could take that to the ground."

"Take that to the ground. Take that to the ground."

"Why are you talking so much?"

Thaddeus looked at her, grabbed the piece of pizza, and dropped to the ground, as if fully understanding.

The others stared at her and then at her talkative bird.

"Does he really understand?" the captain asked in disbelief.

"I would normally say no. However, when he does something like that, it makes me question everything I thought I knew about him," she muttered. "I swear he's just there to torment me at times."

At that remark, everybody nodded, but it was Mack who spoke up. "And to support you and to save you when you get into reckless situations," he reminded her. "Oh, and, when you get depressed and feel low, he's there for you to cuddle."

"Thanks for the reminder," she muttered. "He's a huge part of my family, but he's certainly a mouthy part."

The others all laughed.

"Anyway," she began, as she stared down at the pizza in her hand, realizing that the second order of pizza was getting demolished almost as quickly as the first. "I'll wander around and see what I can find on Arnold's missing Taser, but no guarantees."

"That's okay," Arnold stated. "I feel strange even asking you to help." He looked over at the rest of them. "And you guys will do your best, right?"

"Definitely," Mack replied. "We'll solve this thing, and we'll solve it quickly."

Arnold nodded glumly. "I still feel bad that one of my weapons was used to kill somebody."

"Who's this victim anyway?" she asked curiously. At that, Mack glared at her. She shrugged. "I can hardly look into the stolen Taser case without knowledge of the murder-by-Taser case. Even without your giving me the victim's name, there seems to be no honor among thieves. One bad guy with a stolen Taser probably used it on another bad guy. Obviously the target of the murder by Taser is always part of the answer."

Mack smiled at her. "You're even starting to talk like us."

She smiled at him. "*Yeah*, and I know very well that I'm not one of you, but sometimes I feel a bit as if I am."

"Hey," Arnold interjected, "more times than not, it seems you *are* one of us," he muttered.

She smiled. "Thank you, Arnold. That's a lovely compliment."

Chapter 7

Tuesday Morning ...

DOREEN WOKE THE next morning, her mind racing with options, theories, and scenarios as to what was going on. On the surface it seemed simple. Somebody stole the Taser, hung on to it for a while, got bored of it, was offered some money for it, or had it stolen. Then whoever took possession of it used it in an attack and killed someone.

Maybe that attack had turned into a robbery. According to Mack, who had finally given her a little bit more information last night, the victim's pockets had been turned out, and no identification was found on the body. That sounded like a robbery or a crime made to look like a robbery. Whether the victim had been targeted or was just in the wrong place at the wrong time made for a completely different scenario.

The conversation last night had gone from theory to theory to theory, but nobody really had any idea what was going on. Until more information came to light, all the speculation was just that. No facts, no nothing. While Mack was focused on getting evidence, she knew her gut would lead her in the right direction. It always seemed to.

Quickly up and about, she got dressed and headed downstairs. She smiled when she noted some pizza was left from last night and would be great for her breakfast. Not exactly the healthiest of meals, but she would take it. Particularly right now, when she wasn't sure where she was heading and needed some carbs to maybe top off her energy. At least that's what she told herself to stave off any guilt. She shook her head. The guilt was still a persistent remnant of her ex's voice in her head.

She knew it would take some time to be rid of it, but, even now, just knowing she could have pizza for breakfast—and Mathew couldn't say anything about it—was enough to make her smile.

"Sorry about that, Mathew. Going to miss you … *not*." And she knew that was mean, but, if she needed to say those things for the sake of her soul, that's just where she was at. Groaning, she picked up her coffee, then headed outside.

The animals immediately booked it to the gardens, for one reason or another. She had a litter box for Goliath in the house, but he preferred to go outside in the garden, if he could. By the time everybody had made their way back onto the deck, she was sitting down and sipping her coffee, her notepad at the ready in front of her. She wasn't even sure how to start this case of the stolen Taser, since there was so little to go on. The only place she could really start was with Frankie, Arnold's friend and roommate from ten years ago. Of course Frankie couldn't exactly be called a friend if he was a suspect in the breaking-and-entering at Arnold's house.

Chances were, Frankie wasn't involved, but he may well have known something about it that he didn't share back then. That alone gave him as much of a guilty vibe as any-thing. People often didn't know exactly what was wrong with somebody, but they just knew something was. In this case, Arnold had been a cop for a long time, and he had developed some instincts. At least she would like to think so.

With the animals in tow, she headed to the river. As soon as she had parked her butt beside the flowing water, she pulled out her phone and called that friend.

When he answered, he sounded sleepy, half disgruntled.

"Sorry if I woke you, Frankie," she began.

"Who is this?" he snapped. She quickly identified herself, and a moment of stunned silence followed on the other end of the phone. "What are you doing calling me? And how did you get this number?"

"You came up regarding a B&E at Arnold's home about ten years ago," she replied. "You were one of the persons of interest at the time, and, since that time, the missing Taser has been identified in a series of other incidents—"

"Incidents?"

"Yeah, incidents. Your name came up from that initial investigation."

He snorted at that. "Arnold tried to pin that on me," he snapped into the phone, "but I didn't have anything to do with it."

"Good, then you won't mind answering a few questions." That silenced him, and she continued on. "That's right, isn't it? If you didn't have anything to do with it, it's definitely to your benefit to clear this up, especially so your name is removed from the record."

"It's not as if it'll really be erased from the record," he corrected, sniffing into the phone. "How come you're dealing with this? You're not a private eye, are you?"

"No, not yet, but I'm definitely starting to warm up to the idea." If nothing else it would give her some validity with the cases she was involved in.

"*Huh*, I suppose Arnold put you up to this, didn't he?"

"No, why would he?" she asked curiously. And, by rights, Arnold hadn't. She'd decided to do this on her own.

"Whatever," Frankie muttered. "Look. The only reason he thought I might have had something to do with it is because I came into a bit of cash after the B&E."

"Where were you at the time of the break-in?"

"I was staying with him at the time, but I wasn't there when it happened. I was down at the bar."

"Of course you have an alibi for that, with witnesses?"

"It would have been somewhere around the time I was walking back from the bar to the house. Arnold was on night shift, and we had argued earlier that day. When I got home, … the front door was open, and the place had been tossed."

"Wow. So did you call him then?"

"Sure I did. What else was I supposed to do?"

"Wait until morning?"

"Yeah, as if that would have gone over well."

"No, I don't imagine it would have," she agreed. "Okay, what did you do then?" There was another moment of silence, but she just waited until he spoke.

"What do you mean, what did I do then? After the cops were done looking around, and I finally had a chance to get to sleep, I went to bed. I was pretty darn sober by then."

"Right, nothing quite like that to sober you up."

"*Right*," he muttered, slightly mollified.

She smiled. "And you didn't see anything? You didn't see any vehicle leaving the scene? You didn't see anyone or anything suspicious at the time?"

"No, I didn't see anything, and, of course, that just made Arnold all the more suspicious."

"How far away was the pub?"

"About, I don't know, maybe six, eight, nine blocks. It's not even there anymore, but it was a darn good pub. Everything that's good seems to disappear," he snapped. "They had cheap booze, and that was good in my book."

She nodded. "Do you work now?"

"What do you mean, do I work? What's that got to do with anything?"

"I just wondered where you work now," she replied carefully.

He snorted. "Why? What you're really wondering is whether I'm living a life of crime or whether I'm holding down a steady job, like the rest of you sticks in the mud."

Her eyebrows shot up at that. "I wasn't really thinking along those lines, but, now that you brought it up, I would like to know."

He groaned. "Look. I had a job. I was working at one of the big supermarkets here. Then I got into an argument with the boss, who was an absolute jerk, … and I got fired not too long ago, but it wasn't my fault."

She wondered how many times people could repeat these same things over and over again but never where they were in any way at fault. "Okay, and who was the guy you got into an argument with?"

"Oh, him. If you call him, he'll just tell you a bunch of nonsense," he muttered.

"Let me talk to him. You don't have to worry about the rest of it all. I'll decide if it's lies or not."

"He'll just say that I stole from the place and that I deserved to get fired."

"Did you?"

Yet another moment of hesitation came and then a weak attempt at anger. "That's not a fair question, and, if all you'll do is set me up by asking those kinds of questions, I'm not talking to you."

"That's okay. You don't have to talk to me. I can just hand this over to the police. They can take over for me."

"What are you talking about? … So, you're saying that, if I tell you, you won't turn it over?"

"I might have to eventually, but that depends on what information comes up," she shared, knowing perfectly well she would have to tell Mack about this. "But they may not need to come back to talk to you—unless you're more involved in this than you're telling me."

"I'm not involved," he snapped.

"Okay, so, ten years ago, the money that

you came into that made Arnold suspicious, where did it come from?"

There was another ugly silence. "Maybe I need a lawyer," he grumbled, his tone turning belligerent.

"Well, … if you really think you need a lawyer, you're more than welcome to get one," she replied. "I'm just asking you questions. It's a friendly call, and a lawyer is your choice, but you should realize that will attract attention from the police. So you better figure out what you need to do."

"I don't like the questions," he snapped.

"I can see that, but, if you didn't have anything to do with the theft of Arnold's Taser, a few ugly questions right now seems pretty minor compared to what could happen if they have reason to suspect you're more involved than you appeared to be so far."

"I'm not involved."

"Then tell me where the money came from back then," she repeated. "It's easier to tell me than it will be to go down to the station and do it there."

"Says who?" he snapped. "I'm not talking on the phone. For all I know you're recording this."

At that, she stared down at the phone. "Oh,

that would have been a really good idea, but I wasn't, no."

"Good, but I'm not talking to you if you've got a wire on."

Her face twisted as she thought about it. "And again, a wire would be interesting, but, no, that's not part of my wheelhouse."

"Sure, everybody says that, yet still uses the whole *send you down the creek without a paddle* setup."

She smiled. "So, if you don't want to talk over the phone, where do you want to meet?"

"What do you mean, *meet*?" he asked in alarm.

"If you don't want to talk over the phone, and we can't get the answers the normal way, then we'll need to meet somewhere in person, so I can get the answers face-to-face."

"What if I don't want to meet?"

"That's fine too. I'll pass on this information to the cops, and they can call you, and you can talk to them officially downtown at head-quarters."

"That's not fair," he muttered. "I didn't do anything."

"In that case, it's easy. Just talk to me, give me the answers I need. Then I can carry on with the investigation. If it doesn't involve you, no reason for anybody to come back to you." She hesitated. "Unless of course you think that something will involve you, and you're scared."

"I'm not scared," he snapped.

"Good, with that out of the way, where do you want to meet?"

"Outside, in public. But not where people can see me, yet I can still see who else is around."

"The City Park?"

"Sure, but you're buying coffee."

She grinned at that. "I think I could manage a coffee."

"Good," he muttered. "I haven't had any today."

She looked down at the cup in her hand and nodded. "That can be a rough day then. When do you want to meet?"

"The sooner, the better, so I can get you off my plate, and I don't have to deal with this anymore. I shouldn't have to deal with it at all."

"I get that, and, if you had nothing to do with it—"

"Yeah, but it's not as if you'll listen to me."

"Am I not listening to you now? Let's see

what you have to say."

"Fine, but, if I don't like anything you've got to say, I'll walk away."

"Fair enough," she replied. "I'll see you down at City Park in an hour then."

At that, he ended the call.

She quickly texted Mack, explaining in short form that she was meeting Arnold's friend Frankie for coffee at City Park.

He called her back. "Why are you meeting him in person?"

"Because he didn't want to talk over the phone," she explained. "He's a little on the paranoid side. I think he also feels a little persecuted over this."

At that, Mack snorted. "Yeah, what did he do?"

"He says he didn't do anything."

"*Right.*"

Such disbelief filled his tone that she had to laugh. "Yeah, that's my take too, but I will talk to him and see what he has to say."

"Did he have anything to say?"

"Yeah, up until I insisted on finding out where the money came from around the time of the initial theft that made Arnold suspicious."

"Ah," Mack replied, with a wealth of understanding. "You watch your back when you're down there."

"Will do."

"You do know that the money probably had to do with drugs or something illegal, right?"

"Maybe, but we still need to know, and, if he didn't tell Arnold, that's probably exactly right. He would have thought that Arnold would turn him in."

"Chances were good that Arnold would have."

"And that makes perfect sense as to why Frankie's in this situation now."

"Maybe, yet it's still got to be solved."

"I agree with you completely," she muttered. "I understand what you're trying to say."

He laughed. "Glad to hear it. Now take care of yourself and check in afterward."

"Will do," she murmured, and, with that, she ended the call and loaded the animals into her car and headed downtown.

Chapter 8

DOREEN WANDERED AROUND City Park, heading toward the huge pergola, where she and Frankie had planned to meet. She picked up two coffees and took her time getting there. By the time she met up with Frankie, the coffees would almost be cool enough to drink, or at least she hoped so.

Picking up these coffees when they were so hot meant she had to carry these hot cups for the whole distance. Still, this investigation was going better than she thought it would, at least she hoped so. It seemed a little early to have any real idea of what was going on.

When she arrived at the meeting place, she sat down to wait for Frankie. She waited and waited, the coffee now cooling off in her hands. Then she heard a noise behind her, and Mugs instantly growled. Doreen held tightly onto his and Goliath's leashes.

"Don't turn around." When she froze, the man mockingly said, "Good choice. We don't want people asking questions."

"Yet all I'm doing is trying to figure out if you had anything to do with the burglary at your friend's place."

"Is that what friends do to each other?" the man asked, again with that mocking tone.

She shrugged. "Not my friends."

An ugly silence came after that. "Good point," he muttered, sounding nonchalant.

"If they did that, maybe they're not friends," she added.

"You'll get yourself in a lot of trouble saying that."

"Maybe. Yet, if you're involved in this burglary, you might want to know that something stolen has now been used in several other crimes."

At that came a shocked silence.

She nodded without turning around. "In case you didn't know that." Mugs continued to growl, but the man behind her never mentioned it.

"What kind of crimes?"

"The worst kind," she replied, her tone soft, "and that'll lead to all kinds of trouble." She heard him cussing in the softest of whispers.

She waited and then added, "Any information would be helpful."

When no response came, she asked, "Will you talk to me?" With still no response at all, she instinctively knew that she was alone. Plus Mugs had quit his growling. She slowly turned, and, sure enough, nobody stood behind her. She groaned at that, realizing she had no idea who she'd been talking to. She realized that she hadn't been talking to Frankie, and she had no idea who it was. And still had two coffees in her hands. Frowning she took a drink of one, her mind consumed with the conversation.

"That's not helpful," she muttered, as the animals crowded around her, wanting pets and scratches behind the ears. "The least you could have done was talk to me," she muttered to no one. She saw no sign of anybody, not running away or otherwise acting suspicious. She got up and walked around with her animals. Of course City Park was always filled with people, always attracted tourists to walk around the area, always catered to people simply sitting around, visiting. It was a beautiful morning, and just enough foot traffic was in the park to hide anybody who wanted to slip away unseen, so she found no sign of her source. Finding a bench, she sat down, placing the coffees safely beside her before picking up her phone and calling Mack.

"How'd it go?" She explained and he swore. "Wow, just simple questions, and it blows up."

"I'm not sure it was very simple at all. I don't think it was the same guy."

"What?"

"The voice was different, more mature or refined somehow."

"Sure, but one was a phone call, and one wasn't."

"Still, it was a different voice. I'm certain of it," she insisted. "I'm not exactly sure if I would recognize it again."

"Did he disguise it?"

"No, I don't think so," she replied hesitantly. "But he didn't know anything about what the Taser had been used for recently."

"What did you tell him?"

"I just mentioned that it had been used in several incidents, crimes, and he wanted to know what exactly. When I said the worst kind, he swore, then took off right after that."

Mack pondered that for a moment. "That's not good. But, if he was involved, it could be that he's afraid the heat is coming down on him."

She nodded slowly. "I guess that's possible, isn't it? Something else has to be going on there."

"Oh, something is going on, no doubt about that. The job now is to figure out just what it is and put a stop to it as quickly as possible." She didn't have anything to say to that. "Where are you now?" he asked.

"I'm still standing in the park," she shared, looking around for the man she just spoke to.

"I wouldn't hang around if I were you. No *good* reason for him to come back at this point."

"Right, I hear you," she said. "I have to admit that I'm a little worried about Frankie at this point."

"Why?" Mack asked curiously.

"Because I really don't think it was him just now, and the stranger's warning to not talk about this would have applied to Frankie too."

"And you think that, by contacting Frankie, he's in trouble?"

"I'm not taking the blame if something does happen because obviously Frankie's been heading down a criminal pathway and has been for a while."

"Exactly," Mack agreed. "Do you want me to give him a call?"

"Actually I can give him a call," she suggested. "That would be a normal thing to do if he didn't show up for a meeting, right?" He hesitated and she smiled. "You're right. That's exactly what I'll do. I'll call you back in a minute." She disconnected and quickly dialed Frankie's number.

When there was no answer, she called again, and it went to voice mail. A few minutes later, she decided to call again. When a woman picked up on the other end, Doreen quickly asked for Frankie.

"He's not here," she said. "He headed down to City Park."

"I'm the one he was supposed to meet down here, but he didn't show up." Doreen had a ten-year-old photo in the case file to go by, but at least she had that much.

"What do you mean he didn't show up? He left here forty-five minutes ago, maybe even an hour."

"He's not here," Doreen repeated, "and I've been standing here, waiting, holding a coffee for him."

"Who are you?" the other woman asked suspiciously.

"Somebody asking him questions about a break-in that happened at the place of a friend sometime back."

"Arnold," she muttered in disgust. "I told Frankie that all this sketchy stuff he gets involved in would get him in trouble one day."

"It may have gotten him into trouble right now," Doreen shared. "I don't see him any- where. I'm Doreen, by the way."

"I don't know where he is either," she mut- tered. "He'll come back. He always does. He just runs off scared after he gets himself into trouble, but hopefully he'll get himself out of it again this time."

"I hope so," Doreen replied. "Anyway, if he contacts you or when he gets home, can you have him call me? I'm a bit worried about him."

"That'll be a surprise. I doubt if many peo- ple have ever worried about him," she snapped.

"Are you his partner?"

"No, we share rooms here, but that's it."

"Is it just the two of you there?"

"No, four of us. It's hard to pay the rent in town. In case you hadn't noticed, it's pretty darn expensive."

"You're quite right," Doreen agreed. "And

your name?"

"Tammy. Tammy Farrow."

Doreen wrote down her name, as she nodded. "The rents are high downtown."

"Not that you would know anything about it," Tammy muttered in disgust. "You're probably one of those people sitting high and pretty, with your own little house."

Doreen winced because she did have her own house, but only through her grandmother's generosity had she gotten there. "I inherited one from my grandmother, so, yes, in a way, you're right," she admitted, "but I was without one, without any place to live for a long time, so, yes, I do understand your frustration,"

"*Huh*," Tammy muttered. "Maybe you do understand then. Anyway, if Frankie gets back, I'll have him give you a call."

"Okay, thanks." Doreen rang off. She sent Mack a text, saying there was no sign of him, then wandered toward the boardwalk along the lake. She felt foolish holding the second coffee, but she was still hoping Frankie would show up, and she could hand it over. It may not be worth drinking by now, but it would be a nice gesture.

Finally she sat down on one of the benches and just watched, as the water splashed in front of her. When Mugs barked, she slowly turned and found a man motioning her to come closer. She frowned at that but, snagging the coffees, she got up and slowly walked over. "Frankie?"

He nodded. "Yeah."

"What is going on?" she muttered. "We were supposed to meet up on the other side." She handed him the cold coffee.

He took it and threw back a good portion of it without even breathing. Then he smacked his lips together and said, "I needed that."

She stared at him. "So, who did you send in your stead?"

He stared at her in shock and then horror. "Did somebody come?"

She nodded slowly. "He wouldn't let me turn around, but he basically told me to stay away and to stop asking questions."

He swallowed nervously and looked around. "That had to be Jed."

"Yeah? Who is this Jed, and who does he think he is, coming up and scaring me like that?" she muttered.

Frankie shook his head. "Jed's a scary dude, and you should stay away from him."

"That's very nice to know, but I'm not the

one who approached him," she noted in exasperation. "Where were you, and why didn't you show up on time?"

Frankie frowned, then looked around a little wildly. "I was talking to Jed this morning, and I wasn't sure what he was up to, so I followed him. I lost him in the park here, and, before I knew it, I'd missed our time frame. I saw you wandering around, but I wasn't sure whether you were who I was supposed to meet or not, so I followed you, until I decided it was worth a try."

"It's me," she confirmed, "and your coffee would have been hot if you'd gotten here on time."

He shrugged. "Coffee is coffee. I'll drink it anyway I can get it."

She understood the sentiment, yet she didn't understand anything else he had said. "So, you told this Jed guy about me?"

He nodded. "Yeah, sorry about that."

"Is something likely to happen to me because of it?"

He stared at her in shock. "Most people wouldn't ask something like that."

"Yeah, well, most people aren't me at this point in time," she snapped, her gaze turning hard. "So, did you set me up, Frankie?" At her tone, Mugs began to growl again.

"No, no, of course not," Frankie replied. "Why would you even say that?" He started to back up.

She waved her hands about wildly. "Because this guy showed up in your stead, and, for all I know, you set it up that way."

He shook his head. "No, I didn't, but, once I told him, he told me that I should stay away. He thought you were probably a cop, wearing a wire."

"I already told you that I'm not a cop and that I'm not wearing a wire."

"Yeah, but you can say all kinds of stuff," he declared, glaring at her.

"If you thought that, why did you show up?"

He shrugged. "Because Jed is scary," he muttered.

"So scary that you're afraid he might do something?"

He nodded slowly. "Yeah, he's that scary."

"That's good to know," she muttered. "Not that I want to be in that position of course."

"No, you don't," he confirmed. "You should just leave this alone. Walk away and leave it be. Just let it all go, and it will be better for both of us."

"Why? Because you had something to do

with the break-in?"

He shook his head. "No, I didn't do it."

"You didn't have to *do* it," she clarified, studying him. "But that doesn't mean you didn't give Jed the times or let somebody know when Arnold wasn't home."

He stared at her. "But that wouldn't have been so bad, would it?"

"Absolutely not, unless you did it on purpose."

"What if I didn't know what they would do?"

"You sure didn't help your friend at the time, did you? Arnold could have done something about it back then, and maybe that would have been the end of it."

Frankie swallowed, then looked around. "You don't know what this is all about."

"Maybe not," she admitted, "but, so far, it sounds pretty simple. It sounds as simple as one guy betraying another, resulting in a breaking-and-entering at a *cop*'s house, where they stole something that was later used in the commission of a crime. I don't know how many years somebody hung on to that Taser, but, when they brought it out, they put on one heck of a show with it."

He looked at her. "Did anybody die?"

She nodded. "Yeah, somebody sure did."

His face paled. "But surely I can't be held responsible for that."

"I don't know what they do in these cases," she stated. "I told you. I'm not a cop. And I'm definitely not a lawyer, so I don't know anything about it. But I can tell you one thing for sure. If you do know something now and if you don't come clean, then it goes badly for you. Especially if this Jed is involved. You said yourself that he was bad news so—"

"No, it just goes bad anyway."

"Sure, if you've already done jail time maybe." She frowned at him. "Have you?"

He shrugged. "Not really."

She winced at that. "Look, Frankie. I don't really understand all the details or what kind of trouble you're in, but I've about had enough of the nonsense. So tell me exactly how *not really* applies to jail time?"

He glared at her. "I got off on a technicality."

"Thank you, that makes more sense, and yet I really don't know how that works. I guess it depends on whether you were guilty, and they just decided to not go back and retry you because it wasn't worth it, or if you'd spent enough time in jail already."

He shrugged. "It was a lot of things. I don't

even know why or how it all came down, but I got off and took off, then never looked back."

"Smart move. It seems you should have stayed there."

He nodded, his face glum. "I would have if I could have, but finding a job and all that is hard. There are no jobs for cons."

"I find that hard to believe. There are always jobs for someone who is honest, respectful, and willing to work hard. And the work starts with applying for jobs with a good attitude, until you get one. Regardless I'm certain it's difficult for guys coming out of jail. On the other hand, getting in trouble seems to be pretty darn easy, so maybe getting out of it should be harder. I don't know."

He stared at her. "You still don't know anything about this?"

"No, and, unless you tell me, I won't know."

Suddenly he appeared to make a decision. "Look. If Jed finds out I told you, I'm dead."

"Sounds like a *great* guy to be hanging around."

"No, he's not. He's scary, but he pays the rent, and I've got to live somewhere."

She mentally counted Jed among the four who lived in his house. "Go ahead and tell me. What did Jed say?"

"It's just that he knows what happened to the stuff at Arnold's back then."

"Was he involved in the original theft?"

Frankie shrugged. "I just told him that Arnold was on night shift that night. I didn't say anything else, I swear. They took advantage of that information." He gave her a pitiful glance. "Next thing I knew, I was coming home from the pub, and the place was getting cleaned out."

"Ah. *Getting* cleaned out. So you saw and knew who they were, and you were there during the commission of the theft. That's a little different from what you told me before."

He nodded. "Yeah, I was there, but I didn't plan it, and I didn't have anything to do with it."

"Didn't plan it, didn't have anything to do with it, yet somehow your friend's place got stripped of something of value, … furniture, electronics, anything they could pack off, and you didn't do anything to help Arnold. He was giving you a place to stay, which seems to be a far better situation than what you have now."

He winced at that.

"And that's how you chose to repay his friendship? That is beyond my understanding."

He stared at her. "I needed the money."

"For drugs?" she asked.

He nodded slowly. "But I'm off the drugs now."

"I'm certainly glad to hear that." She studied him. "The thing is, getting off the drugs is only part of the battle."

"Yeah, that's true," he agreed bitterly. "I wasn't really big into it, but it was a way to make money."

"It probably paid better than finding and making true friends, which is a slow and time-consuming process, only to then rip them off when they probably didn't have a whole lot to rip off anyway."

"See? That was the problem. I think they thought that, because Arnold was a cop, he would have an awful lot more than he did. However, Arnold's been paying for his mom's keep for a long time, so he didn't really have much money."

"Wow, this doesn't get any better for you, does it? So, they ripped off Arnold, using intel provided by you, and you didn't even tell the cops?"

"I couldn't. Don't you understand?" he cried out. "If I had told, and those guys found out, then I'm the one who would have been in trouble."

She nodded slowly. "Right, so back to that self-preservation thing."

He glared at her. "When you're already down on your luck, you would do anything you can to get back out again."

"I understand that," she noted, "and I've been through that a few times now." He looked at her oddly. She shrugged. "The more time I spend watching people do the things they do, then listen as they try to justify it, the more I realize just how much humanity in general needs some serious help."

He flushed. "I suppose you'll tell Arnold now."

"It's not as if he's trusted you ever since, has he?"

Frankie shook his head. "No, he hasn't. So maybe he knew some of it all along, and I, ... I felt really bad about it."

She laughed. "Yeah, you felt *really* bad about it."

At that, he started to get mad. "You don't get to preach at me. I made a mistake, but I didn't know how to tell him."

"*Right*. Either you can tell Arnold now or I can tell him. But this is your chance to man up, and he'll want to know about this sooner rather than later."

Frankie's shoulders sagged. "I'll tell him."

"That would be a very good idea, since his career and his pension are on the line right now." At that, Frankie stared at her in horror, and she nodded dismissively. "So, not only is it your life that you've ruined, but somebody else's too."

And, with that, he gave a shudder, took another look in her direction, then turned and ran away.

He was moving like his home was on fire, and she wasn't sure he would do the right thing or not. She hoped, but hope was a fickle thing.

"I guess time will tell," she muttered to herself.

Chapter 9

DOREEN DROVE HOME, setting her animals free, now happy to be out of the vehicle again. Once inside the house, she headed directly for the kitchen and made a sandwich. Almost immediately Mack called her.

"Well?" he asked. She filled him in on what happened. "So, Frankie really was behind the break-in?" he asked in astonishment.

"Yeah, that's apparently what friends do for each other now. I feel so sorry for Arnold."

"Absolutely, but then it may not come as a surprise to him. Arnold suspected Frankie from the beginning, but nobody ever wants a suspicion like that confirmed."

"*Right*. Of course now that the repercussions are growing, Frankie admitted that he lives with Jed. Frankie didn't say anything more about his roommate and took off. So my understanding from part of the conversation was that Jed was the one who did the looting and then dealt with selling the loot."

"Right, so he did the pawning off of whatever they hauled in. So Frankie's been aligned with this Jed then for at least the past decade." Mack muttered, "Birds of a feather."

"I suspect that, after Frankie got kicked out of Arnold's house, Frankie moved in with Jed, but I don't know that it happened immediately," she clarified. "Yet it happened at some point. There were lots of years in between, and Frankie needed money for drugs. He did say he's off drugs now, but I have no idea how much of what he said was true, though I'm confident that some of it was. And, when you think about it, selling drugs was a way for Frankie to make money and to keep his criminal lifestyle going."

"Yeah, and the minute drugs get involved," Mack added, "common sense goes right out the window."

She smiled at that. "Anyway, I'm home and making a sandwich, while I contemplate my next move."

"How about doing nothing more on this one?" Mack asked. "I don't like the sound of this Jed guy at all."

"Me neither, so you may want to have a

talk with the parties involved. I would like to stay out of this, if that's even possible now."

Mack offered, "I'll do it this afternoon."

"Good enough," she noted. "Tammy, the woman living in the house with Jed and Frankie, seemed to know a fair bit about what went on back then too. She's not Frankie's partner, but she knew him well."

"But you don't know what their relationship is?"

"No, just something about sharing a house with four tenants. Jed must be one of them. However, the original theft happened ten years ago, yet she seemed to know at least something about it. So I don't know if she's been there in that house the whole time or how she may have heard about it."

"Right, more secrets."

"Not so much secrets in this case," she noted cautiously, "but I didn't get a chance to ask all the questions that needed to be asked."

"I'll follow up," he told her. "You liked her, didn't you?"

"It's not so much that I liked her but that I understood where she was at. Life hasn't been the easiest for her, and she needed a roof over her head. She was bitter, but that is life. People like that are more than ready to talk."

"Something which you are very sensitive to."

She chuckled. "Yeah, you can bet I am."

"So have you heard from Scott at all about the sale of the antiques?"

"No, not yet, but I plan to give him a phone call in the next day or two."

"If he doesn't contact you, then you should definitely call him," he suggested. "You should be hearing something by now."

"I'm pretty sure I'll hear lots, and it'll probably all happen at the same time. We'll have a big party when that check comes in."

"That's the time when you must be sensible with spending it and saving it," he warned.

"I'll be sensible, but that doesn't mean I won't provide beer and pizza for a few people who helped me get through this stage of my life."

"Got it, and count me in. I'll never say no to that."

She burst out laughing. "No? Even though you just had a big pizza fest?"

"Hey, one can never get too much pizza," he protested.

She wasn't so sure about that because it

wasn't her most favorite food.

What she really did enjoy was a chance to have everybody over and to just chill out and relax. Of course the reason they had been over last time wasn't the best event, but, hey, all kinds of things could be done to make life a little easier. Having friends around was one of them.

After the phone call, she took her sandwich outside onto the deck and just relaxed, with her animals close by. She wasn't even sure that she had an avenue to pursue, except for this scary Jed guy. He was definitely dodgy, and she was really lucky not to have encountered him earlier. The female housemate might have more information. But Doreen didn't have any way to contact her directly.

Pondering that, she quickly sent Frankie a text, asking who the other three roommates were at his place. Doreen didn't get an answer, which was really no surprise. Maybe it was better that way because then Tammy wouldn't get asked about it, although it was probably already too late for that. Tammy seemed she could handle things herself though. Sad to see that people had to be in that position in this day and age.

Still pondering things, Doreen munched

her way through the sandwich. When her phone rang, she looked down to see Millicent was calling. She smiled and answered, "Hey. How's the garden doing?"

"Fussy," she muttered.

"Uh-oh, have some weeds gotten out of hand?"

"They just keep coming back where I don't want them to," she fretted. "Any chance you could give me an hour this week?"

"Absolutely," Doreen stated. "I could come by now, if you want—or at least as soon as I'm done with my lunch," she added, with a note of humor.

Millicent cried out in joy, "If you wouldn't mind, I would really appreciate it."

"That's all right with me," Doreen replied. "I'll see you in about thirty minutes then, okay?"

And, with a much happier Millicent ending the call, Doreen quickly sent Mack a text, saying she was heading to his mom's place to work on those pesky weeds. He sent her a thumbs-up, and she smiled at that. He was still underwriting her bills in a way, something she felt bad about, yet didn't want to feel bad about it. Knowing she had plenty of money on the horizon made it all easier. She gathered her animals to go over to Millicent's and was looking for her gardening gloves, when she got an email. Checking it, she stared at the message in surprise.

It was from the city, inviting her to put in a design for one of the new gardens downtown. She stared at it for a long moment, then pocketed her phone and headed out to Millicent's. While she and her animals walked over there, it gave Doreen time to process what new opportunity had just come in. She knew she hadn't put in for the odd job, so how would they have even gotten her email address?

She figured it was probably from some electronic database, yet it was still curious. It was also exciting and certainly something she was interested in. She just had to figure out which garden it was for. Then she could work out a design that might fit, whatever that meant for now.

Once she'd arrived, Millicent pointed out the various weeds now bothering her, and Doreen set to work. By the time she'd worked for an hour, she was loose, limber, and sweating freely.

Millicent stopped her and waved her over. "That all looks very lovely. I guess that's good enough for now."

Doreen frowned at her. "Are you sure?"

Millicent nodded. "You work way too hard, and I feel bad. I shouldn't have you doing this."

"Of course you should," she murmured. "I've been doing it for you this whole summer and most of the fall now. It's really no bother at all."

"Pretty soon it'll be time to put the garden to bed for the winter."

Doreen nodded. "Not quite yet, though."

"No, not yet," Millicent agreed. Then she gave her a bashful grin. "I really should have the boys do it."

At that, Doreen burst out laughing. "I don't think the *boys* would particularly like it if you had them gardening," she guessed. "It's definitely not something in their wheelhouse. Mack can certainly do all the heavy work, but I'm not at all sure he would want to be involved in all of it."

"No, but they could do it," she argued.

"They could, but the time involved is important. I'm not working, so I have the time to do this."

"Right," Millicent noted. "I just feel bad because you're always so busy helping other people, and nobody is out there helping you."

Doreen raised her eyebrows. "Actually they've helped me a lot," she shared. "I certainly don't feel as if anybody owes me anything. People here have been really good to me." Millicent looked somewhat mollified but still a little worried. Doreen shook her head. "Don't you worry about it. I'm fine."

At that, the older woman relaxed a little more and pointed back at the house. "I made tea. Will you stay for a cup?"

As it was part of their ritual more times than not, Doreen nodded. "Sure, that sounds lovely. Thank you. I can help carry something for you."

Millicent beamed and disappeared into the house.

Doreen texted Mack. **One hour, now teatime.** Then she walked in behind Millicent and stood in the kitchen doorway. "It's still nice out. Do you want to sit outside?"

Millicent nodded. "Every chance I get, I love to be outside. Some of the days are chilly, but outside is way better than inside." And, with that, the two of them sat outside with a pot of tea and some homemade cookies.

Doreen asked, "Did you make these?"

Millicent nodded. "Every once in a while, I get into a baking frenzy. ... The boys seem to enjoy it."

"I'm sure they do," Doreen said, with a chuckle, "I'm sure those two eat anything that you want to fix."

"They're men," Millicent noted, with an eye roll. "The way to their heart is definitely through their stomachs."

"Too bad in my case," Doreen replied cheerfully. "I can't cook worth a dime."

"Yet you are working on it, aren't you?" Millicent sounded almost anxious about it.

"Sure, I am," she shared. "It's just not something that comes to me naturally, so it takes a little longer."

"I understand what you mean there," Millicent stated. "I wasn't much of a cook either when I married the boys' father, but I did learn."

"That's the thing. Cooking takes time. And, while I'm out working on these cold cases, I'm not exactly cooking."

Millicent nodded. "That is very true. We all only have so many hours in a day. Still, it's important in a marriage if you do know how to cook."

Doreen had an inkling of what was coming.

"That might be the norm for most marriages, but it certainly wasn't part of my marriage. Nowadays, I think whoever has the skill and the desire to cook should be in the kitchen. Same thing with yard work."

"Oh right, you were married before, weren't you?"

"Yes. ... Does that bother you?"

Immediately Millicent shook her head. "No, it doesn't bother me at all. I just want to know that the boys are happy."

"Ah, this comes back to the relationship between Mack and me?"

Millicent hesitated but nodded. "Yes, and I'm just an old woman worried for nothing, but it would be nice to see the boys settle down before I pass."

"That sounds very much like a conversation I just had with my own grandmother," Doreen said, with a chuckle.

At that, Millicent grinned. "Hey, you can't blame us. We want to arrange everybody's life just so, more or less, because it suits us to see everybody happy." Then she sighed. "It doesn't always work out that way, though."

"No, it definitely doesn't," Doreen agreed. "Since my ex, Mathew, is no longer in the picture, it's a whole lot easier for me to move forward in a new relationship."

"With Mack?" she asked anxiously.

"With Mack," Doreen confirmed, "but no pushing allowed."

Millicent sat back and nodded. "No, I wouldn't want to do that, and I wouldn't want to do anything to jeopardize it." She patted Doreen's hand. "Mack's done a lovely job in picking you. Now we just have to find somebody for Nick."

"Ah, I would have helped if I could, but I'm not into matchmaking, so don't look at me."

At that, Millicent laughed. "Oh, I don't know. You've picked Mack, so you've done very well."

Doreen chuckled. "That's true, but still it's a bit out of my wheelhouse."

"If you do meet any eligible young ladies who would suit Nick, be sure and let me know."

"And you'll just throw them together somehow?" Doreen asked, with a twitch of her lips.

"Somehow, yes," Millicent replied. "I really do want to see him settled. Of course I want to see Mack settled too," she added, with a sideways glance at Doreen.

"Oh, I got the message," Doreen replied. "However, remember that *no pushing* part?"

"Yes, but remember that *I'm old and dying* part?"

"We're all dying," Doreen noted. "It's just a matter of when."

"It's not as if we get a heads-up when it'll happen either."

"How much easier would life be if we knew?"

"Maybe so, but it's not among our options at this point in time."

Chapter 10

Tuesday Early Evening …

LATER THAT EVENING Doreen received a text that had her wondering who had sent it. She answered it cautiously, but when another text came in right after it, she realized it was Tammy, or at least that is the name she had told Doreen. Tammy's message was simple.

I have information. Where can we meet?

Doreen winced at that but sent an immediate response. **Anywhere and when?**

Now, downtown.

"What is it with you people and downtown?" she asked out loud. Not that it was far away, but it was just one of the areas where Doreen would rather not go alone, especially at night. She sent back a thumbs-up, and they arranged to meet just outside the big monument. After that, Doreen immediately texted Mack.

He phoned her almost instantly. "You're not going there alone."

"That's why I texted you," she said. "I don't like that area of town at the best of times, but at night and all alone? No thank you."

"Good, I'll pick you up."

"Tammy said she would be there in an hour."

"That's fine. I've got to finish up a few things here before I pick you up. So, once I arrive, be prepared to leave right away. I want to take up a spot where I can keep watch."

"Sounds good," Doreen replied. Feeling much better about the whole thing, she tidied up the kitchen and put on the laundry, noting that some of her activity was just plain nerves at work. Tammy may very well have information, but her choice of location was also partly Doreen's fault. She needed to get the full names of Jed and anybody else involved in the original B&E of Arnold's house and then get some research done on them. That way, Doreen would have more information as to what exactly was going on here.

By the time the meeting hour got closer, there was still no sign of Mack. She texted him and asked, **Will you make it?**

He replied that he was just pulling in out front. She quickly grabbed her animals and headed out the front door.

He frowned at her and asked, "So you really need to bring them?"

She nodded. "Yeah, but don't ask me why."

He shrugged. "Those famous instincts of yours. So, if you feel the need to bring them, then you should bring them. What do I know? Nothing about this makes any sense, so trust your instincts."

"I guess maybe that's why I want them along." He didn't say anything else, and she quickly loaded everybody up. Once she got them all inside his truck and tucked in safe and sound, he backed out of the driveway and headed downtown. "I should have suggested a couple options about where to go and not left it completely up to Tammy," she muttered.

"It's probably a location close to her, and, if she has no wheels and doesn't have a way to travel, this is probably the safest and most convenient meeting spot for her."

"Oh, I didn't think of that," Doreen admitted, lost in her head, "but you're right. I have wheels, and she might not."

"Do you know anything about Tammy Farrow? I never got a chance to call her. Sorry."

"That's fine, and this may work out for the best anyway. I am hoping to find out some details, and we certainly need more information on the rest of the housemates or whoever else was involved in the B&E at Arnold's ten years ago."

"Yeah, I'm up for that."

She hesitated and looked over at him. "How did your day go?"

He shrugged. "I was at the crime scene again today for quite a bit."

"Right, and the body was found in a public garden?"

He nodded. "Yes, and then we went to his home today, which is also downtown."

"So he could quite possibly be connected to this whole B&E mess?"

"That's what I'm wondering. In a way it seems that it doesn't have any choice but to be connected."

"Right," she muttered. "Still, any information we come up with could be helpful."

He chuckled. "Yes, that's true. However, it's supposed to be on us, not you."

She smiled. "Got it, though I'm really not

too bothered about the niceties right now. We've got to get Arnold out of trouble."

"I don't think he's in nearly as much trouble as he thinks he is."

"Either way, it can't be terribly comfortable for him to hear that a piece of equipment stolen from him is a murder weapon."

"That does seem to be what's bothering him the most," Mack noted.

"With good reason, and you would feel terrible too, I'm sure. Any of us would be devastated."

He smiled at her. "That's true. I definitely would."

As soon as they got downtown, she asked, "Are there any good places to park here?"

"At this hour of the night there are." He looked around for a safe spot, out of the public eye. "Most of downtown is pretty empty in the evening, except for all the party-goers."

At that, she watched as they headed to one of the large parking lots. She nodded. "I'm meeting Tammy just around the corner here."

"Which is why I thought I would park over here," he shared, "and then we can go for a walk afterward."

"Oh, I would love that," she said. "And the

animals will really love it too."

"*Right,*" he replied in a dry tone.

She chuckled and shook her head. "You know you love them."

"And it's a good thing, since you are clearly a package deal."

She gave him a quick nod. "Glad you realize that."

"Oh, I do," Mack stated. "I take all four, or I don't get any."

"So true."

Once he parked, she hopped out and grabbed the leashes. "See you in a little bit." With the animals in tow, she headed toward the meeting place.

Chapter 11

Tuesday Evening ...

OUTSIDE THE MONUMENT, Doreen headed for one of the many benches in the area. With the animals tucked up close beside her, particularly Goliath, who didn't want to be on the leash at all, she sat down to wait. In a few minutes she heard a woman speak beside her.

"May I?" Tammy asked.

"Yes, sure."

Tammy sat down beside Doreen, staring at the animals. "Good God. I didn't realize who you were, until I saw *them*."

Doreen nodded. "It's one of the reasons why I travel with them. Everybody seems to know who they are, which saves me some time when approaching people."

"They are quite famous," Tammy noted, and a fan-girl moment seemed to be happening here.

Doreen stared at her in the half light. "They're friendly, if you want to pet one or two of them."

Tammy held out a hand to Mugs, who immediately nudged her hand, looking for cuddles. Tammy gave a delighted laugh and smiled. "I do miss having pets," she shared enviously.

"Can't have them where you are?"

"Are you kidding? We can't have anything where we are, especially not a life."

"Ooh, that doesn't sound good," Doreen replied.

"No, once you get into trouble, it's almost impossible to get out."

"If you did get out, where would you go? Where would you want to go?"

"Home," Tammy stated immediately. "I would be on the first bus home."

"Where is that?"

"Ontario," she replied, as a shadow of sorrow crossed her features. "I have family there, and I want to go home. Get a fresh start somewhere and get out of this nightmare, which is only half living, or maybe not living at all. Hopefully find something new to do with my life."

"A bus ticket isn't all that expensive, is it?"

Tammy eyed her with a haunted expression. "The ticket is not expensive, but buying your freedom is a whole different story."

"You need to explain that," Doreen said. "Maybe I can help."

"No, it's better if you don't know." Tammy looked around nervously, obviously jittery. "Jed's already got enough issues right now. I don't want to add to it. He's a mean, mean drunk."

"Yet he doesn't have to be drunk to be mean, does he?"

Tammy shuddered and shook her head. "No, he lashes out first and asks questions later. Hitting people is right up his alley."

"And he apparently has some hold over you?"

She snorted. "Not unlike the rest of the men in my life," she muttered.

"Is he your partner?"

"Jed doesn't have partners. He has a stable."

At that, the tumblers fell into place. Doreen whispered, "Ah, now I understand."

"Do you though? Or are you too high-and-mighty to understand?"

"No, definitely not that," Doreen replied.

"Whether I understand or not doesn't have anything to do with your getting free of him."

"He doesn't let go of people easily," Tammy explained. "Now, if you have a way to get him into jail and to keep him there for a while, and I can get free and clear before somebody else takes over for Jed, then that's a possibility I could entertain."

"That's why you are here, isn't it?"

Tammy hesitated. "Yeah, Jed's out on a business thing, and I'm supposed to be working, which is where I'm going after this. However, my telling him it was a slow evening is one thing, but me sitting here talking to you is another."

"What if he sees you?"

"I can get away with it for a little bit but not for long."

"Okay, then talk," Doreen urged. "Let's not have you getting into trouble over this. Better talk fast," she suggested.

"Unless you can pay me," Tammy noted hesitantly.

"For your time?"

"Yes, I will do all kinds of things for money."

Doreen nodded. "What I really need is information."

"Exactly, so if I bring home some money, then I could potentially fob this off as just being a bad night, but not a terribly bad night. So I can give you good information."

"I'm not even sure I have any money on me," Doreen shared.

At that, Tammy smiled. "We're a little more modern now," she began, and she held out her phone, a little debit machine on her screen.

"Good Lord," Doreen said, staring at Tammy. "You guys really are modern." Doreen pulled out a credit card and very carefully put $50 in.

Tammy eyed her and asked, "I guess you don't tip easily either, do you?"

"No," she declared. "When I told you that I spent a lot of time without a home, I meant it."

"Okay, fine," Tammy muttered. "That's enough to at least get Jed off my back for a few minutes. So, now what?"

"Now you answer my questions." Doreen was still wondering at how easily she'd handed over $50. She could hardly ask Mack to reimburse her for it, when he wouldn't have paid Tammy in the first place. Doreen sighed and began, "It would be better if you do it honestly, especially after I just paid for it."

Tammy chuckled. "That's okay, honey. Enough takers are in this world that sometimes you just have to give a little."

"Or did I just get taken a little?" Doreen asked in a neutral tone.

"If you get information, is it being taken?" Tammy asked curiously.

"I don't know. I guess it depends on what you have to offer, if you have anything that's helpful."

"If you did some checking into Jed, I'm sure you would find something that would take him off the streets," she shared.

"What's his last name?"

"Barry, Jed Barry."

"Okay, and in what direction am I supposed to be looking, outside of prostitution?"

"Pimping and theft of course. Add a little B&E into the mix. He's the go-to guy for pawn shops," Tammy shared. "Not that I've ever seen that part of him in action."

"Of course not. How many women are in the house with you?"

"Just me and one other."

"What role does Frankie have in all this?"

"He's supposed to be running errands and doing all sorts of odd jobs, but honestly Jed's getting pretty fed up with him. If I had to guess, Frankie's likely to get the boot real soon," she told Doreen. "He just doesn't know it yet."

"Will that boot be permanent or just a strong invitation to get out of the house?"

"It should just be to get out of the house," she replied, "but, if he's done anything wrong, I can't promise that."

"Has Jed killed anybody?"

"I don't know," she said.

"Any girls gone missing?"

"No, at least not that I know of. He had four, and he sold two. Now there's just the two of us."

"How long until he sells you?"

"I don't know," she muttered. "It is definitely a concern."

"Can you buy your own freedom?"

"If I had the money, sure," she replied, with a hysterical and bitter laugh. "I did mention it at one point in time, and the price that he told me doubled the next time I brought it up."

"So, in other words, it will likely double again."

"Soon enough I would think so and, for sure, if I mentioned it. It's not so much that he cares. It's just that now, with only the two of us in his stable, we're his source of income.

We pay the rent, and he doesn't have to work."

"Does he do drugs?"

"He doesn't take drugs, no," she clarified.

"Do you?"

"No, I don't."

"Explain to me why, after a really good night, you couldn't just take that money and walk to the closest bus stop and never come back."

"I've thought about it," she admitted, "a lot actually. I just haven't gotten there yet."

"Why not?" Doreen wasn't sure why she was pushing this *leaving on a bus* angle so much when she needed to get answers for other questions, but Tammy, if she were in trouble, needed to explain in a way that Doreen could understand.

"Sometimes you don't realize just how much of a prisoner you are," Tammy said.

"So, Tammy, if I were to give you $400 right now, what would you do?" Tammy stared at her. "I mean, that's all a ticket is, isn't it? A bus ticket should take you across Canada to Ontario, taking two to three days."

Tammy gave Doreen a sideways look. "Are you offering?"

"Not yet," Doreen replied, "but it makes me

wonder if you would even take it because you have that opportunity on a regular basis."

Tammy gave a bitter laugh. "Now you're judging me."

"No, I'm trying to understand you because I was in a similar relationship," she shared, stopping to clear her tightening throat. "I wasn't in a similar situation per se, but I was definitely in an ugly relationship, where I was being hit and belittled and controlled all the time. Yet I only left when I was forced to do so. I'm still trying to figure out why it took me so long."

Tammy stared at her. "You?"

"Yeah, me," Doreen confirmed. "I get that most people look at me and don't see a battered woman, and I work hard to remind myself where she came from. Yet, when you get an opportunity to change, you need to grab that chance and run with it."

"So far you haven't given me that opportunity to change," Tammy pointed out.

"I'm not sure you would run with it."

"I don't know either," Tammy admitted. "It's scary."

Doreen smiled at that. "Now *that* I understand in spades."

"Do you though?"

"I do," she stated. "I get it. An awful lot out there you don't really want to deal with. An awful lot out there is ugly. Watching over your shoulder is definitely not how you would choose to live your life, but do you really think Jed would care enough to follow you back to Ontario?"

Tammy shook her head. "No, he wouldn't."

"Since you have family, did you ever ask them for help?"

"No, I didn't," she said, taking a deep breath. "I don't really want them to know how far I've fallen."

"Do you think if you got back there on your own, you could make a new beginning?"

Tammy nodded.

"Because your family would help?"

"Yeah, they told me to just get back there, and they would be there for me."

"Do you believe them?" Doreen asked.

"I do, very much so," Tammy replied. "It's just hard to think that I'm bringing all this baggage with me."

"Maybe not," Doreen countered. "Maybe you can't bring it with you. Maybe you'll just walk away and leave it here. Then you can start fresh."

"Is that even possible?"

"I think it is," Doreen noted, "but it takes time and effort and maybe some counseling on the other end."

"I would do anything I could," Tammy declared, "but first I have to get clear of this guy. Jed is not one to mess with."

"Meaning, you *do* think he'll come after you."

"Meaning, I would spend a lot of time looking over my shoulder, not knowing how far his reach goes."

"*Right*," Doreen muttered. "So tell me more about Jed Barry."

"I don't know if that's his real name," she began. "He wound up down here at some point. As far I know, he was homeless for a couple winters, then hooked up with some *characters*," she said, with emphasis. "I don't know who they are, but he somehow ended up with one girl, and, with her, he ended up getting enough money to get them both into a place so she had a bedroom where she could bring her johns back to. As the story goes, from that Jed slowly built up."

Tammy took a second and looked around them. The park was empty, and only a few people were in sight, with no one near them. "Jed's not a big player at all. He's a two-bit player really, but the fact that he's a player at all means that nobody is safe because he deals in fear and anger."

"Of course," Doreen agreed. "That's how they manage people, isn't it?" Tammy nodded slowly. "Because you're petrified to do anything wrong, and, no matter what happens, he gets away with it."

"Nothing quite like a fist to keep you in line."

Doreen winced, reminded of her own injuries. "That part I know all too well."

Tammy studied Doreen in the shadows. "Would you really help me?"

"Yes," Doreen stated. "To what extent, I'm not sure. I guess it depends on whether you're serious or whether you'll take my money and just put it into booze and be back out on the streets again. Worse yet would you be supporting this Jed guy with my money, instead of working toward a better future for yourself."

"That's really not my intention, but I can see why you might be doubtful."

"Okay, so we'll have to see how best to proceed with that. What can you tell me about Frankie?"

"Frankie is Jed's lap dog. Frankie's a loser.

He cheats on his friends and does anything for a buck. Anything goes with that one. He can't seem to keep a real job, which is how Jed likes it—I think because it keeps Frankie dependent on Jed. The fact that Frankie will be on the streets really quick will be bad news for him. He's not that well equipped for it."

"Why? What'll he do if that happens?"

"In his case, it won't be pretty, but he'll probably end up rummaging through garbage cans again, looking for meals, sleeping under porches to get out of the wind, and eventually he'll start stealing and doing anything he can to get some money. That's my best guess."

"So, he'll sink right back down to that level again."

"Exactly. In that way Jed's been good for Frankie because he's cleaned up his act a bit."

"Did Frankie ever screw over Jed?"

"If he hasn't, he will," Tammy declared. "That's just who Frankie is."

"*Nice*," Doreen muttered.

"Not nice at all, but I'm not a fool, and I do recognize Frankie for who he is."

"I got that same feeling too," Doreen replied, pondering it. "How much longer do you have with me out here?"

"Not much," she said, looking all nervous again. "I need to go. Fifty bucks doesn't get you much time in this world." She looked over at Doreen, gave her a half a smile, and added, "Unless you want to kick in another fifty bucks."

Doreen shook her head. "Nope, I've already hit my limit, but you've got my number. So anytime you're serious about getting out, and you want to head back to Ontario and leave this all behind, text me."

Tammy hesitated.

Doreen studied her. "If I gave you bus ticket money and found out you stayed here, found out you took my money and used it instead of taking on a john, as much as I'll understand, it won't make me happy. And you might find yourself in trouble with the police for doing this kind of work."

"We do a lot to ensure that doesn't happen," she replied.

"Does Jed pay anybody to keep you guys out of trouble?"

She shrugged. "Not that I know of, but we're constantly on the move. You do know there are bigger organizations, bigger stables in town," she pointed out. "So, as long as we stay out of trouble, the cops generally leave us alone. No one pays us any mind at all."

"It's hard to believe this has been going on here all the time. I've never caught wind of it."

"Are you kidding? It's in every town, everywhere. Those are just the facts of life, and, if you think differently, you're wrong." With that, Tammy got up and left as quickly as she could.

Doreen sat here and watched Tammy disappear around the corner, thinking how her animals had all easily accepted Tammy. Maybe Doreen could too.

Chapter 12

Tuesday Late Evening …

DOREEN SLOWLY WALKED toward Mack, knowing where he was, having texted him that her meeting with Tammy was over. She continued to ponder Tammy's words. "Is the world so messed up that prostitution really is everywhere?" she asked Mack, as soon as she filled him in on Jed's stable in Kelowna.

He nodded. "It's pretty well in every town, in every country. Some places it's a bigger industry. Some places it's smaller. Some places it's legal, and they're set up with protection. In a lot of places, you'll find they're on the streets, on the corners, trying to turn a trick or two, either for their next fix or to keep their masters off their backs," Mack explained, shaking his head, keeping an eye out around them. "It's a sad world out there."

She nodded. "You don't really realize how sad."

When they got to a large green expanse, away from any traffic, she unleashed Mugs and Goliath. "Come on, guys. Let's run." She had a bit too much energy coiled up inside her after that disconcerting conversation with Tammy. So Doreen ran and raced around, tossing sticks, and generally kicked up a storm, while the animals kept up their antics around her. When Doreen finally collapsed, they bounced on top of her. And Thaddeus on top of them.

Mack was laughing at her by now. "I don't know what brought that on," he said, "but that's a side of you I don't really see that often."

She smiled. "It's a side most people don't see," she admitted, with a chuckle. "I just had to release some energy. After that conversation, I needed it."

"Apparently you did," he agreed, with a bright smile. He bent down to give her a hand up, when they heard a *crack* overhead. He immediately dropped on top of her and whispered, "Don't move." She cried out for the animals, and he placed a hand over her mouth. "*Shh*," he whispered. "I don't know if that was meant for us or not, but it sure could have been." When a second shot splattered the tree above their heads, he nodded, quickly bounded to his feet, and pulled her along with him, behind the tree.

She stared up at him, her eyes huge as she stared at him. "That was definitely meant for us," she whispered.

He peered around the tree and nodded. "Sounds like it." He already had his phone out, calling for backup.

She sank into a pile at the base of the tree. "Good Lord," she whispered. "What was that all about?"

"I don't know for sure, but it was likely about the conversation you just had."

She stared at him. "I hope not because that means Tammy is in trouble. She won't last long if Jed is shooting at us."

"Oh, I'm sure, if she's not working and doesn't have an alibi by now, she's in trouble," Mack confirmed. "Nothing good comes out of these kinds of conversations, if you're expected to be somewhere and are lying about it."

Doreen winced. "Yet she seemed to be quite comfortable doing it," she muttered.

"Maybe she's serious about getting out—or

maybe not," he said. "For all we know, she's the one shooting at us right now."

Doreen gasped. "I really don't want to think about that."

"Maybe not, but it doesn't change anything though," he stated.

She nodded and waited, but no more shots were coming their way. She looked up at him. "Is it safe to leave?"

"No, not yet." Moments later, they heard sirens in the distance, and he smiled with a grim satisfaction. "Now it should be safe. That should put a stop to our shooter."

"Yeah, but that doesn't mean anybody saw anything."

"No, but you can bet that we'll be all over Tammy now."

"Great. That's hardly what she needs."

"Maybe not, but, if Jed's got something going on that we need to shut down, then we need the information to do it. That means we have to nail him. If this tasing is how he deals with interference in his life, that'll come to a stop really soon as well," Mack declared, his tone hard. "I don't care where he came from or how hard his life was. You don't get to keep people as prisoners to do your will just because you feel like it. Jed should get a real job and live a real life."

"I think they do have prisoners," Doreen agreed. "Guys like that always seem to think they're owed something."

"Yeah, we need to find Frankie as well and have a little talk with him."

"Yeah, good luck with that. Tammy seemed to think that Frankie would get the boot pretty fast, and from Jed."

At that, Mack turned and frowned at her. "Seriously?"

She nodded. "Frankie's apparently not been doing his job or not holding up his end, whatever you want to call it. No idea when this might happen, but Tammy seemed pretty certain that Frankie wouldn't be living there much longer."

"We need to pick him up now then," Mack announced, placing another call. Soon he disconnected and returned his attention to her. "Okay, so we've got an order out for Frankie to be picked up. I've also put out an APB on Jed, and I'll go pick up Tammy right now." He eyed Doreen and asked, "Can I trust you to go home and to stay there?"

She smiled. "I've got no problem going home at this stage, but won't I need to stay here and make a statement first?"

"We'll catch you tomorrow."

With that said, he escorted her to a police cruiser parked near Mack's truck. He gave the uniformed officer instructions for her to be delivered home. The officer just nodded, and she got into the back with the animals and watched as Mack slammed the door on the black-and-white. Then he strolled off and was soon out of sight.

She groaned. "Sure doesn't feel like this is over."

The cop in the front seat nodded. "Correct, this is just beginning."

Chapter 13

Wednesday Morning ...

THE NEXT MORNING, Doreen's mind was in overdrive, still waiting for Mack to call and to fill her in on what was going on. She was going stir-crazy, and the fact that he hadn't called was starting to get to her. It's not that she was afraid for his safety at this point, but she wanted answers, and yet she knew he was not prepared to give her any. That also drove her nuts.

So she'd already scrubbed the bathrooms, washed the floors, and put on laundry again. Having nothing else to do, she changed the bedding and even now was wiping out the inside of the cupboards. When her phone finally rang at ten o'clock this morning, and he asked what she was doing, she quickly gave him a rundown.

After a moment of shocked silence, he

asked, "Seriously?"

"Yeah, I clean house when I'm waiting for you to call and to fill me in." The frustration in her tone could not have been more evident.

"I can't tell you very much," he replied.

"But you can tell me more than you have, which is nothing."

"Yeah, that was the plan," he admitted, "but, at this moment in time, all I can tell you is that we have no sign of Jed or Frankie anywhere."

"What about Tammy?"

"She's disappeared into the woodwork too."

"That's not cool, Mack," Doreen snapped.

A long silent moment came from the other end. "Leave it alone," Mack said finally.

"*Sure*," she muttered. "I'll leave it alone all right, but we need answers, and we need them now, or I'm afraid we'll find Tammy's or Frankie's body, or both of them, dumped somewhere."

"Let's hope not," Mack replied. "We are working on this and are doing everything we can."

"I know," she conceded, "and I'm not blaming you. I'm still a little rattled knowing someone was intentionally shooting at us last night. That puts the whole thing in a whole different light."

He hesitated, then replied, "Listen. I didn't say anything last night, but that sounded an awful lot like a police-issue gun last night."

"What?" she asked, her heart stopping. "Do you think one of the cops is after you? Is that what this has come to now?"

"No," he stated. "I don't. … It could be yet another stolen police weapon in the wrong hands."

With his tone so firm, she relaxed slightly. "That would really not be cool. It's bad enough that Arnold is dealing with this, without having more cops dealing with more issues like this."

"I agree with you there," Mack said, "so we're not going in that direction."

"Yeah? I'm not sure what we're supposed to do about it right now then," she said, "because it sure seems we're heading in that direction. And it's too soon for you to be sure a police-issue gun was used, right?"

"No, but …"

"Right, I get it. What about someone retired or anybody kicked off the force? Somebody who maybe ran into trouble and is looking for some payback or got into some trouble and now is being forced to cover somebody's tracks?"

"All are possibilities that we're looking into. My department looked for a stolen police gun but found nothing, even going back years and years. One of the guys is checking in Vancouver, just to see if maybe a police gun had been stolen over there. We're not holding out much hope, just checking two departments. This is where that nationwide database would come in helpful," Mack complained. "However, this is where you back off, and we take it a step up now."

"*Ha*." She snorted. "The minute there's any danger, I'm being told to back off."

"Of course you are," Mack agreed in exasperation. "We want to keep you safe, remember?"

"Of course you do," she muttered in frustration, "and I want to keep you safe."

After more silence on the other end, he replied, "I'll count that as progress too."

She groaned. "You know perfectly well that no progress is required on that front."

"I'm not sure about that," Mack countered. "I don't think you're fully into this relationship thing yet."

"I am," she declared. "I definitely am."

His tone brightened. "In that case, we have a few things to talk about."

"No, we really don't," she stated nervously, "unless it's got to do with this case?"

"Oh, no, you're not holding me hostage on *any* case. Not when I'm *not* allowed to hold you hostage to keep you safe. I'll call you when I have something that I'm authorized to tell you." And, with that, he was gone.

She groaned as she stared down at her phone. How was she supposed to get more information? At that, she immediately picked up the phone and dialed Nan. "Do you know anything about a Jed Barry, Frankie some-body, or Tammy Farrow—or maybe a cop who got kicked off the force for any disgraced or dishonorable discharges?"

A shocked silence came on the other end. "Good Lord," Nan muttered. "I hadn't realized you had another case, and obviously it's important."

"Well, let's see. I was shot at downtown last night, twice," Doreen began. When her grandmother gasped in shock, Doreen winced. "Don't worry. It wasn't as bad as that sounded." She quickly explained further.

Nan replied, "But that sounded way worse than what you originally told me. What the devil is going on here?"

"I'm not sure. All I know is somebody broke into Arnold's place ten years ago. By the looks of it, they stole some things, including his Taser, and now that Taser has showed up at a crime scene where some poor guy was basically zapped to death. Probably the guy your delivery people were talking about that you overheard."

"Good Lord," Nan muttered.

"So I went to Arnold's friend Frankie, who had been living with Arnold back then and yet not at home at the time of the B&E, who supposedly had not seen a thing. Yet, not only had Frankie seen an awful lot, he had basically blabbered to some unsavory acquaintances all about the fact that Arnold was working the night shift, so his place could be emptied. As you can imagine, they ripped off Arnold, and Arnold's *friend* all but arranged it."

"Of course," Nan noted in that ironic tone that she was so good at. "That's what friends are for."

"Exactly. That led me to Jed, some scary roommate of Arnold's and Tammy's. Both work for this Jed guy, paying off what they owe, with Frankie running errands and Tammy working the streets for Jed."

"Oh my," Nan muttered. "Wow, you've really had a night of it."

"Yeah, it's turned quite ugly once the shooting started."

"I didn't see anything about it in the papers," Nan said cautiously.

"Maybe Mack had something to do with that. I don't know. As of this morning, he doesn't have any more information, and nobody they've been looking for has been picked up yet."

"But, as long as they're looking to pick them up, that should be some progress."

"Sure," Doreen conceded, "but, in the meantime, somebody shot at us, and I want more information. I'm just restless, and I can't let it go, Nan."

Her grandmother sighed. "I can understand your being a little upset about that," she murmured, "but maybe this is one that you need to let Mack handle. On other cases, any shooting came somewhat later, but, by the looks of it, you were barely on this case a day and were already shot at."

"I would let it go if I wasn't already involved and if Tammy wasn't half ready to leave this Jed guy and get a life for herself."

"And, of course, somehow you feel responsible." Nan seemed exasperated.

"Not responsible," Doreen clarified, "but, if I can do something to help, then I want to help."

"And you really think you're the person to do the helping?" Nan asked curiously.

"I certainly understand what she's going through."

"Yes, I can see that. What is it you want to do, dear?"

A wealth of understanding came in Nan's tone. "I don't really know. I guess I was hoping there would be a way to get the $400 to give her a bus ticket and get her out of town."

"Will that really get her anywhere?"

"I researched on Google and got that as the average bus fare. Tammy told me that she has family to go to, but she doesn't want them to know what she's been doing. She wants to make a fresh start and not take any of this mess with her."

"Of course not," Nan agreed. "That wouldn't be much fun. Obviously, when you start fresh, you don't want to carry that kind of baggage along."

"Exactly," Doreen replied, "yet I don't know whether she's ready to leave Jed or not."

"Interesting that somebody in such a mess isn't ready to leave him."

"Yeah, interesting, but maybe not that surprising."

"Explain, please," Nan said, her tone sharp.

"It's easy for me to put myself in that same place, before I ended up separated from Mathew," she began. "I found it very difficult to even contemplate or to accept that I had a problem. However, once I did, getting out was too much to consider. At least Tammy knows that she's in a bad spot and wants to get out."

"So, of course, you want to help her."

"Yes, I guess I do."

"Nothing wrong with wanting to help, my dear. It's a matter of making sure that the help is of value and isn't something you'll end up regretting."

"I don't think I'll regret it," she replied, "but I don't really have a whole lot of money."

"But you do have a lot of money coming."

"Exactly, but it's just not here yet."

"I can help a little bit, but …"

"Right, *but*."

"Okay, why don't you call and see how much a bus ticket would cost if we were to send Tammy back to her family. Then, if she does seem 100 percent invested in that new life, we'll at least know for sure how much money is needed."

"Right," Doreen muttered.

"While you're doing that, I'll head down to the kitchen to see what I can snag for tea, and you can come on down, and we'll talk more about it."

"Okay, thanks, Nan. I didn't really mean to bring you into this."

"Of course you did," she said immediately. "That's what I'm here for. It's important that you have the opportunity to contact me whenever it's needed, particularly when it comes to stuff like this. My life wasn't always so sweet and sunny that I don't understand how, when trouble comes, sometimes you need a little help."

"I knew that anyway," Doreen stated. "You've always been there to help me."

"And now you want to be there to help somebody else. I get it," Nan said. "We just have to ensure that the help we provide is the help she needs." And, with that, Nan disconnected.

Doreen quickly looked up the prices of a bus ticket to head back to the other side of the country, and it wasn't cheap. They could get it on sale potentially for just over $600. That sounded like a hurdle, but if Tammy could manage the food along the way, then that would at least get her home.

Pondering that, Doreen packed up the animals and headed over to Nan's place. Not seeing Nan on her patio, Doreen walked inside. Nan sat at her kitchen table, pondering a pad of paper in front of her. She looked up and smiled. "There you are, child."

Doreen gave her grandmother a hug. "Hey, I didn't mean to worry you with all this."

"If I don't have something to worry about, I just create something to worry about. So better to have a real problem to solve," she declared, with a smile. "Now, do you really feel Tammy was serious about leaving?"

"Yes. I do think she's serious. I just don't know if she's ready."

"There is a big difference, and that makes sense to me."

"Unfortunately, just because she says she is, it doesn't mean she's all in."

"What do you think it'll take for her to get there?"

Doreen studied her grandmother for a moment. "I would think understanding that her situation is hopeless and going downhill, while knowing a ray of sunshine is out there waiting for her."

"Right," Nan replied. "I would agree with that."

"What are you thinking?" Doreen asked her.

"I think we should buy the ticket, so she doesn't use that money elsewhere. I have a little bit of money, and if a couple hundred dollars can make a difference in somebody's life, then it's worth spending the money on Tammy," Nan added, looking at Doreen intently. Then she raised her glasses, put them on her nose, and looked over them. "I also know that, once you head down this pathway, you'll want to help more people like this."

"Is that wrong?" she whispered.

"No," Nan stated, giving Doreen a beautiful smile. "Charity, particularly for those in need, is huge, but it can come at the expense of your own safety, which is not optimal. We've come so far to get you here, and putting you at risk now seems questionable."

"It certainly won't be Mathew who comes after me," Doreen stated, "and I do understand what it's like to have somebody like that in your life. I have lived that life, Nan."

"That's why you want to help, and I'm all for your helping," Nan said. "Don't get me wrong. I just want to ensure that the help we give is help that'll give the best benefits with minimal risk."

"I hadn't really thought about that," Doreen admitted, "and it's something that we do need to consider. Just because Tammy says she's ready, we don't want her to turn around and spend that money on drugs. So I agree with your suggestion that we buy her ticket. It's $600 plus, by the way, for the bus fare," she shared. "That's the cheapest rate I could find, and Tammy still has to have money for food. It will take several days to get there."

"Of course it will. You can drive across Canada in three days but don't plan on sleeping while you do it."

"Have you ever taken that trip?" she asked Nan curiously.

"I have, but it was decades ago." She waved her hand, as if of no consequence. "It might be nice to do that kind of traveling sometime, but I would do it better the second time around," she noted.

Doreen frowned. "We have such a huge country, and I haven't had a chance to really enjoy it or explore it."

"One day you may get that chance," Nan said, "but not now. Soon though, very soon."

Doreen smiled at her grandmother. "What makes it *soon*, Nan? Do you expect Mack to take me on a road trip to see more of Canada?"

"He could. Yet I wouldn't want you to leave while I'm still here," Nan admitted. "So I'm being selfish when I say that."

At that, Doreen frowned and patted her grandmother's hand. "I have no intention of going anywhere for a long time, and I certainly don't want to envision my life without you either."

"Good. I'm just selfish enough and greedy enough to want to keep you to myself," Nan admitted, "but I'm also fully aware that you and Mack need time alone to grow your relationship together. I support that, so that I don't have to worry about you." Nan gave her a beaming smile. "As I mentioned before, if I could arrange life to suit me, you and Mack would be married tomorrow and staying put locally, with lots of *Nan time* involved—or something along that line." Nan chuckled. "Life isn't quite so simple."

As soon as the tea was ready, she poured two cups, while they discussed the options of helping Tammy. "You do realize that once you help one …" Nan began, looking over at her granddaughter.

Doreen nodded. "I know. I heard you the first time. Now, depending on how much money is coming in soon with the antiques and whatnot, I was wondering …"

Nan immediately nodded. "It's important to give back, as long as you first ensure that you're safe and secure financially," she stated. "So, when all that money finally lands, we'll look at what options you have and how much money you can free up in order to help some of these people. I'm right there with you, understanding what you want to do, even if you don't."

"I don't really know what it entails," Doreen admitted. "I mean, helping is something that I think I can do, but I don't know how I would do it. So that's still a bit of a challenge."

"Challenge is a good thing," Nan agreed, chuckling. "Do you think Mack will have a problem with it?"

"No, I don't think so. And the more situations we can help like this, it might clean up the streets that much more."

"Oh, my dear," Nan replied. "You do realize that in our society, as soon as you clean up one of these problems, another one immediately pops up."

"I understand," Doreen replied, staring around the gardens. "I'm not naïve. I just want to see the world as a rosier place."

At that, Nan beamed at her affectionately. "Understood, so let's start thinking about a plan." And that's what they did, the two women huddled over tea and conversation, talking out how they could possibly help Tammy and any others like her.

Chapter 14

Wednesday Noon ...

WALKING HOME, DOREEN was in a much happier place. She hadn't realized just how much she felt the need to help somebody else who hadn't been quite as lucky as Doreen had been. Not everybody had a grandmother like Doreen had, and most certainly not everybody had a houseful of antiques that would bring her a huge payday. Or the fact that Doreen's marriage and divorce—or what should have been a divorce—had an awful lot of money and property coming her way too. Between Mathew's and Robin's estates, Doreen would eventually come close to being filthy rich. She had been blessed in ways she had no idea were even possible.

So, if a few hundred dollars could make a difference to someone else, then Doreen wanted to make that happen. It would take some effort, some time, and some legal woolgathering and research in order to figure out just what Doreen could do. She would probably need to bring Nick on board to sort it out in a legal sense, but there was time for that. It's not as if Doreen needed to or even could jump on it right now. Not until her other legal affairs were settled, and she fully understood her financial position anyway. But, in Tammy's case, there wasn't a whole lot of time to wait.

Doreen also wanted to confirm that Tammy was sincere and ready. People would say one thing and do another, but it didn't always have anything to do with the real truth of the matter.

Now at home, Doreen stepped inside through the kitchen back door, letting the animals off the leashes. Mugs immediately started tearing around, barking and barking like crazy. She froze and realized she hadn't armed the security system. She walked gingerly through the main floor of the house, but Mugs didn't find anybody. He continued to bark though, obviously distressed. That got to her because Mugs acting this crazy had to be bad. Goliath's fur was fluffed up as he stalked through the house, sniffing the air. She headed back to the kitchen, and, sure enough, the window was open.

She groaned, staring at it. "I didn't open that. I know I didn't."

She took a moment to really consider it, but she never opened that window. It wasn't that easy to get to, but somebody had obviously opened it and, with her luck, had come inside. Now, she turned and stared around the rest of the house warily. Were they still inside? That was the question, as she knew the house had way-too-many hiding places. The last thing she wanted was to have somebody jump out at her. She quickly pulled out her phone and called Mack.

"I'm really busy, Doreen."

"Yeah, of course you are, but it seems I had an intruder in the house. Based on the way Mugs is acting, they could still be here."

"Crap. I'll be right there."

She had to smile when he ended the call and dropped everything to come to her rescue. It's not that she needed the rescue, mind you, but it was sure nice to know that, when she was in trouble, he would be there, no questions asked. She headed outside and stayed in the backyard as she waited. It was a beautiful day, and sitting outside wasn't exactly a hardship, which brought up the question of how somebody had known she wasn't home.

Richard popped his head over the fence and frowned at her. "What's the matter?" he asked suspiciously. "You look like you've been through the spin cycle."

"Did you hear anything going on at my house?"

"Yeah, sure. Heard you were doing some banging around. I was about to ask you what was going on, but my brother phoned, so I talked to him."

"I wasn't home," she stated bluntly.

He stared at her, his eyebrows shooting up to his hairline. "What do you mean, you weren't home?" He was confused.

"I just now got home," she stated, "and my kitchen window was open, as if somebody gained entry that way."

He glared at the house. "Is somebody inside?"

"I don't know. I called Mack."

He gave a sage nod. "Nice to know you've got a cop on speed dial."

She snorted. "Not sure he's all that happy about it."

"No, I don't imagine he is," Richard agreed calmly. "Yet it's a good deal for you."

Just the way he said it made it sound as if he wouldn't get such a good deal. "It is the cops, Richard," she explained. "They come when anybody calls."

He snorted at that. "But they come to some places faster than others. That's all I am saying."

She glared at him. "I'm not doing anything to get special attention."

"Don't think you have to at this point," Richard stated, with that wiser-than-thou expression of his. "Pretty sure you're on everybody's speed dial at this point."

She snorted. "It would be nice if I weren't on a *criminal's* speed dial list. No matter what, I want some privacy,"

At that, he burst out laughing. "Now that's a good point. You do seem to get more than your share of intruders, don't you? I wouldn't want to be on their list either. What have you gotten yourself into now?"

She shrugged. "Somebody's in trouble, all right?" she shared. "So naturally I was asking a few questions."

He gave an eye roll at that. "Just a few?"

"Yes, just a few," she snapped and glared

at him. "I don't try to cause problems."

"You don't have to try. It happens naturally around you."

He did have a point there, and she seemed to piss off people these days. All without even trying the tiniest bit. "I wasn't trying to upset anyone," she muttered.

"Good because I can't really imagine the havoc you could create if you were actually trying," he replied, with a gleeful snort at his own joke. "I hear the cops."

"How can you tell? There's not exactly a siren."

"No, but, hey, with all the stuff going on right now, it wouldn't be the worst thing in the world if they would use one."

"Sometimes it's hard on me though. It seems everybody is always coming here."

"*Ya think*?" he asked, with another snicker.

He was right. She heard a couple doors slam out in front, and she walked to the side yard and called out, "Mack, I'm in the back."

He came around to the side fence and looked her over and asked, "Are you okay?"

She nodded. "I'm fine. I've just been back here, talking to Richard." She turned to look back, and Richard, of course, had disappeared. He always scrambled away before any authority was near enough to ask him anything. "Well, I *was* talking to Richard," she clarified. She pointed to her kitchen window and then noted Chester had come with Mack. She smiled at him. "Hey, you're probably just here to see if there's any leftover pizza."

He grinned at her. "That's not the primary purpose of the visit, but if you happen to have any—"

"Nope, sorry. I pretty well ate up all the leftovers."

At that, Mack nodded. "She's not lying either."

Chester frowned at her. "You don't look like you eat very much at all."

At that, Mack laughed out loud. "This girl can put away the groceries just fine," he muttered, as he studied her kitchen window. He turned to her and asked, "Did you go upstairs?"

"I didn't go upstairs or down into the basement. I pretty much stayed outside after calling you."

He winced at that. "Fine." He looked at Chester. "You want to check downstairs?"

Chester nodded, then he headed to the side door of the garage. Mack went in through the kitchen door and headed upstairs. She sat down on the deck and waited.

Mack was down and back out first. He took one look at her, and she shook her head. "No Chester yet." Mack immediately disappeared.

She stood up, holding back Mugs, who definitely wanted to follow Mack. Goliath was nowhere to be seen at the moment. Thaddeus had been really quiet, worrisome even. She looked over at him, seated on her shoulder. "You okay, bud?"

He looked at her. "Thaddeus is fine."

She stared. "You can't possibly know what you're saying," she muttered.

"Thaddeus is fine," he repeated, then gave a quick nod, before he turned and looked off defiantly in the other direction.

"Are you upset with me?" she asked. "It's not as if I've done anything to piss you off lately."

"Thaddeus is fine."

She wasn't sure who he was imitating, but she was worried it might be her. She sighed. "Okay, so I've upset you somehow, and I'm just not sure how." Thaddeus didn't respond this time. She did remember mentioning Big Guy to Thaddeus a few days ago, and she had yet to bring Thaddeus to visit Big Guy. That could very well be why Thaddeus was upset with her. She vowed to do that soon, but she couldn't do that today.

Before she realized it, Mack was returning, and Chester was with him. She sighed with relief. "Chester, when you didn't come back, I was afraid somebody was down there, holding you hostage."

He shook his head. "That's a heck of a basement you've got there. Too bad you don't have access from inside the house."

"Yes and no," she replied. "So far, having access to the basement would not necessarily have been good, considering the number of times I've had people here, inside my home, wanting to do me harm."

"That's a good point," Chester agreed. "You do have a tendency to piss off people."

She raised her hands. "Apparently even Thaddeus seems to think so right now."

Mack looked at her. "What's wrong with Thaddeus?"

"I don't know, but he's kind of off."

At that, Thaddeus gave her a look. "Thaddeus is fine." And, sure enough, he got the emphasis just right.

Mack started to snicker. "I don't know, buddy. It doesn't seem as if you are doing very fine at all."

Thaddeus walked over and hopped from Doreen's shoulder to his. "Thaddeus loves Mack."

Mack gently brushed his feathers and said, "That's all right, buddy. I love you too." And the two of them just sat here and had a mutual admiration circle going on, while Doreen and Chester watched.

She shook her head. "Even my bird has fallen in love with Mack," she muttered.

Chester looked at her, then grinned, and said, "It's a good thing."

She nodded. "It is a good thing. It would be a little hard if they didn't like him. Of course, it's not that easy if they like him too much either."

"Surely you can't be jealous."

Such astonishment filled his tone that she had to laugh. "No, I'm not jealous at all. I know what this crew is like, and, as soon as you think you understand what my animals are up to, they completely surprise you."

Chester chuckled and turned his attention to Mack, as did Doreen.

"So," she asked, "the house is safe?"

"It's safe," Mack replied. "I don't know whether we should try fingerprinting this window or not."

"I doubt it would be worth your time," she muttered. "Chances are whoever was here used gloves."

"But we don't know that," Chester pointed out. "The minute they start getting cocky, that's when we have a chance to capture them. I think we would be better off to check for fingerprints." And, with that, he dashed out front, then came back with a small kit. "I've been packing this around all the time, hoping I could use it." He looked over at Mack for permission.

Mack shrugged and said, "Sure, fly at it."

Within minutes Chester crowed and cried out, "Look at this."

They walked over, and, sure enough, with a dusting of the black powder, a fingerprint was found on one of the window edges.

She sighed in joy. "I don't remember ever touching this window, so it shouldn't be my fingerprint. Any chance we can figure out who this is?"

"I hope so," Chester replied, as he carefully set down a piece of plastic and picked up the black-dusted print.

"That's awesome." She rubbed her hands together. "It would sure be nice if nobody would get away with this for once."

"Hey, nobody's gotten away with anything so far," Mack reminded her. "You've done pretty well at getting everybody caught."

"Yet here we are, with a sloppy break-in and getting shot at. Did you find any of the people you were trying to pick up? Any sign of Jed, Tammy, or Frankie?"

Mack shook his head. "No. So far, none of them have shown up."

She frowned at that. "You know what I didn't get to do yet, don't you?"

He asked, "What's that?"

"I didn't go to the Taser crime scene, and I need to do that."

"Not right now," he stated.

"Why not?" she murmured. "Maybe we'll find something." Still, with the guys here, even if Mack wasn't cooperating, the relief washed over her all at once, and she sat down with a hard *plunk* on the patio chair. "I'm glad you came anyway, even if I can't go to your crime scenes," she muttered.

He frowned at her. "Came *anyway*? Really? Obviously somebody tried to get into your house and may very well have succeeded," he pointed out. "The question is, what were they after?"

She shrugged. "I don't know. It's not as if I

have much. Everything that's important is in a safe deposit box or scanned, if it's related to the cases I've worked on. Some of those files of Solomon's are probably the most important things I have here." She watched Mack, as he tried to control a burst of laughter and failed miserably. She stared at him in aston-ishment. "What's so funny about that?"

"We've been to an awful lot of break-ins over my career, and the women are typically worried about jewelry, clothes, shoes, hand-bags, money, furniture, and God-only-knows what else," he explained, still chuckling. "And here you are, worried about somebody steal-ing your case files."

She understood his outburst and respond-ed with a sheepish grin, "Those are all scanned in too, so, even if somebody did take them, I have digital copies of it all."

"Right," he muttered, with a nod, no longer smiling. "So, the next thing we have to con-sider is that they were looking for you."

That statement wiped the smile off her face as well. "They were after me?"

Chapter 15

Wednesday Early Afternoon ...

WHEN CHESTER LEFT with the fingerprint from the window ledge, just Doreen and Mack remained. She sat outside on the deck, with a calming cup of tea, while Mack drank coffee.

"Do you really think the intruder was after me?" she asked. "And does that also mean the shooter was after me too?"

Mack sighed. "I'm not sure. I'm still trying to come up with a reason for that."

She nodded. "I guess it's almost to be expected at this point, isn't it?"

"I was hoping it wouldn't be," he stated. "The fact that you live alone doesn't help either."

She looked over at him, and her lips twitched. "Does that mean you want to move in?"

He eyed her in surprise, then smiled. "No, that's not what I was saying at all. Not that I would say no, if the invitation was there. That would definitely be something to consider. However, if I thought the danger was any worse than this, I *would* move in, and you wouldn't get a choice."

She laughed out loud at that. "At that point, I wouldn't fight you or argue about it either. If somebody is determined to come after me, I'll hardly turn down the assistance. Although, I will say, the animals have held me in good stead so far. They may be ready to fight even *you* off of me."

"You wish, but we can't count on that, particularly when Thaddeus appears to be in a snit over something."

"Yeah, if only I knew for sure what he was mad at me about," she muttered, with a headshake.

"Could you find out?" he asked her curiously. "It seems Thaddeus has his own agenda to whatever it is he's working on."

"I don't even know if it's so much his own agenda. Sometimes, when I don't take him down to visit Big Guy, or if I don't do something that he thinks I should, he gets miffed at me."

"*Miffed* is par for the course with animals and people," he noted. "So, is it more than that?" he asked gently.

She shrugged. "I don't know. Has he seen something or did I not do something? It could be anything or all of those things. … I thought I was doing well learning his language, but he's the one learning mine," she admitted.

Thaddeus flew from his perch in the living room to join them on the deck, perhaps hearing his name mentioned. He landed on Doreen's arm and soon settled on her shoulder.

"I think that's probably pretty common," Mack noted, as he gently stroked the African Grey's feathers. Thaddeus ruffled up, then looked at him and walked from Doreen's shoulder, down her arm, and over to Mack.

"He definitely likes you," she pointed out.

After a moment of silence, Mack gently spoke. "Does that bother you?"

She shook her head. "No. I see our role as loving custodians of the animals, and, if we're lucky, they love us back. Plus I think it's good for Thaddeus to have a more rounded repertoire of people in his world, and you've been a mainstay for many months now. No wonder he loves you."

"He's become part of my family too."

At that, Thaddeus rubbed his beak against Mack's cheek.

Doreen smiled. "Did he just whisper to you?"

"I'm not sure," Mack noted, looking at the bird with a frown.

"I think he's imitating us and doing the best he can to enunciate words. However, maybe he can't hear or understand all the nuances of a whisper."

"Thaddeus is fascinating, no matter what." Thaddeus settled onto his shoulder, making Mack smile. "Honest to goodness, the acceptance by your animals is lovely."

She looked at him, and her heart melted at that. "Acceptance is lovely, and that's something I'm slowly adjusting to."

"You'll have an awful lot to adjust to and fast, between Scott—Did you ever get a hold of him?"

She shook her head at that. "I've left a couple messages, and he's left a couple messages with me. So far we're just playing phone tag."

"You didn't have your phone with you?"

"I was gardening, I think, and another time I had the ringer turned off." She shrugged.

"Even if Scott's sold everything, it'll still be a while before I see any of the money from the sales."

"Maybe so, but you've come a long way, and maybe some of it was sold sooner."

She smiled. "Maybe. I don't know yet. Of course I'm very curious. However, I don't want to get my hopes up."

At that comment, Mack chuckled. "That's also what you said about the divorce and look how that turned out? I don't know anybody who's had as much financial good luck coming to them as you've had of late. It's not just selling the antiques—and you really needed that money—but now you'll also have money and assets coming from possibly Robin's estate and definitely from your ex's. Some of his stuff you should get pretty quickly because your name was already on a lot of his properties."

"Which may mean a lot of taxes are owed and probably immediately due," she muttered, her tone turning dark. "For all I know, that's why he left it all to me, knowing that I would struggle to pay for it."

"I'm pretty sure he didn't plan on leaving it in your hands. Pretty sure that he fully intended to take it away from you," Mack pointed out, his tone serious. "But, if you do run into that kind of trouble, you can get help in order to make those payments."

"I would imagine that property taxes aren't due for another year. So, if Mathew had paid everything up to date, maybe I'm good to go for now. I can ask Nick to look into it."

Mack smiled. "We do need our lawyers and Nick too, even if they seem to be taking their sweet time."

At that, her phone rang. "Look at that. Speak of the devil. Hey, Nick. I'm sitting outside on my deck with your brother, and we were just talking about you."

"Good," he replied briskly. "I need to confirm your bank account and safe deposit box numbers and everything else, so we can get all your paperwork and legal matters handled."

"What do you need the bank accounts for?"

"I presume you want all the money from Mathew transferred to your account and taken away from any accounts that have his name on them. Technically nobody should have access to those accounts of his, but just to be safe ..."

"Oh, I definitely want to move it all," she

stated.

"Okay, as soon as we get everything into your name, we have a bunch of paperwork to handle. Plus we need to set up a proper will."

She winced at that. "Right. Just in case somebody succeeds in knocking me off." Her tone went dark again as she mentioned that.

Nick's tone was sharp, as he snapped back, "Did somebody attack you again?"

Mack reached for her phone and put it on Speaker and answered his brother. He let him know of the latest shooting incident downtown and the break-in at Doreen's house as well.

"Good Lord, that's just a little too depressing to hear."

"Yeah, lots of things in life are depressing, Nick," Doreen interjected. "According to your mother, the fact that you don't have a partner is also depressing."

Silence came from Nick's end, but Mack burst out laughing.

"Unfortunately Doreen is quite right about that," Nick admitted, "but I am not sure you two are in a position to throw stones."

"Mom appears to be somewhat okay with Doreen and I having some kind of a future," Mack shared, sending an odd look at Doreen.

"So, that means you've become Mom's next project."

"Good Lord," Nick muttered, his tone a bit jittery. Then he laughed too. "I guess that's part and parcel of living closer to home, isn't it?"

"Exactly," Doreen agreed. "Yet it might make it easier because she'll see you on a regular basis, and that might push away some of her concerns."

"Or bring them right into focus," Mack countered, with a smile. "But, hey, as long as the focus is on you and not me, I am very okay with that."

"*Right*. Thanks for that, bro. Doreen, I'll call you in the morning. Or maybe let's just set up a meeting … around ten or so?"

"Sure," she replied.

"Okay, so I can come down to you. We'll collect all the information I need, and then we'll start sending some documents through."

"Is this to do with Mathew's estate?"

"Both Mathew's and Robin's estates are involved here, and I'm the one dealing with the lawyer. Therefore, as long as you sign the documents authorizing me to do all this for you, we can get it sorted and the cash wired into your accounts. After that, we can then start the transfer process for the rest of the properties and other non-cash assets."

"Right, and then what about the stuff that my name isn't on?"

"Everything was left to you, so that part is pretty clear. We haven't had any claims as of yet or any disputes about property ownership, but we will consider that, if it happens."

"That's lovely," Doreen muttered, a bit sarcastically. "I very much want to be free and clear of all this stuff relating to Mathew's estate and would prefer that it happen sooner rather than later."

"You'll be a very wealthy woman after this, and remember that being free and clear comes with another set of responsibilities."

"I know, such as property taxes that may be due," she muttered. "I need to talk to you about something else, once we get all this done too."

"What something else?" Nick asked curiously.

"Just what my options are for spending it. Optimal investments and all."

"Are you worried about the groceries again?" Nick asked, a note of humor in his tone.

"No. … I was wondering, and then talked

to Nan about it, how I can best help Tammy and other women get off the streets."

"Who is Tammy?" he asked cautiously.

At that, Mack stepped up and explained, staring at her with an expression of amazement and wonder, as if seeing her for the very first time.

"Ah," Nick replied. "Once we get this paperwork straightened away and assets distributed, we can talk about what to do with the money and how to help other people. In the meantime my current advice is to not do anything at the moment. I've already got a lot of paperwork that needs to be completed, without adding more. We can discuss it once it's all safely moved into your accounts." And, with that, he wished them a good day and rang off.

Mack smiled at her. "You didn't tell me about Tammy."

She shrugged. "I'm not exactly sure what to do yet. I literally just talked to Nan about this right before I came home to this intruder mess. If all Tammy needs is just a bus ticket, it seems too simple. It's not fully addressing her problem."

His smile spread across his face and blossomed into a huge grin. "Says the woman who didn't have two pennies to herself for all these many months."

"I know, and maybe that's partly why I want to help. The value of just a simple helping hand has already been proven out by Nan. If she hadn't given me this home, I could have ended up where Tammy is." Mack stared at her in shock. She shrugged and didn't shirk away but spoke the truth, as simple as it was. "I had no visible means of support, Mack. No skills," she added slowly. "It's not at all out of the realm of possibility to realize that I could have ended up in a very bad state. Nan is the reason I'm not in that distressing scenario. So, if I can help somebody else get out of the scenario she's in, and, with a small sum involved, such as a bus ticket to Ontario, that's fine. The problem is trying to figure out if these people are serious and whether Tammy will stick to the plan, and that's my job to determine."

"Meaning?"

"Meaning, do I just help and then walk away? What if I did offer the help, but they take that money to buy drugs or something? Do they not get any more help? Do you see what I mean?"

"I do," he said, with a gentle smile. "I think

charities the world over have that problem."

"Right," she muttered. "It's so sad to think that we can't quite make a decision on the future because we don't know how people will react."

"I think when it comes to cash money, you have to give it and let it go. That's all you can do. Now for a bus ticket, you just buy it for her."

"That's one of the concepts Nan and I were discussing," Doreen noted, now with a smile. "Nan is quite willing to fork over any money I can't quite manage. If it's only a few hundred dollars—"

"A few hundred dollars times how many women? That could add up quickly," Mack reminded her.

"I know, and at the moment it's only about helping Tammy, but I can see that it could become an avalanche very quickly."

"When you get all this other paperwork done, maybe talk to my brother about setting something up. I don't know if a *charity* is quite the right word, but a trust or a foundation or maybe an endowment is what you need. You could set aside a portion of the money you are getting and use it to provide that support to people in a way that's safe. However, you should also consider doing it in a way that could offset your tax liability a bit."

She winced at that. "Seems I have an awful lot to learn."

"You're smart, and you're quick on your feet," he declared. "Plus you have the benefit of time, and you have my brother there to help you out."

She beamed at him. "Yeah, turns out you were a very good find for me." She gently stroked his cheek. "Not only did you teach me how to cook—and regularly come to my rescue—but your brother is keeping me afloat in all these other areas. What would I do without you two?"

Mack chuckled. "I don't think that's quite what Nick intended. He was mostly trying to help you divorce that ex of yours."

"Yeah, and somebody else took care of that in a much faster way."

He nodded. "But we won't dwell on that part."

"No, we won't," she agreed, as she patted his hand. "With everything else lining up to provide a comfortable living for me and my animals—way more than I could have imagined—plus with the long-awaited antiques money coming along, it'll all be a fair bit to deal with. I appear to be entering a whole new stage in life."

At that, he couldn't say a whole lot more, except to remind her that she was up for the challenge. He looked back to the house. "How satisfied are you with your alarm?"

"Not as much as I thought," she murmured, "but then I'm not sure any sensor was on that kitchen window anyway."

"No, there wasn't," he confirmed. "I already called the security company, and we definitely need to boost up your system."

"It'll take a day or two, I presume."

He nodded. "Most likely. Since the shops are closed for the day now, I'll talk to them in the morning and see if we can get a rush on it."

She smiled. "And in the meantime?"

"In the meantime, you'll take care of yourself, and you'll be very cautious."

"Sure, I always am."

His tone grim, he looked at her with a serious expression. "You get into situations that require a high level of caution, so you'll have to up your game on that."

She didn't say anything, but he was right. Chances were, at some point in time, she would get into a scenario that wasn't good. It had happened too many times to count now, and she couldn't always trust in her animals being there to rescue her—although they'd done a heck of a job up until now. She reached over to Thaddeus, still seated on Mack's shoulder, and gently stroked his beautiful feathers. "Doreen loves Thaddeus."

He looked over at her and immediately responded, "Thaddeus loves Doreen."

Chapter 16

Thursday Morning ...

THE NEXT MORNING, Doreen woke to Mack texting her and realized it was already eight. "Wow," she muttered, "I slept in."

She'd had a hard time getting to sleep last night, after all his comments and the lecture about being more careful and needing to boost her security system. Even now as she read his text, she realized he'd already run with it and was letting her know to expect someone from the security company at nine this morning to assess her home for enhancements to the system. Which meant she needed to get up and to get moving to have a clear head before this security person arrived.

She raced into the shower, and, when she came out, the animals were all waiting for her.

"Right, I slept in, and you didn't get break-fast or a chance to go out. Sorry, guys." She quickly dressed and headed downstairs. There she let them outside, put on coffee, and got their food ready. With that done, she felt better, as she always hated when she slept in to the point where they were waiting for her. They did so much to enrich her life, so the least Doreen could do was provide meals and their basic care on time.

She laughed at that. "You guys really don't have it so bad," she noted. Mugs had already inhaled his food and was ready to race out-side again. She propped open the door, so that everybody could come in and out. As soon as the coffee was done dripping, she grabbed a cup and headed outside herself, where she sat down, still yawning and trying to shake out the vestiges of her bad night.

She checked her emails and gasped. She had really been late this morning, and quite a few emails were already stacked up. Several came from Nick about their meeting at ten today, and thankfully he wanted to push it back a little bit. She immediately okayed that, then moved on to various other issues that she still had to deal with as well.

One email came from Scott. She immediately opened it, just to find his request that she call him. It seemed everything would be even better than he'd originally expected. She phoned him, and, when he answered, he seemed distracted. Yet he immediately perked up when he realized she was on the other end.

"Doreen, hello."

"Hey, Scott."

"You won't believe it, but we've had several of our long-term customers step up and buy quite a few of your pieces before the auction date," he began, quite ecstatic. "Now we've only got about four pieces left unsold."

"Wow, so it won't go to auction after all?"

"They were willing to pay more to preempt the auction."

"They can certainly do that as far as I'm concerned," she stated, with a laugh.

"Exactly. At the moment you're at well over one million, seven-hundred thousand."

She stopped and stared. "How much? I thought you said, one million, seven-hundred thousand dollars."

"You heard me right, and we still have a couple of the larger pieces left that we're dealing with, so you should do very, very well."

"Is that one million, seven-hundred thousand for me or one million, seven-hundred thousand before expenses and your cut?"

He burst out laughing. "Oh no, that would be your take, and honestly I'm really hoping we'll get over two million for you."

"Me too," she muttered. Even after their phone call was done, she remained stunned. She had always hoped the antiques would bring in good money, but even one million dollars didn't seem possible. And now, between everything else going on, it looked as if she would be okay after all. Then she burst out laughing and gave herself a talking to.

"Doreen, you're an idiot. Nobody would see that antique money as simply *being okay*." With a little bit of solid investment advice, she should be good to go for the rest of her life, and that was something worth cheering for. She looked around at her home and her garden, realizing it was all due to Nan. Doreen would call her grandmother soon to share the good news with her.

Right now though, Doreen just wanted to sit and savor this moment, realizing that all that fear and insecurity about her future was now a thing of the past. She knew she wouldn't get the money for a bit yet, although

Scott had promised to facilitate it as quickly as possible. Once he ended up selling all the pieces, the money could come in multiple chunks.

Not that she needed it right away, not with Mathew's estate being processed fairly quickly. According to what Nick had told her, some of Mathew's bank accounts and properties were already in her name, or had her name on them, so no probate or other legal issues would need to be dealt with. She would be in a far better financial position than even her wildest dreams could have imagined.

Some of that was due to her ex, despite his unfortunate intentions, but a lot of it was due to Nan. Any one of these items or events would have set her up, but all of them? Wow. Now it was a whole new world of financial independence for Doreen, and she still didn't even know what to think.

She sat here, basking in joy, with her cup of coffee, when Nan phoned. Doreen quickly told her what Scott had shared.

"That is absolutely perfect," Nan crowed in delight. "We'll definitely celebrate."

"Oh, we absolutely will," she replied, "though I have no idea what that might entail." She laughed at that. "But, if you want to go anyplace for a holiday or a dinner out or anything at all, you let me know, and I will be more than happy to make it happen."

Nan chuckled. "My traveling days are over, but that doesn't mean I won't take you up on lunch out. Is Mr. Woo back up and running?"

"Yes, he sure is. Maybe that's what we should do. Maybe we'll go down and see him today."

"Oh dear, it just occurred to me that he may not be all that receptive to seeing you."

"I sure hope he is," Doreen replied in confusion. "Why wouldn't he be?"

"Some people would look at you as bad luck at this point."

Doreen snorted. "A lot of people consider me to be bad luck, but usually they're the ones looking at jail sentences as well." That brought a huge guffaw of laughter from Nan, as if Doreen had made the best joke ever. Honestly it wasn't even so much a joke as it was the truth.

"Why don't you come down and have tea with me?" Nan asked. "Or are you sitting outside having coffee?"

"That's exactly what I'm doing. I didn't have a great night, after I had an intruder in the house yesterday afternoon."

"Oh my," Nan muttered. "That isn't good."

"I'm waiting for the security guy Mack arranged to come take a closer look at the security system here. The intruder came through one of the windows, and I didn't have sensors on it."

"Right, and you'll certainly need to have sensors on every window if you keep handling cold cases and stay in trouble all the time. Now with the new case—"

"I wasn't planning on inviting any trouble at home," she muttered.

"No, you might not plan it, but that doesn't mean other people won't make it happen."

Not a whole lot Doreen could say to that. She talked to Nan a little bit more, then shared, "As soon as I'm done with the security people, I have a meeting with Nick. So, maybe this afternoon I can come down for a visit."

"That sounds good," Nan replied, and, with that, they made plans for later in the afternoon. Just as Doreen disconnected, she got another phone call.

"Hey, this is Chris from the security company. Mack asked me to stop by and take a look at your system this morning. I'm calling because I finished up my last stop sooner than planned and was wondering if maybe I can head over to your place now."

"Not a problem. Come on over. I'm just enjoying my coffee."

"Okay then, I'll be there in about five minutes or so."

And, with that, she ended the call and walked back inside. "Well, guys, it looks as if our day has started."

By the time she'd hit midafternoon, she needed to phone Nan and push back their tea. When Doreen called, Nan was unflappable as usual.

"Oh, don't worry about that, child. You come down whenever you're ready. I'm happy to see you anytime. I'm sorry it's been such a busy day though. That can be tiring."

"Very tiring," Doreen muttered, "but it's all good." In fact, it was very good. She signed the authorization for Nick to act on her behalf. So now Nick would contact Mathew's attorney and Robin's attorney, sharing bank account numbers and other information as needed. Doreen sighed. They could finally get a bunch of this stuff taken care of.

By the time she gathered her animals together, they were all more than ready for a walk and a visit. "Let's go down to Nan's."

Mugs raced to the river, and Doreen was laughing as she finally caught up with him. "I'm glad to see you're ready to see Nan but wait up for the rest of us."

She frowned as she noted that Goliath had already run ahead and was waiting a good one hundred yards down the path. Even Thaddeus was half-hopping, half-flying his way down. He would call out to Nan, then pick up his feet, fly a little farther, then land and do it all over again. Doreen smiled. "Your antics are something else," she muttered.

She was very amused, and it was nice to see them so eager to see her grandmother. As she headed toward Rosemoor, she tried not to rush it but to settle down a bit, since everything in her day so far had had an underlying sense of urgency about it. When she got to Rosemoor, she found Nan sitting outside, waiting for her. Doreen stopped for a moment and savored the feeling of knowing what it was like to have family who cared, family who thought far enough ahead so a financial safety net had been put in place, something there specifically for Doreen, just in case she ended up in trouble. Sure enough, trouble had found her, but Nan's gift had been so much bigger than actual money.

Doreen's throat already choking with emotions, she stepped onto Nan's patio and hugged her grandmother gently. "I don't even know how to thank you."

Nan just patted her gently on her shoulder, as the two of them stood here, caught in a warm embrace, not saying a word.

Until Thaddeus broke the silence. "Thaddeus loves Nan. Thaddeus loves Nan."

Nan stepped back, looked at the bird, and smiled. "Did you get left out of the cuddle?" His head bopped up and down, up and down. Then he walked over to Nan and cuddled his way right onto her shoulder. Nan sighed and held Thaddeus close. Not to be outdone, Mugs put his front paws on Nan's lap, as if to say, *Don't forget me*. Nan chuckled. "I'm not sure what's going on with these animals of yours."

"I don't know either," Doreen admitted. "They've been a little bit crazy lately. I don't know whether Thaddeus is mad at me or just tired, but he's been off a little lately."

"*Lately*?" Nan asked, with a dry look. "I would say they're always a little bit on the crazy side. And Thaddeus, he doesn't like winter. So if you can't fix that for him, he's going to be mad at you."

Doreen snorted at that. "It's not as if I can control the weather," she protested. Still, as she considered his behavior of late, she realized Nan could likely be right. Regardless, as long as everybody was doing okay, Doreen was happy. And Thaddeus would get out of his funk soon enough. Although just thinking about it made her shake her head and want to laugh, but she couldn't because it would hurt his feelings.

Goliath even waited until Nan was free of Mugs before he walked over and hopped up and settled on her lap, making her cry out in delight. "Goliath doesn't do this nearly as often as I would like."

"Well, he's a cat," Doreen pointed out, with half a smile. "The fact that you've been chosen to be where he wants to nap right now is an honor in itself."

Nan burst out laughing, as she gently stroked his beautiful fur. "They are something, aren't they?"

"Absolutely," Doreen agreed, "and sometimes they are everything. They're my family and my friends," she declared. "They comfort me. They make me laugh. They're just such a special part of my life."

"That's another thing," Nan added. "You

can thank me for everything I've done, and believe me that I'll take all the kudos coming there," she noted, with a beaming smile. "Yet you also made it happen. Not everybody could have done what you've done so far. Lots of kudos go right back to you."

Doreen chuckled. "So, we'll have a mutual admiration society today then?"

"Absolutely, let's call for the minutes," Nan declared and pounded the table, with a big grin. And that's how the visit went. The animals were curled up, sleeping peacefully, yet Nan was looking tired. Doreen hopped up and announced, "This has been so much fun and just what I needed, but I'll take these guys home, and maybe we can just relax at home, until Mack stops by later on."

"Yeah, you must have dinner plans or a heavy date or something, don't you?" Nan teased, waggling her eyebrows.

"Pretty sure he'll stop by and check on the security system," Doreen replied, with a laugh.

"I won't argue with that," Nan noted. "I rest a little easier knowing that he cares as much as he does and looks after you."

"I do know that he cares," Doreen stated, "but it hasn't quite translated to what you want it to."

"Oh, it will soon enough," Nan declared. "You just have to give it time."

"That's what I've been saying all along," Doreen pointed out gently.

"Give it time." Nan eyed her shrewdly. "It may not take quite as much time as you think. He won't wait around forever."

At that Doreen went cold inside. "What do you mean?"

Nan shrugged. "I wouldn't be at all surprised if he wasn't planning something."

Doreen immediately frowned and shook her head. "No, he wouldn't do that."

"Really? Why not?" Nan asked, looking at her granddaughter in amusement.

Doreen frowned. "Maybe he would, but he knows I'm not quite ready."

"Maybe, but I'm not sure we're ever ready for these things. Sometimes we just have to let them happen and react accordingly."

"Of course." Doreen agreed with that.

With the newly jumbled mess of thoughts in her head, she headed home with her animals, content and happy on the inside in a way she hadn't even realized she needed. But, with the sales of most of the antiques finally coming to fruition, and knowing that all the legal things were being transferred and dealt with, she experienced a level of joy that she hadn't felt in a long time. It was a massive sense of relief that both overwhelmed and liberated her as she walked home, and halfway there she started to sing.

By the time she got to her place and walked up the creek pathway, Richard popped his head over the top of the fence and asked, "Who's caterwauling over there?"

She stopped, then frowned. "Was my singing that bad?"

He harrumphed. "It wasn't that it was *bad*," he clarified, studying her curiously. "I just don't think I've ever heard you sing before."

"I don't think I've ever had any reason to sing before."

His eyebrows shot up. "So, I guess that means good news?"

"Oh, absolutely good news," she confirmed, beaming. "Sometimes life gives you good things, and it seems as though I've had a whole pile of them lately."

He nodded. "When you get all that money that's coming your way, ensure you spend it wisely, or, better yet, don't spend it at all, so that you'll always be provided for, and you can eat more than peanut butter sandwiches." He rolled his eyes, sarcastic and stoic as ever.

She stared at him. "How did you know I was eating peanut butter sandwiches?"

He snickered. "I've heard some of the conversations between you and Mack in the backyard. Maybe now you can at least get some jam to go with it." And, with that parting shot, he hopped down and went back into his yard.

Chapter 17

Friday Morning ...

DOREEN WAS STILL in bed the next morning, trying to get herself back into the mind-set of the missing Taser investigation. Yesterday had been one chaotic thing after another, but absolutely nothing had moved in her cold case investigation. She had to admit that now, with some things settled, she really wanted a ton of other things to get settled too. Lying around, she pondered just what that would mean in terms of this case, until she was interrupted by a phone call. She picked it up and answered it cautiously. "Hello?"

At first, silence came on the other end, and then a woman asked, "Is this Doreen?"

The voice was so soft, almost fragile. "Yes," she replied, and recognition dawned. "Tammy?"

"Yes," she said, her voice even fainter.

"Are you okay?" More silence came. "Tammy, talk to me." Doreen bolted to her feet. Tammy started to sob. "Do you need medical attention?" Tammy just sobbed even harder.

Not sure what to do or how to get her to talk, Doreen paced her bedroom, just trying to calm down Tammy. "If you need me to call somebody, you tell me," she suggested. "I can get help there within a matter of minutes." She could if she needed to, and she knew it, but, so far, Tammy wasn't capable of talking. The sobs were real though, and they were heartfelt, which, in a sad way, made Doreen feel better about whatever was going on in Tammy's world. When a break in her tears finally came, Doreen asked, "Where are you?"

"City Park."

"So you can walk?"

"Yes, yes, I can walk, but I don't want to go back to the house."

"I'm coming down to you at City Park, so just stay there. Meet me at the big pergola with the wisteria. Do you know what I mean?"

"Yes, I know where that is." Tammy hesitated to get more words out. "I just don't want him to see me."

"No, I don't want him to see you either," Doreen murmured, "but I'm on my way. So, if you do see him, hide, just let me know where you'll be." Tammy ended the call, and Doreen raced to get dressed. She called for the animals, and they all came running. "Come on, guys. Rescue operation time." And, with the animals in tow, she headed for her car.

As soon as she was in her car, she backed out of the driveway and headed toward City Park. She wondered why everybody always wanted to meet there. It was public and all, but, in a situation like this, did Tammy really want to be out in the open? Or was she not that badly injured and mostly just scared? Doreen hated the doubts that kept creeping in, but she'd seen just enough these last few months to make her wonder about anybody's motives.

She phoned Nan on the road and explained what happened.

"Oh dear Lord, that poor child."

"That's why I'm heading down there right now. I'll let you know how it turns out."

"Of course, of course, and remember what we talked about."

"I know," she murmured, "but we still have

the problem of trying to figure out whether this is for real or not."

"Or whether Jed is just using Tammy to bring you in," Nan suggested in a worried tone.

"Let's hope not, but we'll find out soon enough," Doreen noted, "because I'm only a few minutes away." With that, she disconnected and quickly parked in the same parking lot that Mack had used. Realizing that it could get ugly really fast here, she quickly sent him a text, letting him know where she was and what was going on. As she headed to the boardwalk, knowing she had a few minutes before she reached the pergola, she wasn't at all surprised when Mack phoned her.

"What's going on? That wasn't a very clear text you sent me."

"No, I'm sorry, but Tammy contacted me, and she was in tears."

He hesitated. "That's not necessarily all that unusual."

"No, it isn't," she agreed, recognizing the truth of his words. "She sounded quite desperate though, and almost at the end of her rope."

"That may be, but she could still be setting

you up."

"*Great*," she muttered under her breath. "That's exactly what Nan said."

"Good. I'm glad Nan's got her head on straight. ... I suppose you're already down there, aren't you?" he asked, his tone resigned.

"Already parked and I'm walking toward the pergola."

"*Great*," he muttered, then hesitated. "I'm just about to walk into a meeting."

"I'll be fine."

"Yeah, I've heard that before too," he muttered. "Call me as soon as you see her. And, if you're doing anything with her, you'll let me know, right?"

"I will," she promised, and she intended to keep her promise, if at all possible. She just didn't know what she was supposed to do if Tammy was looking for some real serious escape help right now. It's not as if Doreen had any secret underground network where she could stash her.

As she walked at a staid pace toward the huge wisteria pergola, she pondered what Tammy's options were. It wasn't for Doreen to judge how Tammy had gotten here or what she'd done. It was a matter of trying to figure out what serious help could be offered in a way that would give Tammy a realistic chance to get out of this. Doreen hated to admit it, but she didn't really want to get taken either. After all her years of dealing with Mathew, and all the other cons that had gone on, Doreen definitely didn't want to see herself getting ripped off.

If she lost a few hundred dollars, that was one thing. It still wouldn't be nice though because Doreen was slowly regaining her faith in people. Finding out that some weren't willing to be truthful and honest had been a bit of an eye-opener. Still, Doreen had met enough good people in her world throughout this process, and she knew that not everybody could be painted by the same brush as Mathew. Even now she wondered if he was rolling in his grave because she would inherit everything and would be helping abused women with his money.

Feeling a sense of urgency, she almost broke into a run, so she was out of breath when she got to the meeting place. The animals had run alongside her. As soon as she stopped, they came to a dead halt and just collapsed. She looked around but saw no one here. Her heart sinking, it could have been a ruse. Yet her next thought was more hopeful that Tammy could simply be on her way. Maybe Tammy wasn't sure at all how this would work.

As Doreen walked forward, she saw a bench up ahead. She sat down to catch her breath, waiting and looking around.

When she heard a whisper of movement behind her, she bolted to her feet and spun around. But instead of just Tammy standing there, a stranger was with her. A stranger with a hard look on his face and a pistol in his hand. Doreen took a deep breath and reached a hand down to calm Mugs, who was even now barking and snarling. "Jed, I presume," Doreen said calmly. "Is that a police-issued gun by chance?"

One eyebrow shot up, and he gave her a twisted snarl. "Seems you are a little too smart for your own good, aren't you?"

She tilted her head to the side. "I don't know about that. Sometimes I'm not quite smart enough." She looked over at Tammy with a hurt expression. "Did you arrange this?"

Tammy gave a tiny shake of her head, and Jed laughed. "She was acting weird, so I knew she was up to something," he stated.

"Figures she would be talking to a no-good busybody like you," he muttered.

Doreen stared. "Why am I a no-good so and so? What have I got to do with anything?"

"Oh, don't tell me lies," he muttered. "You're trying to help her escape."

Doreen's eyebrows shot up at that. "So, you *are* holding her prisoner then."

He stared at her and declared in disgust, "The only reason I'm here was to track down Tammy. Now that I have her, I'm taking her away with me, and you can't do anything about it."

Doreen gave him a knowing smile. "I wouldn't count on that, if I were you. If you had anything to do with any deaths, that will be a whole different story."

He stared at her. "I didn't have nothing to do with any deaths."

"Right, so you're only worried about making sure that your meal train stays healthy enough for you to continue to work her at nighttime, *huh*?"

"I don't care when she works, nights, days, mornings. I don't really care. All I'm concerned about is making sure she works. If she doesn't work, I don't get any money, and

I want my money."

"You could try getting a job yourself. Even better, why don't you put your body out on the street for anyone to buy?" she suggested, with a wry smile. "Afraid you wouldn't get any customers?"

As Doreen mocked Jed, Tammy's eyes widened.

Jed stared down at Doreen in disbelief. "I don't know who you are or who you think you are," he snarled, "but Tammy's done with you. If she ever talks to you again, I'll kill her. Do you hear me?"

"Yeah, I just heard you threaten her," Doreen declared, staring at him intently, try-ing to figure out how to defuse the situation and how to get Tammy away from him. "That will never go over well."

Jed barked, "Doesn't matter if it does or not. She's done with you, and, if she can't do that, then she's done with life."

"Do you always make threats like that? Are they idle, or will you really kill people? You just told me that you didn't murder anyone, so it doesn't make sense that you would make a threat now and have me believe it."

Jed silently stared at her.

Doreen shrugged. "I'm used to being

threatened these days, and yours doesn't sound particularly awe-inspiring. Maybe you should give it another go."

His face turned ruddy, as fury overcame him, and he took several steps toward her. Immediately Mugs started to bark and growl. Goliath, who was no longer on a leash, sauntered around behind Jed.

Doreen winced. "You probably should be a little nicer to me right now," she suggested, staring him in the face. "Otherwise you might end up with a repercussion you're not happy with."

"I don't know what you're playing at, or who you think you are, but nobody tells me what to do."

"Right, so it's back to that control thing." She brushed her hair away from her face. "I'm really hot and sweaty from the run down here. I thought I would be late. Then I show up, and there's no Tammy." She studied the look of true panic in Tammy's gaze and was relieved to see that Tammy had not set this up. "Look at Tammy. You've got her absolutely terrified."

"Good," he muttered. "She should be."

"Why? So you can just beat her up and make her life miserable again? What kind of a human being are you that you can't even get a job yourself, but you have to terrorize other people into supporting you, just so that you can get some free money?" she asked. "The least you could do is put your own sorry butt out on the street instead. Why do you have to torment Tammy into doing it?"

"Because that's not the way the world works. It's all about power and who's got control."

"And what happens when I have somebody wrest control away from you? Then what?" Doreen asked.

He laughed. "That ain't happening, so don't get any ideas, sweetheart."

"Yeah, I'm no sweetheart, Jed, and I sure wouldn't want to be in your position right now. The cops are looking for you already. Did you know an APB is out for you right now— actually for both of you, so that's an interesting twist."

"But the cops don't know I'm here," he declared, with a smile.

"No, but they do know that *I'm* here, and they know that Tammy is here," she replied calmly.

"So then what?" He just stared at her, more fury working alongside his nervousness, as he glanced around several times, as if afraid the cops would jump out of the bushes. But, when nothing happened, he just relaxed and laughed. "Not bad as fakes go," he said, with a chuckle.

Yet nothing was funny about the words coming out of his mouth.

Jed added, "Still, you should really find something better to do than try to trick me. I really don't like people playing games."

"Neither do I," she stated. "Particularly when it's guys like you, who live off women and don't even give them decent food, a nice place to live, or a percentage of the profit. If Tammy was doing this because she wanted to, and she was getting a fair percentage of the profits, that would be a whole different story. But the fact that you're holding her hostage and that she has no choice in the matter, that's got to stop."

"Who'll stop it?" Jed asked in shock. "You?"

"Yeah, I think so," Doreen declared, with a nod. "I was talking to my grandmother about it, trying to figure out just what our options were."

"Your grandmother?"

He didn't seem to have a clue what she

was saying, and she probably didn't either, if she were honest. It's not as if this was a conversation she had really planned on sharing with anybody. Doreen nodded. "Yes, my grandma."

He shook his head. "Look, lady. I don't know who you are, what you think you're doing, or what game you're playing, but Tammy is out of your league. So you leave her alone and stay away. Understand?"

"I understand what your words are saying," she replied. "I can see the fury in your gaze at the thought that you might lose your breadwinner, but Tammy needs a life. She needs a chance to be herself and to get away from you. She needs to choose what she wants to do, whatever that is. Maybe she'll go back to school. Maybe she wants a career. Hey, maybe she wants to get married and have a family."

He snorted at that. "Who'll want her now? She's used goods."

"That's saying the same thing about every woman who's had a prior relationship, isn't it? Very insulting I would say," she pointed out, staring at him. "I mean, you're also used goods, and nobody wants anything to do with you. So, from that perspective, I can understand where you're coming from."

At this point in time even Tammy stared at Doreen as if she were crazy.

Doreen gave Tammy a reassuring smile. "But, Jed, you can make things a lot easier on yourself right now if you just walk away and leave Tammy alone. I'll take her with me, and you won't see her again."

"But that ain't happening, remember? The whole point of coming down here is so you understand that she's mine, and she doesn't get a choice in this."

"You're wrong. She does get a choice in this," Doreen stated emphatically. "This is her life, and she gets to decide. Now, what choice she wants to make, that's a different story. A woman who has been beaten and abused tends to not necessarily make the best choices because already so much fear has been ingrained into her mind."

"Exactly. So even if she chooses to go with you, or would have a choice right now, she wouldn't make it," he replied, with a beaming smile. "She's under my thumb, and that's where I intend to keep her."

"Oh, right. Because you're afraid that she'll leave you, if you give her a choice."

"She won't," he said. "She's smart."

"But she could, otherwise you wouldn't be so panicked about her having a choice."

"She does have a choice, and she's choosing to stay, aren't you, Tammy?"

"How can Tammy make a real choice if you're squeezing her arm like that?" Doreen asked. "You are nothing but a bully, using force."

He immediately dropped Tammy's arm. "See? Look at her. She knows exactly where her bread is buttered," he said.

And, with that, Doreen looked at Tammy, raised one eyebrow, and replied, "Your choice."

Tammy immediately booked it, racing to Doreen's side. "Lady, you're crazy, but you're my kind of crazy." She turned and faced Jed. "I don't want to work for you. I don't want to be a prostitute, and I don't want anything to do with you ever again."

He stared at her in shock, then a look of absolute fury crossed his face. "You get your skinny butt back over here," he yelled, pointing to the ground beside him. "And maybe, just maybe, I won't beat you within an inch of your life. Or kill you…"

"Yeah, *that'll* work to encourage her," Doreen snapped, crossing her arms.

He lifted his gun to her. "You're responsible for this."

"Actually it's all the abuse you've heaped on Tammy that's done this. Even animals turn on their abusers, and that's where you're at right now. So, you can shoot me. You might even kill me, but Tammy will run, long and hard." Doreen handed Tammy a piece of paper with Nan's name and phone number. "If he kills me, you get a hold of this woman, and she'll help you."

Then she turned to face Jed. "Now, of course you realize that this is happening all in clear view of the city cameras. So the local authorities will know exactly what went on here. Don't forget about the cops already knowing I'm here."

"So you say," he sneered. "Nobody'll believe you, and, if Tammy doesn't get back over here right now, I'll shoot her."

Doreen glanced at Tammy, who was terrified. So Doreen stepped in between Tammy and Jed, whispered, "Tammy, just run away, and I'll see you in a little bit."

The woman shook her head and whispered, "He will shoot me and you both."

Just then a familiar voice called out, "No, he won't."

Doreen looked over to see Chester and one of the other cops she didn't know quite as well, both standing behind Jed, staring at them all. "If Jed does shoot, he'll take a bullet himself," Chester announced, holding his own handgun on Jed. "Now, drop the weapon."

At that, Jed glared from the cops to the women and back again.

Doreen added, "If you don't cooperate, Jed, the cops will shoot you. I know that for sure. So, what'll it be?"

"You really did bring the cops?" he asked.

"Of course I brought the cops. Do you think I'm an idiot? You're out here, forcing this poor woman into prostitution, not to mention the other woman you've got back at your place. We'll have to free her as well."

He stared at her and blurted out, "I won't have any money then."

"Oh, I'm so sorry. Well, you've still got your body to sell, so maybe you can make some money off that." Then, giving him an up-and-down look, she shuddered. "Or ... maybe not."

At that, Chester grinned. "Not bad, Doreen."

"Hey, I'm working on it," she muttered, and she watched as Jed slowly lowered his handgun, while Chester and his partner disarmed him. As soon as Jed was safely in cuffs, Doreen turned to look at Tammy. "I wasn't kidding when I said that the cops have an APB out on you."

Tammy stared at her in shock. "Why me?"

"Because they were worried about your safety." It was as if the shocks just wouldn't stop hitting the poor woman, who clearly didn't understand. Doreen introduced Chester. "Chester, this is Tammy."

He nodded. "Ma'am, I would like to take you down to the station. You will be safe there, and we need to ask you some questions."

She gripped Doreen's hand tightly. "Will you come?"

"Of course. I practically live there these days."

At that, Chester laughed. "Come on then. Do you have your vehicle?"

"I do. Did Mack tell you that I was down here?"

He nodded. "Yep. He said you were heading into trouble again. Man, I have never met anybody who's got an eye for trouble the way you do."

"I think I come by it naturally."

Chester nodded. "Yeah, you sure do. My mama would have told me that you are trouble all the way."

"I am, I suppose, but not to everybody, only to the idiots in the world who think they can abuse other people."

Chester smirked. "Yeah, you're on our side, and that's the reason I'm here. Man, oh man, if you ever choose to go on the other side, we're all in trouble."

Chapter 18

Friday Afternoon ...

NOW AT THE station, Doreen parked, looked over at Tammy, and asked, "Are you ready?"

Tammy shuddered and shook her head. "I've never been here before."

"This part's easy," Doreen told her. "You just have to tell the truth. Let's go on in and talk to them."

"But what if they arrest me?"

"Did you do anything wrong? Did you have anything to do with murder or theft?"

Tammy immediately shook her head and stared at Doreen in shock. "No, of course not."

"Then I'm not sure what you would be arrested for."

She lowered her voice. "I work as a prostitute."

Doreen nodded. "As of now, that's your former career," she pointed out, "and, since you didn't get caught soliciting, can they charge you with that?"

"Do you think so?" Tammy nervously chewed on her bottom lip, wondering just what her options were.

"Pretty sure they can't charge you for something they haven't seen you do. Have you ever been picked up before?"

Tammy shook her head. "No, I've come close a couple times, but I've always run away."

"Smart. Learning to run at the right time is always a good idea. Come on. This time you have no need to run." She hopped out, opened up the vehicle, and let Tammy and the animals tumble out. She quickly scooped up Goliath and clipped him onto his leash.

"I don't think I've ever seen a cat on a leash before," Tammy said, staring down at Goliath, who was not looking too happy.

"He prefers *not* to be on the leash, but, where he can get into a lot of trouble"—she tilted her head toward the station—"such as here, then I keep him on a leash. Come on, Goliath. Behave yourself." But he threw himself on the ground and glared at her. She took two steps, but he wouldn't budge. She tried to move a little bit forward, giving him a slight tug, and he just stared at her, while she dragged him forward a few feet. She stopped and raised both hands. "That won't work."

Thaddeus started to cackle on her shoulder.

At that, Tammy smiled at her and her animals. "They really do control this, don't they?"

"You mean me?" Doreen asked, with an eye roll. "I try not to let the world know how much control they have over me, but I'm kidding myself if I think I can hide it."

Tammy chuckled. "I haven't seen anything this funny in a very long time, so keep at it."

"Yeah, you'll find that Doreen has a lot of amusing moments," Mack interjected from behind her.

Doreen turned and glared at him. "You could help out and call to Goliath."

He walked over, leaned down, and gave her a big kiss. Then he looked at Tammy, reached out a hand, and greeted her. "Hi, Tammy. I'm Corporal Mack Moreau."

She stared at the hand proffered and then slowly reached out.

Doreen nodded. "Remember that you are a human being. I don't care what job you had or how Jed thought about you. You are not less than anyone. You are certainly as deserving of a handshake as anybody else."

Tears came to Tammy's eyes. "After you've been treated as if you're so much less for a very long time, you forget what anything else is like."

"You do," Doreen agreed, "but you will remember soon enough." Tammy stared at Doreen, and she nodded. "Yeah, unfortunately I do know what I'm talking about, but thankfully my situation has completely turned around, and I am no longer under the thumb of an abusive man."

"What about him?" Tammy asked, with a nod toward Mack.

"I'm not under his thumb either," she replied, with a mischievous grin, as she faced Mack. "I don't think he wants me under his thumb."

"No," he muttered, with a heavy sigh, "although there are definitely times when I want to tell her to stay put and would like to know that she will, but she doesn't do that very well either." He burst out laughing at that. "Come on in. We'll have to ask you some questions." At that, Doreen went to move forward, and Goliath once again laid there and stared at her.

She let out a breath very slowly, very carefully, and muttered, "Goliath, you are testing my patience today."

Mack crouched down in front of him. "Hey. Buddy. I haven't seen you all day. Where were you?" Goliath immediately hopped to his feet, bounded forward, and jumped into Mack's arms.

Doreen glared at Mack. "You could have done that from the beginning."

"Yeah, but it was much more fun to watch Goliath get the better of you," he teased.

When he reached out his arm, she thought he would put it around her shoulders, but instead he was reaching for Thaddeus, who immediately walked up onto his shoulder and tucked up against him.

"Thaddeus loves Mack."

She groaned. "See, Tammy? This is what I put up with."

But Tammy was laughing, the delight obvious on her face. "Oh my, you guys are great together."

"I keep telling her that," Mack stated, "but she's still not convinced."

At that, Tammy looked at Doreen in surprise.

Doreen shrugged. "I just came out of an ugly divorce."

"Yeah, but that's *out* of an ugly divorce, not into one. This guy is amazing," Tammy noted, having lowered her voice. "You really should snag him up before somebody else does."

"Thanks for the words of wisdom," Doreen muttered, with a groan. "You and everybody else keep telling me the same thing."

"So maybe you'll wise up and listen." And, with that snappy retort, Tammy quickly stepped behind Mack and followed him into the station.

Chapter 19

Friday Mid-afternoon ...

Back Home Again later that afternoon, Doreen put on coffee, then looked over at Tammy, who even now sat on the patio outside. "Do you want coffee?"

"Yes, please," she replied. She was fixated on the river. "I can't believe how beautiful this place is, even though the house needs some updating, but wow."

"I know. This was my grandmother's house, and she left it to me when I got into a bad situation with my marriage. She was so happy when I came back."

"Holy... she gave you a house?"

Doreen nodded. "I know, right? She's living in a senior home right now, down at Rosemoor. So she couldn't remain here and enjoy the house, but didn't want to sell it and didn't need the money from it, so she gave it to me instead."

"You are blessed."

"Yes, I sure am," Doreen agreed. "I am very appreciative of everything my grandmother has done for me."

Tammy shook her head. "It's truly amazing."

Doreen smiled. "How bad was the police station visit?"

"It wasn't bad," she said, "but it was very strange."

"Why is that?"

"Being treated like an equal," she whispered.

"You're human, so that makes you an equal," Doreen stated. "We all make mistakes. We all get into trouble, and we all need a little bit of help sometimes to get back on track."

"I don't dare go back to the apartment again, so I'm not sure what I'm supposed to do from here," she shared, staring around at the backyard. "I feel like asking you if you have a tent that I can pitch in the backyard."

"You would be welcome to, if *you* had a tent," Doreen teased, with a chuckle. Just then her phone rang. "Hey, Mack. Problems or a social call?"

"You tell me. Is everything okay?"

"Yes, I just put on some coffee. Everything here is okay. You?'

"Yeah, I'll be done here soon and plan to run by and talk to you both."

"Good idea," she replied. "I don't know that either of us have answers about anything else at this point in time. We're pretty tired, but otherwise we're all good."

"Good enough. I'll be there is about twenty."

She ended the call to see Tammy eyeing her in surprise.

"You really do have a relationship with him, don't you?"

"Yeah, I sure do. I just haven't quite figured out what to call it yet."

"You don't have to call it anything. The fact that you're even with somebody like him is amazing."

"He's amazing all right," Doreen agreed, with a smile, "and I do know it, but I'm coming out of a pretty-rough divorce, from a pretty-ugly marriage, and I'm just not too eager to jump into something new without … some time to … How do you trust in your own judgment again?"

"Oh, yes. I understand that all too well."

Doreen nodded. "Which is also why I haven't really been working too hard at nailing down our relationship."

"I don't think you need to nail it down. It's obvious he's very much in love with you."

"Is it?" she asked, looking at her in surprise.

"He's absolutely smitten, and you're really lucky."

"What do you want to do now that you're free and clear of this Jed guy? Where would you like to go, and what would you want to do?"

Tammy shrugged. "I want to go back to my family."

"Have you contacted them?"

"No, not yet, and I don't really have any way to get back there."

"Have you thought about asking them for money?"

"I didn't want to do that," she said, her voice turning faint. "Yes, it would get me back there, but it wouldn't exactly be the kind of return I would prefer. Besides, I wouldn't want them to all see me as this sad person who needed help to get home."

"Right, well, we're looking at some of the costs involved in transportation, but you still need some money for food and such on the journey. Plus you need some clothes too. You came away with nothing."

"Right. As for food, I don't eat very much. I can go without food for a while. As for clothes?"

Doreen chuckled. "I don't think either will be an issue. We can go to the thrift store and find clothes for you. I can make you some peanut butter sandwiches to take with you. I'm willing to front you the bus ride home, if you're willing to go home and make some changes in your life, so you can have your life back again."

Tammy stared at her in shock. "Seriously?"

"Absolutely." Doreen smiled. She hadn't even finished discussing these plans, when she heard a *Yoo-hoo* from the river. She looked over and pointed. "Perfect timing. Here comes Nan."

At that, Nan walked up, gave Doreen a big hug, then looked over at Tammy. "Hello, you must be Tammy. My granddaughter told me all about you."

Tammy frowned from one to the other. "She did?"

"Absolutely, and, yes, she told me all about it, so relax, and please don't feel ashamed."

Tammy sagged in place. "I hope you're the last person who knows what I *used* to do for a living," she noted, with a deliberate emphasis on the past tense usage.

Nan chuckled. "We all have a history, dear, and burying that history so you never have to be tied down by it again is hugely important. So, did Doreen tell you about the bus fare?"

"Just now, Nan," Doreen said, with a smile.

"Good. She'll pay the bus fare, and I'll front you some clothes at this end and a few hundred dollars so you can get started on the other end. It won't take you very far though, so you'll need to have a place to land when you get there, plus find a job pretty quickly to get you some cash. I presume you can live at home in the interim."

Tammy stared at the two of them, tears in her eyes. "Seriously?"

Doreen nodded. "Yes, we don't want to see you going back to what you were doing."

"I don't want to go back to that either," she stated fervently.

Studying her intently, Nan added, "It's also an easy lifestyle to fall into if you're desperate for cash and short on other experience."

"I used to type and do office work, so I don't know if I can get a receptionist or clerical job right away, but believe me that I will take any honest job at this point in time, if it will pay for my living expenses. And I can probably get some help from my mother with that."

"Maybe you should find out if and when they can pick you up from the bus station."

Tammy again stared at them, almost as if she were afraid to make the phone call and to hold out any hope.

Doreen handed over her phone. "I have long distance on mine, if you want to use it."

Tammy snatched it up and quickly dialed a number she obviously knew from heart. She got up and walked a little bit away. "Mom?"

At that greeting, there were tears on both sides of the conversation, from the little bit Doreen could hear. She sat down, looked over at Nan, and smiled.

"You've done a good thing," Nan declared.

"I hope so. I really want to give her that chance to start again."

"And that's what you're doing," Nan stated. "What she does with that chance, you have no control over, and you'll need to let it go."

At that, Doreen winced yet nodded. "That's the thing, isn't it? You can only help some-body by showing them where the water is, but you can't force them to drink."

"No, you can't, and, in this case, you'll give her the tools so she can start again."

The phone call lasted at least another ten minutes. By the time Tammy rejoined them and returned the phone to Doreen, Tammy had wet streaks down her face, but shining out beyond the tears was hope in her gaze.

"I'm to call Mom back and let her know when the bus is due to get in, and she will pick me up. She also told me that they're looking for an assistant where she works, and she would put in a good word for me—if I was interested in staying for a while. I didn't tell her that I was hoping to move back home because I didn't have a job or a place or anything."

"Did she offer you a place to stay?"

"Absolutely," she replied, with a beaming smile. "She offered and sounded really happy that I'm coming home, like over the moon."

"Of course she is," Nan declared. "When we love our children, we love them forever, not just for the good times or not just when we like them. Enough times you guys get to go off and make your own decisions, but, when you remember your family, they'll do anything for you."

Tammy smiled. "It sure sounds like it. Do you know when the next bus leaves?"

At that, the women sat down and started to work out the details. When Doreen found a bus going to Toronto, Ontario and leaving tonight, she looked over at Tammy. "Are you ready to make that change now?"

"Absolutely," she stated fervently. "The sooner I'm out of this town, the better. It's never been a good place for me," she admitted. "When I came here, I immediately got hooked on drugs. I managed to get myself off the drugs, but I couldn't get away from Jed." She shook her head. "Now that I am rid of him, and he's in jail for a while, I want to get while the getting's good."

"I couldn't agree more," Doreen said, as she looked to Nan, who nodded.

Nan added, "Take her to get some clothes and a backpack or something. Then straight to the bus station and buy the ticket." Then she got up, fetched a small wad of bills from her pocket, and handed it over to Tammy. "You'll have to leave now to get any clothes because the bus leaves in about an hour and a half."

Tammy looked shocked, then gave Nan an ever-so-gentle hug. "Thank you, thank you, thank you," she whispered.

Nan just brushed it away. "Just remember that we're counting on you to make a whole new start out of this and to make something out of your life. It doesn't have to be fancy. It doesn't have to be anything other than the fact that you allow yourself to become the really good person who you are and to stay off the streets."

"Got it." She brushed the tears from her eyes. "I'm ready to go, so I know this is for real. Plus I sure hope they don't let Jed out early."

"Come on then." Doreen asked Nan, "Mack will be here soon, did you want to come too?"

Nan shook her head. "No, I'll stay here with the animals until you get back, the sooner, the better."

Doreen got up, snagged her purse and keys, and, with Tammy once again in her car, the two women headed to the thrift store. Soon they were at the bus depot.

As she pulled in and parked, Doreen said, "Come on, let's go get the ticket." They walked up to the cashier, then quickly asked to book a ticket.

"You're just in time. We're doing checks on the bus right now."

Doreen and Tammy stood at the station, until the bus could be boarded. Doreen gave her a hug and whispered, "You've got a second chance, so make good use of it. When you step on that bus, remember it's the first moment of the rest of your life. A life you can be proud of."

Tammy gave her a big hug and then raced onto the bus, taking a window seat on Doreen's side.

For whatever reason, Doreen felt she needed to stay. She stood here until the bus pulled away, the two of them waving the whole time. Something was incredibly rewarding about helping someone else.

As she slowly turned toward home, her phone rang. "Nan?"

"Yes. Is Tammy on the bus?"

"She's on the bus, and I'm heading home."

"Good enough," Nan said. "You should probably hurry along."

"Why is that?"

"Because this man sitting beside me has a gun. He says he'll wait right here until you come home. So, sooner would be better." And, with that, Nan ended the call.

Chapter 20

"MACK, MACK, ARE you there?" she cried into the phone.

"Yeah, what's the matter?" he asked.

"Are you on your way to my place? You should have been there ages ago??"

"I was, then I got held up at work. Everything okay with Tammy?" When she quickly explained about Nan, he muttered, "Good Lord. Are you sure she said he's got a gun?"

"Yes, no doubt, and I can't get there fast enough."

"I'm already on the way, so, if you're coming from the bus station, I should get there before you."

"Good to know. I should never have left her at home."

"But you left her with the animals, right?"

"Yes, not that it'll help much against a gun," she cried out. "Oh my God, I can't believe a gunman is holding Nan at my house."

"I'm not completely surprised, considering you had a break-in, but I'm not at all impressed that they're bothering Nan."

"Yeah, you and me both," Doreen agreed bitterly, as she quickly turned another corner, tires squealing.

"Hey, hey, hey," Mack cried out in alarm. "Let's get you home in one piece. Slow down. I can hear your tires through the phone."

"Oh, I'll get there in one piece," she muttered. "But I can't guarantee I'm leaving whoever is holding a gun on my Nan that way."

"Ouch. Come on now. We can't have you going crazy in there."

"Yeah, you ain't seen crazy yet, but you're about to," she muttered. "Who on earth terrorizes innocent old women?"

"That's what I'm afraid of. I'm on the way, and I should be there ahead of you."

"Maybe not," she replied. "I'm not very far away."

"I hope you're a little farther than that at this point. I'm pulling into the driveway."

"Good. I'm guessing they're in the backyard," she suggested. "Maybe you can get inside the house and go out that way."

"Did you lock it?"

"No, I don't think so," she said, her heart slamming against her chest. "I really don't think so."

"Take it easy. I'll go check it out. Please don't come barging in." And, with that, he disconnected.

It was all she could do to stay calm enough to keep driving. She took corner after corner, willing the miles to disappear. By the time she jerked her car into her driveway, she had barely stopped the vehicle before she was out and racing around to the back.

When she came to the patio, nobody was there, so she burst into the house and cried out, "Nan? Nan, where are you?"

Mack came down the stairs. He shook his head. "They're not here."

Her heart sank. "What do you mean, they're not here?"

"They're not here. I've already called for backup and forensics."

She stared at him in shock. "Somebody took her? Somebody took Nan?"

He nodded. "That's how it appears, but we can't jump to any conclusions right now."

"Sure we can," she snapped, staring at him. "Somebody kidnapped Nan."

He winced at that. "And the animals apparently."

She stared at him in horror. "Nan and the animals? All of them?" She called out, "Mugs, Mugs, where are you?" But no answer came. "Thaddeus," she cried out. "Thaddeus, are you here?" And again no answer. Calling for Goliath was almost useless, but she had to try. When she turned to face Mack, she stared at him and whispered, "They've taken everybody who matters to me."

He nodded, his face grim. "I know, and I'm pretty sure it was deliberate." From the expression on her face, it was clear she was about to crumble. He opened his arms, and she raced into them.

"How could somebody do something like that?" she cried out. "Nan's never hurt a soul." He didn't say anything to that. She looked up and frowned at him. "Okay, she may have made a bet or two, but she wouldn't have hurt anybody."

"I know that, sweetheart. Tell me again what she said on the phone."

Doreen struggled to remember the exact conversation and gave him the gist of it. "Just that somebody was here with a gun, and I needed to hurry back."

"He didn't make a sound the whole time?"

"No."

"Which means that she made the phone call with this guy's permission. As a matter of fact he might have been the one to force her to say that."

She nodded numbly and stared at him. "What does that mean?"

He shook his head. "We don't know that it means anything yet, except that he wanted you to show up."

"If he wanted me to show up, why isn't he here then?" she asked, spinning around in a circle. She bolted over to the fence, pounded on it, and yelled, "Richard, Richard, are you there?"

It took a moment, then she heard a chair slammed up against the fence, as he climbed up and scowled at her over the top. "I am now," he snapped.

"Did you hear anybody over here in the last hour?" Before he could respond with his grating answers, she went on. "Somebody's kidnapped my grandmother."

He stared at her in shock. "From your backyard?"

She nodded. "Yes. Did you hear anybody?"

He shook his head slowly. "No, I didn't, but I just now have come outside."

"You didn't hear anybody?"

He looked from Mack to Doreen and then back again. "No, I didn't. I swear." He frowned. "I didn't hear anything."

"You didn't hear them leave? You didn't hear Mugs barking?"

"Sure, I heard the dog barking like crazy," he said, then frowned. "I did hear somebody. I guess maybe it was your grandmother, calling for Mugs to come with her."

"Where did her voice seem to come from?"

He frowned, then looked toward the river and pointed. "I think it was down that way."

She stared at him in shock, took one look at the river, and bolted in that direction.

Mack called out behind her, "Doreen, wait!"

But there was no waiting for her, not right now, not when somebody had taken Nan and her animals. There was absolutely no life for Doreen after this if she didn't get all of them back. As she raced to the water, she stopped on the pathway and studied it. She couldn't read tracks—something that would have been useful right now—but right ahead on the left, as if heading to Rosemoor, was a fresh pile of dog poop. It was about the right size and shape for Mugs, although she couldn't guarantee that it was his. But she wanted desperately to believe that it was, and, with that in mind, she bolted toward Rosemoor, calling back to Mack, "I've got to search for them."

As she raced toward the home, she kept looking from side to side of the creek, wondering where the gunman would have taken Nan and why, or was she just at the wrong place at the wrong time? And how mean was that when she was just there holding down the fort, until Doreen got back?

Gasping for breath as she bolted around the corner of Rosemoor, she noted that nobody was up ahead. She scrambled to Nan's patio and made her way inside Nan's small apartment, but it was empty. Trembling now with the fear racking all the way through her, she bolted out to the hallway, where she saw Richie. "Have you seen Nan?"

He shook his head. "She was going up to your place. Didn't she get there?"

"She did, and a gunman was at my house apparently. She told me that he was holding a gun on her and to get home quickly. I did, but she wasn't there."

By then, a crowd had gathered around

them, and they all started to talk at once.

"Mack has backup coming, but we're looking for Nan. It looks like they came down the river."

"They didn't make it this far," Richie stated, with a defined clip of his head. "But don't you worry. We'll search this place. You go outside and search for her there."

She raced outside because, if the intruder had taken Nan this far, surely somebody would have seen her. As far as Doreen was concerned, that could only mean that they made it partway down the river but hadn't made it to Rosemoor. With that, she headed back up the river.

Chapter 21

DOREEN WALKED THE river again, checking both sides of the water, looking for more signs. No way that Mugs wouldn't have left her a sign if he could have in any way. Of course she didn't even know if he was still alive because, if this guy carried a gun and took elderly hostages, shooting a dog would be a minor offense in his mind. If he was trying to bring maximum pain to Doreen, he had absolutely everything he possibly could in terms of who she loved—except for Mack, and she winced at that.

The last thing she wanted was for Mack to get hurt too. She didn't want to contemplate how quickly her mind had added Mack to this equation because he was definitely on her radar as somebody she didn't want to lose. And, yes, if she had time and a minute to contemplate the issue, she would admit quite freely that she loved him. She didn't know how or when, but he'd snuck into her heart and had taken hold in a way she hadn't expected.

At the first house on the creek, she stopped, checked the fence, and found no sign of anybody having jumped over it. She could hardly imagine Nan jumping over it or the animals. She didn't find a gate on this property. At the second house, she also stopped and checked carefully over its rear fence but found nothing suspicious.

At the third house, she took a closer look and noted a little swathe of dirt at an angle to the fence. Sure enough, she found a gate of just planks, no hardware, so essentially hidden, but she pushed it open and stepped through, looking into the backyard. Another poop spot was right in front of her, hopefully telling her that Mugs had been here too. He would stay close to Nan and would hope that everybody else was coming to help. Of Goliath there was no sign and no way to know.

As she took several more steps forward, not sure if this guy had gone through the backyard to the front of the house, she heard a meow. She froze, then turned slowly, and there was Goliath. He raced toward her, and she scooped him up into her arms, hugging him tightly. With him safe, she quickly texted Mack where she was. At least now it was clear Nan had come this far. The gate behind Doreen was closed, yet Goliath hadn't jumped over it. He had remained here the whole time.

She whispered, "Where's Mugs, and where's Thaddeus?" Goliath wiggled out of her arms, jumped down, and led the way to the back of the house. She slowly approached, not sure that it was safe to go up or in, but she wouldn't leave her grandmother to face the gunman alone. When she reached the back door, she hesitated, but Goliath stretched up on his back legs, pawing at the door, so she pushed it open. She felt strange entering somebody else's house, but not strange enough to want to call out. If something was going on here, the last thing she wanted to do was let them know she had arrived.

As she slowly stepped inside, Goliath raced around the corner in front of her. She headed after him, coming around the corner to a living room. She froze. There in front of her was Nan, sitting with a cup of tea in her hand. She looked up and smiled.

"Hello, dear."

Chapter 22

DOREEN GASPED AND raced forward. "Are you all right?"

"I am," she replied, "but this gentleman is a little distraught."

Doreen stared at Nan, then slowly turned to look, and there was a guy, staring at her, the gun in his hand.

"There you are," he said, his tone harsh.

"Yeah, here I am. Now what is it you wanted so badly that you kidnapped my grandmother at gunpoint?" Doreen straightened and glared at him, as he approached, but the glare on his own face was pretty amazing, twisted in fury.

"*You*," he spat. "You're the one behind this whole mess. This used to be a nice peaceful town."

She stared at him. "Really? Because I didn't do anything but help bring cold-case crimes to light. That was it. This town had a few bad apples who did what they did. Not me."

He nodded. "But still, you had a big hand in it."

"I solved a bunch of cases and put a lot of criminals behind bars. So you think you can come into my yard and kidnap my grandmother?"

"I want you to reverse it."

"Reverse what?" Doreen asked, staring at him in shock.

"All of it," he bellowed. "I want it to go back to the way it used to be."

"Sure. So just how do you expect me to do that? Build a time machine?"

He stared at her for a moment, then shrugged. "I don't know. Not my problem. It's your mess, so deal with it." Then he waved the gun at her again.

"You do realize there are penalties for waving a gun at people, right?" He just glared at her, and she nodded. "You can't expect to get away with this. Just the fact that you're sitting here, holding a gun on my grandmother, will get you in more trouble than you've figured out."

"I'm not in any trouble," he snapped. "I

didn't do anything. You did."

There was just no sense to his words. "So what is really going on here? Were you affected by somebody who was in one of these cases or something?"

He snorted. "*Ya think*? How about lots of somebodies?"

"You're just pissed off about all of it in general, aren't you?" She turned to look at her grandmother. "Nan, did you get anything out of him? Anything that explains this madness?"

She nodded. "Yes, earlier he explained it much better than he is doing right now." She looked over at him and said, "Jethro, come on. You told me how much you loved this town and how you wanted all that peace and quiet brought back again."

"I do," he bellowed, "and she needs to make it happen."

"Wow," Doreen muttered, staring at him, but some sense of relief washed over her as she realized that maybe, just maybe, they would get out of this alive. "Where's Mugs?" She turned and looked around. "Mugs, come here, Mugs!" She stopped and stared at the gunman. "If you hurt my dog, you're—"

He glared at her. "I didn't hurt anybody,

and I didn't even know you had a dog."

At that, she turned and looked at Nan. "Nan, where is Mugs?"

"He followed us, honey, but I don't know where he went from here. I was a little busy." As she spoke, she motioned toward the *gentleman* still brandishing the gun in her direction, which just pissed off Doreen even more.

She walked over to him, her hands on her hips, and glared at him. Almost nose to nose she asked, "Where is my dog?"

He thrust his head toward her in a pugnacious manner and repeated, "I didn't touch your dog."

At that, she realized that maybe he was telling the truth.

When the kitchen door opened, and Mugs came racing toward her, she sighed with relief, then bent down and hugged him. "I don't know where you were, but I am really glad you're here now."

At that, the gunman frowned at the dog and asked, "Where did he come from?"

Nan smiled. "Oh, he was with us the whole time." The gunman looked at her in shock. She nodded. "He's just really good at hiding."

"Where was he hiding just now?" Jethro

asked, turning and looking around.

"Is this your house?" Doreen asked.

He stopped and glared at her. "Yes, and it was a nice and peaceful neighborhood, … until you moved in."

At that, she winced. "You might have a point there," she muttered. "Still, it's not my fault so many crimes were happening around this place that somebody had to come in and clean it up," she snapped. "How do you figure you'll get out of trouble on this one, especially after kidnapping my grandmother with a gun?"

He gave her another glare, then turned to look at Nan.

"Wait. Are you the one who broke into my house?"

He had the grace to look sheepish at that.

"*Great*. So I got stuck paying an extra security bill because my neighbor couldn't keep himself out of my own property."

Jethro added, "I'm gonna hold it against Richard too. He's a nutcase. Not to mention that ghostlike wife of his."

"Ghostlike?" she repeated, wondering about Jethro's sanity. Should he even be living alone in his condition?

"Yeah, ghostlike, as in, I'm pretty sure

she's been dead and gone for many years."

Doreen thought about all the times she had heard voices on the other side of the fence. "So, where are all those voices coming from?"

Jethro snickered. "Pretty sure Richard talks to his dead wife and then answers himself."

She glared at him. "I don't know about that," she replied. "I've heard different voices over there."

"Sure you have," Jethro scoffed.

"Regardless, if Richard wants to talk to his dead wife, he can talk to his dead wife. At least he didn't break into my house and then come back and kidnap my grandmother by gunpoint."

Jethro glared at her again. "I want you to stop."

"You want me to stop what?" she asked, raising both hands in frustration. She sensed Mack in the kitchen, instinctively realizing that was how Mugs had gotten in. She didn't know where he'd been outside, but having him at her side even now was a huge relief. But where was Thaddeus? She turned back to her grandmother. "So, we've got Mugs and Goliath, but where is Thaddeus?"

Nan shifted slightly, and there was Thad-

deus, curled up against her shoulder, snooz-
ing.

Doreen stared at the bird. "Wow. He's
sleeping through all this excitement?"

"I did wonder about that. You really do
need to give him more time to rest."

She snorted at her grandmother. "I can
give him some time, but am I responsible for
this mess keeping Thaddeus awake? No,"
she snapped. "I go to the bus station, simply
doing a good thing for somebody, and I come
back to this." She spun around to glare at the
gunman.

"Jethro, you really should put down that
gun," Nan stated, as she sipped her tea.

"Yes, *Jethro*," Doreen said in a hard tone.
"You really should put it down. Either put it
down or shoot me." He immediately lifted it in
the air, causing her to back up a step. "Or
don't shoot me and just put it down."

He gave her an evil grin. "All this noise and
the constant cacophony, see? It used to be a
quiet neighborhood." He was bellowing like a
maniac by the end of his sentence.

"Maybe it's time for you to move," Doreen
snapped.

He glared at her. "It's time for you to
move!"

"I've got news for you. I'm not moving," she snapped. "I have my grandmother's house, and I love it. I'm not moving."

"I'm not moving either," he growled.

"Except you're bound to be moving to the jail, at least for a while, over this little stunt you pulled today," Doreen declared, with an evil grin of her own. "So maybe the city will just sell your house on you."

He stared at her in horror. "Why would you say that?"

"You're standing here with a gun on my grandmother and I," Doreen yelled. "Nobody will believe you did that for no reason."

"Of course I did it for a reason." He looked over at Nan. "Besides, we haven't had tea together in a very long time."

Doreen snorted. "Really, Nan?"

In a serene tone, Nan replied, "We used to have tea every once in a while."

"And is that all?" Doreen asked cautiously.

Nan snickered, amused at the question. "Yes, dear, that's all."

Doreen sighed. "That's *some* good news."

Jethro glared at her. "I want you to stop this."

"What? Stop what, you psycho?" It was now her turn to raise the roof.

He hesitated, then Nan looked at him and nodded. "Go on. Tell her. She can't solve this if you don't explain it better."

"Solve what?" Doreen asked again, feeling even more frustrated. "I've got so many things going on right now. I don't know who's doing what anymore."

"This is why you need to solve it, dear."

"*Great*. Wouldn't it be nice if I knew what you were talking about?" When Jethro snorted, Doreen asked once more, "What? This is getting very frustrating, and I don't like it."

"I don't like a lot of things," Jethro said, "but I really don't want all the traffic coming down the river."

Doreen frowned at him. "What traffic?"

"People."

"Actually in the river or on the pathway?"

"On the pathway … at nighttime."

She stopped, "Are they cutting through your yard?"

He looked at her and nodded. "Sometimes, yeah."

She pondered that. "I don't know what any of this is related to, and right now I'm full up on cases, but you're supposedly asking me for help in this bizarre way is off the deep end."

"That's too bad," he snapped. "You need to figure this one out, and then you need to stop it."

"And I need to do that, why?" she cried out, eyeing him in frustration.

"Because it's what you do." And, with that, he slowly put the gun on the sideboard. "So now you need to go do that for me." Moving to the other end of the sideboard, he poured himself a cup of tea, then turned and shooed Doreen away. "Now … go off and do it."

"Wow, what a nice way to ask for my help, *not*," she snapped, as she turned slowly to stare at Mack, who was standing in the door-way, glaring at the tableau in complete frustration.

"Seriously?" Mack asked, his low tone lethal for anybody who didn't know him. "You kidnapped a woman at gunpoint because you wanted Doreen to solve something?"

"She's the one who's made all these things happen, so it's her mess to begin with," Jethro growled. "It only makes sense that I want her to stop it."

"Yet you haven't told me what it is, except for foot traffic by the river."

"Yeah, traffic on the river path, people at odd hours of the night, walking up and down and making so much noise all the time."

"Are they going somewhere or just checking out the neighborhood?"

"I don't know. … Going somewhere. But I think they're going through the neighbor's yard."

She turned and looked at the neighbor closer to Rosemoor.

He shook his head. "No, the other one."

At that, she mentally pictured the one place she hadn't had a chance to check out, and it was one that she hadn't seen anybody at in a while. "Who's living there?" she asked cautiously.

"A woman and she brings men in all the time."

Such a note of disgust filled his tone that she frowned at him. "So is that jealousy talking or something else?" He just glared at her. "Fine. Do you ever see any other women?"

"No, just the one."

Doreen pondered that, looked over at Nan, and asked, "Did you know about any of this?"

"No, I never heard about it. You haven't seen anything going on at the river, have you?"

Doreen shook her head. "No, I've never seen any such activities up and down the river. Sure, there's always been a few people walking by the river, but I'm farther up."

"Exactly," Jethro declared.

"So, why is she bringing people through the back way?" Doreen muttered.

Then she got it. She pulled out her phone and quickly sent Tammy a text. She had no idea if she would get it, if she had internet or if it would have to wait until she came to a bus stop. But when she got a response back a few minutes later, she quickly asked her several more questions. Then she turned and looked at Mack. "This may be related to Jed Barry and his operation." She held up her phone, so he could read the messages. "This is Tammy, and she's on the bus right now. They've stopped to pick up more people."

He nodded. "For these cross-country bus trips, they pick up people here and there along the way. She's in for a long bus ride if you're sending her all the way back east."

"I am," Doreen confirmed. "She wanted out."

"Good. As long as she really meant it."

"I hope so, but I have no way to know for sure, except she did say that another woman was involved with Jed and had a place up by the river."

"If she's got a place, why is she turning tricks?" Nan asked, then burst into laughter. "Unless she's making good money."

"Or she's got a deal with another ring around here," Mack suggested. "Just because Tammy was downtown doesn't mean that this other woman here was part of Jed's stable."

"No, it doesn't, or she's—" Doreen stopped and winced. "Or maybe she's the one behind all this." Mack frowned at her. Doreen shrugged. "There are madams who run prostitution rings too. So far, we have no idea if Jed is just muscle. I'm not sure he's got the brains for what's going on here."

Mack considered that. "How do you link all these random events to the one death? Did Tammy mention another woman? Did Tammy ever tell you that the other woman was the boss lady?"

Doreen shrugged. "No, but Tammy hadn't said a whole lot about the business end of things." With that, she phoned Tammy, but the phone call wouldn't go through. She sent another text and asked Tammy for the name of the other woman involved with Jed. It came back with a single name.

Julie.

Doreen immediately texted back. **Do you have a photo? Where did she live?**

Tammy responded. **No pictures. She never allowed them.**

The text conversation went back and forth, as Doreen asked questions and Tammy replied. Apparently this Julie didn't live with them now, yet had before. Sometimes she was there for meetings with Jed.

Seemed this Julie didn't have the same arrangement that Tammy did. As she pondered that, Tammy sent back another message.

I think she was more involved than Jed was.

Doreen pondered that and replied, **In what way?**

In all ways.

She winced and muttered, "That doesn't really confirm it." Yet in a way it did.

"Why wouldn't Tammy have told us this before?" Mack asked.

"Because I think her motto up until now had been, *say nothing, do nothing*. Talk to Jed. We need to figure out if this woman has anything to do with Jed and the dead guy."

"What dead guy?" Nan asked, with interest.

Doreen turned to her. "The guy shot with the Taser, the guy I still don't know anything about." Mack just glared at her, and she shrugged. "At this rate, we'll have it solved before I ever get his name. I still need to go down to the garden to see the crime scene," she muttered in frustration.

"Yeah, and you can now. Forensics and everybody are done down there now."

"I presume they were done days ago, and you didn't tell me, trying to keep me safe," she muttered shooting him a look.

He grinned at her. "They probably were done earlier."

"Not funny," she said.

"You were busy anyway," he reminded her. "It's not as if you needed to go there."

"It's a garden, and it's downtown, which would have put it in the proximity of Tammy. However, I don't know that it really has anything to do with whatever is going on here at the river."

"The river may have nothing to do with this," Mack reminded her. "Just because this guy has a beef about the noise level doesn't mean that the neighbor lady is involved."

"No, it doesn't," Doreen conceded thoughtfully. "I haven't seen or heard anything. But then I'm on the other side of this and further down." She pondered that. "I'll have to ask Richard when I get back home."

"But he's on the other side too," Mack pointed out. "I'll go have a talk with the neighbors on the other side here." He walked over to the sideboard and picked up the old man's gun and then waved over Chester, who had come in with Mack.

At Mack's exit, Chester walked over to the old man and said, "Come on, buddy. We need to take you downtown."

"I didn't do anything," he protested.

"Told you this would get you in trouble, Jethro," Nan declared. "You really shouldn't point those things at people." He just glared at her, then gave her a bright smile. "So tea next week?"

"Love to," Nan replied warmly.

And, with that, Jethro quite willingly walked out to the police cruiser with Chester.

Doreen stared at her grandmother, feeling as if she'd just dropped into some *Alice in Wonderland* rabbit hole. "Seriously, Nan, what was that all about?"

"Oh dear, child. He was just so frustrated and angry because he hasn't been able to sleep, always thinking that these people are coming into his backyard."

"But was it one person, two people?"

"I think it's a steady stream, and they bring

things. Sometimes he hears things clicking all night long."

"Oh good Lord," Doreen muttered, as she stared at her grandmother. "I think he needs to be in a home where someone is looking after him."

Nan nodded. "Probably so."

Doreen shook her head, still thinking over the new development. "So maybe the creekside activity has nothing to do with prostitution. Maybe she's some fence or money launderer or something."

At that, Nan eyed her with interest. "A fence over the fence," she quipped, with a bright smile.

Doreen closed her eyes. "That sounds like something I would have said," she muttered.

Nan burst out in laughter. "Yes, you definitely would have." She got up carefully, with Thaddeus still on her shoulder. "Jethro does make a mean cup of tea."

"That's always important," Doreen quipped and gave her grandmother a gentle hug. "I'm really glad you weren't hurt, but it would have been nice if I had known Jethro was more harmless than he first appeared."

"You never really know who's harmless or not," Nan declared. "I wasn't at all sure myself, even once you got here. I wasn't sure which way he would go. Particularly when you don't get any sleep, which can make people crazy."

"I hear you," Doreen muttered. "Come on. Let me walk you back down to Rosemoor and get everybody calmed down. They're all looking for you as well."

"Oh lovely," she exclaimed, with a bright laugh. "I'll have something to tell them, that's for sure."

And, with that, Doreen escorted her grandmother back to Rosemoor. If Mack wanted to talk to Nan, he would know right where to find her.

Chapter 23

Friday Late Afternoon …

OVER AN HOUR later Doreen made it to her place again. She collapsed on the patio, all the animals with her again, and all safe. She reached down and hugged Mugs. "Thank you, buddy. I guess you followed them on your own, *huh*?" She knew she wouldn't get any answers from him. With Thaddeus curled up on her shoulder again— as if he had no intention of ever leaving—she had no intention of ever leaving him again either. Also she felt he had forgiven her for whatever she had done to upset him.

She kept petting him and smoothing his feathers, as she tried to calm herself down too. It had been one heck of a day, and she hadn't had any further check-ins with Mack yet. When she heard footsteps coming across the kitchen floor, she tensed but then relaxed. "There's no coffee," she called out.

"We can change that," Mack replied, with a note of humor.

She smiled over at him, through the open back door. "I don't know about you, but I'm pretty tired."

He nodded. "Nothing like finding out that your grandmother has been escorted away at gunpoint, *huh*?"

"Right? I still don't really get that."

"I don't either, but I guess Jethro was making some sense to her. According to Nan, he was really grumpy and hadn't slept in days because of the nocturnal foot traffic. Why was he blaming you though?"

"I don't know if he was so much blaming me as he thought that I could fix it," she muttered. "I think he was blaming the fact that I brought so much attention to Kelowna with all these cases that he thought maybe the traffic was a result of that. Nan did share a little bit more information, as I took her home. So, if you need to talk to her, you could head to Rosemoor, but she's pretty tired as well."

"No, it's fine for now. I will need to talk to her, but Darren is on his way over there now. He can do the initial questioning. I figured you probably had as much information as anybody."

"I would like to think so," she muttered, "although sometimes I don't know much of anything anymore."

He gave a heavy laugh. "Right. That's exactly how I feel around you sometimes. You come up with stuff so fast and without anybody really having a full understanding. Then you leave the rest of us in the dark, gasping at the speed with which you've gotten things rolling."

"Not this time," she corrected, "but the good news is, Mugs stayed on Nan's tail the whole way. Even with Thaddeus on her shoulder from the time I left the house, Mugs wouldn't leave them alone, and Goliath stayed at Jethro's gate to let me know which house to search."

"Which in itself is absolutely fabulous," he noted, as he reached down to pet both animals. "You've certainly got them well trained."

"I don't have them trained at all," she admitted. "That's the part that scares me. I don't have them trained, and they can do all kinds of stuff, maybe even more than this, but I wouldn't know. Or maybe they're trying to do more, and I have no way of knowing."

"I wouldn't worry about it right now," he

said, brushing the hair off her face. "You've had quite the day."

"I have," she agreed, with a yawn. "What about you? Did you find anybody at Jethro's neighbor's house?"

He shook his head. "No, I sure didn't, but we've got a sentry posted to keep an eye out. If Julie's got any activity going on tonight, we'll find out."

"Good. In that case, after this, when you go home, I'm crashing. Hopefully not to wake up until halfway through tomorrow."

He smiled. "I hope so for your sake," he muttered. "Honestly I could hope for that for myself too."

"Thanks for showing up,"

He gave her a mock look of horror. "As if I had a choice."

She laughed. "No, you really didn't have a choice in many ways, but I still appreciate the fact that you were there."

Mack squeezed her fingers. "You sent Tammy home on a bus, *huh*?"

"Yeah. It didn't even occur to me that may-be she should stay in town until we sorted out this mess for good."

"I was wondering about that too," he shared, his tone suspiciously neutral. "I guess we know where she is at the moment."

"I really hope she isn't part of this," Doreen murmured. "It makes me feel bad to consider that I might have let her disappear. Not only let her but helped her."

"I don't know for sure either way, but it would have been nice if you'd given us the heads-up."

"But you told me that she was in the clear, and she was only being questioned related to Jed."

"True, at that time," Mack noted. "However, as we found out later, she knows a lot more about other things too."

Doreen sighed at that. "Hopefully she'll continue to answer questions as she travels across Canada," she added, with a smile.

"Considering you paid for her ticket, let's hope she remains on the bus."

"I paid for the bus ticket, and Nan bought her a few outfits from the thrift store. Nan gave her some running-around money too. Enough to buy a few meals and get back to her mother and her family."

"That was a good thing that you did," he stated. "I know times haven't been easy on you, but you're always thinking about other people."

She smiled at him. "I hope you still think so at the end of this," she muttered, "because if Tammy turns out to be part of it …"

He nodded. "If she is part of it, nobody'll be happy that you helped an accomplice to murder escape."

Chapter 24

Saturday Early Morning ...

THE NEXT MORNING Doreen woke with several texts from Tammy. Doreen smiled as the woman kept her updated with her progress. It was an interesting thing to decide to take a bus instead of flying. Yes, it was cheaper for Doreen to manage, yet Tammy's reasoning was also very enlightening. When the subject of travel options had been brought up, Tammy had said that she would prefer the time to undergo some mental changes, taking that time to adjust to and to become the person her family expected her to be, and to leave all this behind. She couldn't do that on a flight, but she was hoping that, over so many days of traveling, she could slowly evolve into the person she used to be.

Doreen had been fine with whatever mode

Tammy had chosen and found it interesting because she could relate to Tammy's reasoning behind it.

As Doreen was poring through Tammy's messages, Doreen realized that she'd slept in again. She shook her head at that. She never used to be allowed to sleep in, and the few times it had happened always came as a bit of a shock. Now it was kind of nice, and she enjoyed the freedom to just stay in bed for a while. She smiled and yawned. She didn't have any particular reason to get up. She didn't have any reason to do anything really.

Apparently her good fortune would bring enough money to her that she would be just fine in the future. All she had to do was figure out what she wanted to do as she grew old.

She burst out laughing at that. Talk about blessings. Nan had given Doreen a gift that she could never repay. Not that Nan wanted repayment, but it was just amazing to think of Nan having done such a thing, having planned this out decades ago. Of course Nan hadn't known that life would leave Doreen this way, but to have put some thought into what would happen if it did, and so many years ago, had been just amazing.

She got up, dressed, and headed downstairs, wanting that first cup of coffee. As she took a look around the kitchen, she realized she could bring in more food and stock up on pet food as well. That would make the animals happy, she was sure.

She opened the back door for them and proceeded to fill up all their food bowls, giving them the choice of eating first or going out first. Mugs immediately chose food. As soon as he was done, he bolted outside and headed to the garden. She smiled at that. "It's a beautiful house and yard, isn't it, Mugs?"

Once the coffee was on, she rustled up a simple breakfast for herself and took it outside to eat. With the animals now interested in her food, she groaned. "I just fed you guys."

Mugs gave her that typical woebegone look of his. After all, his dry meal was just one of many that she was willing to provide. She did know he would get overweight fast if she gave him unlimited food. She'd had a run-in with a strange situation a while back, when he started gaining weight abnormally. Luckily she discovered pretty quickly that Thaddeus had been handing out treats behind her back. With some extra laps, Mugs was doing better. He even often stopped eating when he was full, but maybe the issue was the type of food the animals preferred. She would look into more options for them.

She sat in the fresh air, shutting her eyelids, as she felt the breeze lift her hair and gently blow it back. It was truly a beautiful day. She knew it was just the calm before the storm, literally before everything broke loose. At least that had been her experience. She smiled at that, but almost immediately her phone rang. Stifling a groan, she looked down to see it was Nan. She quickly answered it. "Good morning. How are you doing?"

"I'm fine," Nan replied in a brisk tone. "Jethro's not though."

"What do you mean?"

"They're thinking about charging him," she wailed, her tone quite upset.

At that, Doreen sighed. "He pulled a gun on you, Nan. He held you against your will and even took you away at gunpoint."

"It wasn't real though," she snapped.

Doreen stared at the phone. "What? The gun wasn't real?"

"No, it wasn't. He just wanted to make his point, to ensure that somebody would look into all the comings and goings in the area and figured you would be the best person for the job."

"You've got to be kidding me. So he marches you at gunpoint down to his house instead of just asking for my help?"

"I had turned him down for tea several times recently," Nan added. "I guess he got tired of hearing no for an answer."

Doreen didn't even know what to say to that. Her jaw opened, then slowly closed again. "I'm not sure what they would be charging him with, but I don't imagine he'll get off completely."

"But he should," Nan argued.

"Nan, he created quite the stir when you and the animals all went missing, and the police don't take kindly to people wasting resources. I don't think you can do much of anything about it."

"I'm heading down there now," she declared. "I want to talk to him."

"Did they keep him overnight?" Doreen asked.

"Yes, they did. I guess somebody, … somebody was quite upset at my disappearance."

"*Everybody* was upset, naturally," Doreen declared. "Nan, this isn't something to fool around with. We have an awful lot of serious cases right now that are possibly coming together, causing even more trouble. Whether Jethro was part of any of that or not, I don't know, but it's up to the police to figure that out."

Nan gasped. "Since when do you leave stuff like that to the police?"

She winced. "When I find my grandmother has been kidnapped by a crazy gunman," she snapped. "Worse yet, kidnapped over tea."

"He didn't mean to hurt anyone, and he certainly didn't hurt me."

Doreen sort of understood where Nan was coming from. She shook her head, not at all sure how to make any of this easy on her grandmother.

"It doesn't matter what he did, since I'm okay and back home now. So I'm going down there to talk to the cops now." Nan ended the call abruptly.

Doreen sat here, staring at her phone, then decided to call Mack about it.

When he answered the phone, he was clearly distracted. "Doreen, is it important? I'm really busy."

"Nan's on her way down to the station. She doesn't want Jethro charged."

A moment of shocked silence came. "What?"

Doreen quickly explained the little bit that Nan had told her.

"Yeah, we found out the gun wasn't real last night, when we arrested him," Mack confirmed. "However, all that time *before* we found her, we didn't know that. He's lucky that he wasn't shot. Pulling a stunt like that can get a guy hurt."

"Exactly, and whether Nan knew it at any point in time before this all came to an end, I don't know."

"This is getting out of hand," Mack grumbled. "We can't have people kidnapping each other in order to bring our attention to a neighborhood problem."

"Particularly when I didn't even know Jethro existed, and nobody had ever talked to me about the problem at the creek at night," she pointed out.

Mack groaned. "Look. I'll talk to Nan when she gets here, but I'm not sure we can do anything. It sends a bad signal to the community if we let some man waving a gun around be accepted as the norm in Kelowna."

"I know. I just wanted to give you a heads-up."

"Thanks for that," he muttered. "How's your bus traveler?"

"She's doing much better," she shared. "I woke up to a series of texts from her. In one of them she told me that she had picked up a journal and is working on some of her issues."

"Good. ... Sorry. I've got to go." And, with that, he was gone.

Doreen wasn't sure whether that meant Nan was already at his desk, about to berate him for what he'd done, or if something else had happened. Still, Doreen couldn't imagine that this would be an easy time for Mack. Maybe this Jethro guy would get off with a warning. If he'd had a clean record all his life, maybe they would chalk it up to poor judgment under difficult circumstances and a lack of sleep.

Doreen didn't know his history, and he might have had forty-seven zillion parking tickets and may have refused to deal with any authority issues. Who knew? She had no clue what Nan's involvement in all this would mean for Doreen or if it should mean anything at all. But it would, of course, because the minute Nan got involved, everybody was involved.

Doreen scrubbed her face, then picked up her coffee and tossed back the rest of the cup. She definitely would need a second one at this point. She headed back inside, got herself some more coffee, and returned outside, all the while wondering who would phone her first, Mack or Nan.

When her phone rang, it was somebody she wasn't expecting at all. She stared down at the phone in pleasant surprise. "Hey, Bernard. What's up?"

"I hear you're back in trouble again already."

She snorted. "Wow, good news travels fast, doesn't it?" His laughter peeled out, putting a smile on her face. "Besides, I'm not really in trouble. It's just life, you know?"

"If you're out rescuing prostitutes and going up against the local madam, that's a whole different story." At his use of the term *local madam*, her eyebrows shot up.

"How do you know about the local madam?" she asked hesitantly.

He chuckled. "Not in that way," he clarified. "I've never needed to pay for sex in my life."

"No offense was intended, and I'm certainly glad to hear that. It's wonderful to know you don't suffer in that department," she replied, her tone filled with mirth. "So, what do you know about her otherwise?"

"I did hear that she had moved recently, something about the increased rental prices."

At that, Doreen closed her eyes and whispered, "Oh, that would explain it."

"Explain what?" he asked.

Doreen ignored his question and instead asked one of her own. "Do you have any idea where she moved to?"

"No, I just know that she's not downtown, not since the last little bit."

"Any idea how long ago?" she asked.

"*Hmm.*" He pondered that. "I want to say in the last month or two."

"Okay," she muttered, exasperated, yet understanding. "That would potentially explain one of the problems we have going on right now."

"You always have so much action going on in your life," he said, almost with a note of envy in his tone.

She burst out laughing. "That's true, but it's not necessarily a good thing."

At that, he chuckled. "No, I guess that's a fair point. It's just easy to look at your life and to realize how much more exciting it is than mine."

"Bernard, your world is very exciting," she stated in astonishment. "I can't imagine you missing out on anything, the way you live your life."

"Maybe, but it is an odd thing to realize that I'm out of the loop a bit. Maybe that's why I'm calling, just trying to figure out if I can do anything to help."

"You could confirm the location of the madam for me."

He burst out laughing. "That's just a matter of a phone call."

"Make it then. I definitely don't want my number on any madam's phone list," she added, with a chuckle.

"Okay, give me a few minutes," he said. Then he quickly rang off.

She stared down at the phone. "Is it really that easy?" Then Doreen realized that Tammy was probably the best resource that Doreen had on this particular industry. So, she quickly sent off a series of texts, knowing that Tammy would reply when and if there was an internet connection she could utilize. Traveling by bus had to be iffy at the best of times, depending on the mountain passes. Doreen didn't know how much usage Tammy's cell phone had available either.

Doreen didn't really want Tammy to disappear into the other side of this, but Doreen couldn't really blame Tammy if she did. Doreen would represent a part of Tammy's old life, and she may well want to cut all ties. Doreen was still worried that, at some level, Tammy might have had something more to offer in this case. Doreen just didn't want it to be something terrible, like *commission of crimes* kind of terrible. Particularly since Doreen had gone to bat for Tammy.

By the time Doreen finished working out all the questions she wanted answered, she then apologized for not having thought of going through all this while they could talk in person. Doreen chastised herself for not having more of an idea where this was going, but how could she have? Everything had been so up in the air, and it had seemed more important to just get Tammy out of Jed's grasp and on her way, before it became a bigger problem.

Plus even Mack didn't think all these disjointed incidents—dead man in a community garden, prostitution ring in downtown Kelowna, Jethro's complaint of noisy nighttime activity on the creek—were all connected. Yet Doreen's gut kept telling her that. And so she reminded Mack of that often.

Still, the local authorities were working on it, and, as long as someone was willing to go to bat for people, just as Doreen and Nan had done, life would stay interesting. At the thought of Nan, Doreen pictured her down at the police station, giving them trouble over Jethro. Doreen should probably get Bernard invested in some of these problems, since he was bored, had time and money, and could certainly become a force for good, if anybody wanted him involved.

Maybe that was the problem. Nobody wanted him involved because, once involved, he would quite likely take over. She chuckled at that thought because he was who he was, and definitely somebody she could use on her cold cases.

Just as she was finishing off her coffee, Bernard called back.

"She's out near you," he greeted her.

"Did she just tell you that?"

"No, obviously I have a few other avenues at my disposal," he replied. "I definitely didn't phone her and ask, nor did I make an ap-pointment, getting her address in the midst of said hypothetical transaction. However, I do have a friend who utilizes some of her exclusive services."

"Does he utilize other services, other women?"

"No, he was very particular about her, just her."

"So, he pays a higher price, I assume?"

"Exactly, but she did move recently and is renting a house not all that far from you."

"Do you know if she's involved in anything else?"

"Like what?" he asked curiously.

"Fencing of stolen goods has been a thought."

He hesitated. "Kelowna doesn't have great numbers of high clientele, and she's aging, so it is quite possible that she's been looking at other business avenues."

"Right. So, there have been complaints about increased activities at a house not very far from me, noises at nighttime," she murmured, "and we wondered if it was her."

"Seems it's quite possible," he noted. "I know my friend would be pretty upset if she went out of business."

"If he cares that much for her, maybe he should convince her to get out of the business and to do something else," she suggested, with a note of amusement.

"He's tried, several times, in fact, but I think she's one of the few who actually likes it."

"Which can only mean that she's not getting beaten up and abused."

"Exactly, but she's been controlling things on her own for quite a while."

"Do you know anything about Jed?" She then took a moment and explained who he was.

"No. I don't really know too much more about it than the odd snippets here and there that I've heard from my friend. Frankly it's not exactly the circle of people I'm used to dealing with."

She laughed at that. "Except for a certain friend of yours, who likes to use an escort service."

"They're not cheap either," he added.

"Yeah, just out of curiosity, how much is a night with her?"

"When she was commanding her top prices in Vancouver a few years back, I understand she was easily getting five grand a night."

Doreen's jaw dropped at that. "Seriously?" She squeaked out the word, dumbfounded.

"Yeah, some of the top girls get incredible money. She moved up here—though I'm not

exactly sure how many years ago, ten perhaps—because she was getting older, facing
a lot of competition, and wasn't able to com-
mand the same prices. Out here, the choices
for escorts are limited, shall we say, and she
found her niche. She stayed pretty private,
using only referrals for the longest time."

"I'm just trying to figure out if she has anything to do with Jed Barry's prostitution
operation," she shared.

"My understanding was that they were trying to expand the industry and get more girls,
but I don't think she particularly likes working
with Jed."

"He's abusive and quite the bully, so I don't
know why she would. I really don't even know
why she would need him."

"Because he had girls. I think that's probably how she would put it."

"I guess she's probably not open to talking
to me, is she?"

"No, particularly not if you're interested in
pinning something on her."

"Which we might be, I don't know," she
admitted, with a groan.

"What's this got to do with anything anyway?"

She explained about the missing police

Taser used in a recent murder.

"That Taser went missing about ten years ago?" Bernard asked.

"Yes," she said, then gasped. "Oh no, that's an interesting coincidence."

"What?"

"She moved up here about that same time and is potentially involved in moving stolen goods."

"I don't know that she was doing that back then—or if she is at all, for that matter."

"She may have just gotten into that sideline by way of Jed," Doreen murmured. "After all, Jed was already into B&Es back then, it seems."

"Maybe, I don't know." Just then his phone buzzed. "Hey, I've got another call coming in. I've got to run." With that, he quickly disconnected.

Doreen wondered if any of this information was helpful or if, once again, it was just a lot of speculation with no proof of anything. And without Nan or Mack getting back to her, Doreen had no idea how any part of this whole scenario was going. Though it wasn't long before Nan called her back.

"Jethro's out," she announced, almost a crow of triumph in her tone.

Doreen stared at the phone. "Oh?"

"Yes, I paid his bail."

At that, Doreen winced. "Oh my, do you think that was a wise thing to do?"

Nan hesitated. "I don't know whether it was smart or not, but I really did feel a little bit guilty for what he was doing in the first place."

Doreen groaned. "Why? All this because you turned him down for tea?"

"Yes. He's really a nice man. He's just lonely."

"*Right*," Doreen muttered, followed by a sigh. "So, where are you now, Nan?"

"Home, and he's coming over for tea. I don't think it's good for him to be all alone up there. He really should be in a place like this, with the rest of us. If he were here, he wouldn't be quite so lonely."

"Maybe not, but I can't imagine how much trouble the two of you could get into if he was there with you."

At that, Nan burst out into delighted laughter. "Why don't you come down?" she asked. "It would be good for you to meet him under better circumstances."

"Really? I'm not so sure about that. And what will Richie think?"

"Come on," Nan repeated, but her invitation sounded more like an order.

Doreen wasn't at all sure that she wanted to go, but finally she relented. "Fine, I'll come down just for a quick visit. It'll probably do my nightmares good to see him in a totally different light."

"Exactly," Nan agreed. "He's a very nice man."

"*Nan*."

"Oh, stop. I know exactly what happened, and I know why. Whether you choose to believe it or not, he never intended to hurt me."

She sighed at that. "Fine, but I'm still not convinced."

And, with that, she ended the call.

Chapter 25

Saturday Mid-morning ...

DOREEN GATHERED HER animals, getting ready to go to Nan's place, when Mack phoned her. "Hey," she greeted him. "I guess you had a fine morning, with Nan on the rampage."

"*Not*," he snapped. "After failing to talk anybody into releasing him, your grandmother posted bail for the guy."

"I know. She just told me. I'm about to head to Rosemoor to see her. Apparently she's invited him for tea."

"You're what?"

"I know. I know, and you don't want me to go see him, I'm sure."

"No, I don't," he roared. Then he sighed. "Absolutely no point in trying to talk you out of it either, is there? You or Nan."

She winced. "We won't get into trouble."

"Yes, you will."

She groaned. "No, we're not trouble. We're just more complicated. But you like complicated, right?"

He growled now. "Apparently, though I must need my head examined. I can't believe you're willfully going down to see this guy."

"I wanted to confirm that Nan was okay because I don't trust Jethro. However, she wants me to meet him *under different circumstances*, so I know that he's okay. ... I guess that doesn't make a whole lot of sense."

"No, it doesn't. None of this makes any sense at all," he snapped. "At least call me when you're down there and let me know that everything is okay. And please stay in touch. I don't want another scenario like yesterday."

"If he kidnaps Nan again, you can lock him up and throw away the key."

"*Great*. That's like shutting the door after you let the horses out of the barn." With a loud sigh, he disconnected.

She stepped into her backyard with her animals, still considering the madam living nearby. Would she entertain clients there? Yet why not? She lived there. "It makes sense. Why would you pay for a hotel or another location?" she asked herself, as she walked to the creek.

Maybe Richard knew something. She stopped at the corner of Richard's fence and called out to him. "Richard, are you there?" She looked around the side just in time to see Richard's head pop out over on her side of the garden. She called to him and walked up closer. "Hey, do you know anything about your neighbors down there?"

He frowned at her. "Which neighbors?"

She sighed. "Yeah, that would help, wouldn't it?" She just nodded and muttered to herself, "It sure would."

"What's going on with you?" Richard frowned.

"You missed all the excitement yesterday." She quickly filled him in, and he sighed, shaking his head.

"Yeah, Jethro lost his wife a few years back. I heard at one point he was pursuing some other woman rather heavily."

"Yeah, apparently that may have been my grandmother."

He stared at her and then laughed. "Wouldn't that be justice?"

"What would be so *just* about it?" she asked.

He smirked. "Everything has a way of coming back to you, it seems."

"Hey, not on purpose though. It's not my fault."

He glared at her. "To hear you tell it, you're not at fault, and you don't have anything to do with other people's lives … ever."

"That's not fair," she said. "Up until now, everything had been independent of Nan's personal life."

He shrugged at that. "I'm not sure you can really say that," he pointed out.

"Whatever. But regardless, is Jethro dangerous or not?"

At that, Richard immediately shook his head. "No, I wouldn't say so. He's pretty harmless. He's just been very lonely. However, this sounds a little over-the-top, even for him." Richard shrugged. "But maybe not. I've noticed a bit more noise from down there myself, but I just ignored it. After all, living next to you has made me immune to crazy happenings at all hours."

"I haven't heard anything at all," she muttered as she looked down in the direction of those homes. She talked to Richard a little bit more, not learning anything else of value, so she waved off. She immediately picked up her pace and headed down the greenway. The animals got into the spirit of things again and raced down to Nan's.

As Doreen got closer to the potential madam's home again, she wondered at a lifestyle like that. It wasn't for Doreen, but if Julie had found some sense of control in it, who was Doreen to argue? It wasn't legal in Canada, but there were definitely lots of places in the world where it was. She wondered at the woman's decision to continue working, always on the wrong side of the law, where you had to look over your shoulder all the time. That couldn't be terribly comfortable for anyone. Most people didn't see the law as being anything to worry about, but, as Doreen had discovered, an awful lot of people were looking over their shoulders on a constant basis.

She had never tried to make law enforcement look foolish, and she'd certainly done her best to give them the credit when she could, but it had also been an eye-opener to understand just how much crime happened in Kelowna, and how little of it law enforcement could stay on top of.

The first problem was the lack of manpower. The second problem was just the lack of time available to properly handle each and every case. She also knew from Mack just how frustrating that was for the department as well.

She felt sorry for them sometimes because they did so much. Then, out of the blue, something else went wrong, and somebody had to work late, even after they'd already worked all day. She had thought maybe she could become a cop or a detective, but now she knew better. From time to time she even considered becoming a lawyer, but she wasn't really up for that either. She sighed.

"Honestly, Doreen, it sounds as if you're just lazy," she mumbled to herself. And yet that wasn't right either because she wasn't lazy, though she did have to be motivated. So whatever her goal, it had to be big enough that it really mattered, and, in her life, solving these crimes really mattered to her. The fact that she appeared to be decent at it was just an added bonus.

Mack had mentioned a couple times that the way she thought and processed information was unique. While she wasn't sure about that, so far it had worked out to everybody's advantage, so she was good with it. Besides, it was nice—after years of feeling completely ineffective and useless—to realize she had some redeeming value and something to offer society. Not conventional in any way, shape, or form, yet, for all the families she had helped, surely she would get a pass for some of the things she'd done wrong. And, if she got a pass, maybe others, like Jethro, should get a pass too. She groaned at that.

"Fine," she muttered, as she approached Nan's home at Rosemoor. "Maybe he'll get a pass, but I'm not so ready to say that yet."

As she walked over to the patio, her normal spot had already been taken by Jethro, and Nan? … Darned if she wasn't primping in front of him. Doreen sighed as she walked up. When she caught Nan's eye, her grandmother immediately bounced to her feet and beamed at her.

"You did come," she exclaimed. "When you took so long, I was afraid you'd changed your mind."

Doreen shrugged. "It's not that I changed my mind, more that I was waylaid on the way." Nan looked at her with an inquisitive expression, but Doreen just shook her head. "Nothing to worry about."

"Oh good," Nan said, "we have enough things to worry about."

Doreen gave an eye roll at that. "Yeah, *ya think*?" Then she turned and gave Jethro a good frown.

He stood up and stumbled, almost falling over, yet trying to recover. He reached out with a hand to shake hers, even though she hadn't offered her own. "Thank you, thank you, thank you."

She glared at him. "Thank me for what? I still want to give you a swift kick for what you did to Nan. You kidnapped the only family I had, and you pointed a gun at her. Do you know how freaked out I was for all that time? Plus my animals were missing too."

Jethro looked at her, then at Nan and shrugged. "She knew I would never hurt her."

"Maybe. Did she know your gun was fake? I don't think so. Not for a long time. I sure didn't. I didn't know that at all."

At that, understanding crossed his face. "You were worried about her, weren't you?"

"Of course I was worried about her. Nan is very special to me. I don't like it when people come in and take her, even with fake guns. You say you weren't planning on hurting her, but I had no way of knowing that. I don't even know you."

"No, of course not," he agreed, then

grinned bashfully. "She's always been a real good friend of mine."

"If that were truly the case, you wouldn't have done what you did."

He shrugged, sat down again, and nodded. "That was yesterday, and, at our age, yesterday is over, and we're already onto the next thing."

"Is that because you lost your memory already or because you figured out that life is too short, and you want to move on and try something new?"

"Both," he replied, looking at her with a nod of understanding. "I see that you do understand."

"It doesn't make me very happy, but I do understand."

Nan burst out laughing at that. "Doreen is very, very good," she declared, patting Jethro's hand. "She'll solve your problem, so don't you worry too much."

Doreen glared at Nan. "Maybe I'll solve his problem, and maybe not."

Nan just waved her hand, as if to completely dismiss Doreen's concerns. But the conversation was so completely normal for the two of them that Doreen was dragged into a weird sense of normalcy very quickly. Finally she sighed, sipped her tea, and said, "If you want me to solve this, you need to tell me more."

At that, Nan crowed. "See? I told you, Jethro."

Doreen glared at her grandmother again. "*No promises.*"

Jethro looked at her with so much gratitude that it felt as if she'd been kicking a puppy up until now. She sighed heavily. "What noises have you heard? What time of night does this happen, and have you actually seen anything?"

He shook his head. "I'm not the kind to stand out there and watch," he noted stiffly.

She nodded. "That's too bad because, if we had some idea of what she was doing, maybe we would have a way to stop whatever it is that's bothering you. Because just being noisy won't be nearly enough to make that happen."

He frowned at her, and she frowned right back. After a moment, he sighed. "Your grandmother already said as much to me."

"Good, I'm glad to hear that she's trying to talk some sense into you," she muttered. She looked from Nan and back to him again. "Just because whoever lives in that house now is causing some noise—and the neighborhood has gone to the dogs or whatever, as far as you're concerned—it doesn't mean that it comes to a stop just because you say so."

He nodded. "I get that. I really do, but the noises I'm hearing are not the same."

"Then you need to tell me about them."

He hesitated. "Muffled voices, banging, and sounds of people grunting, as if they're moving heavy items."

She nodded. "What else?"

"Phones ringing, like all night long."

"But the creek is a pathway," she pointed out, "so people could be walking back and forth, using it as a way to get wherever they want to go."

He stared at her. "But, as you well know, there aren't a whole lot of places to go along my stretch of the creek. Just houses, not businesses."

"That's true," she muttered. "I walk along the creek all the time, but I can't say I've seen or heard any of that commotion. However, I am walking in the daytime."

"The disturbances are relatively new," Jethro added.

"Like in the last what? Day? Week? Month? Year?"

He thought about it for a moment. "The last month maybe? It just started to get really bad recently."

"That time line certainly fits with the woman moving in about a month ago, but it doesn't mean that *this* woman had anything to do with the traffic or the noises or that she was doing anything wrong."

As Doreen started to realize, just by being close to Mack, people could do all kinds of things that others didn't like, yet were still legal. They weren't in trouble over it at all just because someone didn't like it. That didn't give them the right to try to put a stop to freedoms that we all had. Complaining was one thing, but actively doing something constructive to change the scenario and in such a way that was illegal was a whole different story. Like drawing a gun on Nan.

As Doreen sat here sipping her tea, she thought about anything else she might ask. "Have you ever seen her?"

"No. … That's another thing I thought was weird. Is she hiding on purpose?"

"What about at the front of the house?"

He shrugged. "It's not really my street."

At that, she studied him, then realization dawned. "Right, it's another cul-de-sac, like on my street. You're just farther down. So I get that your view out the front isn't the same as hers would be," she muttered. As she sat here, quiet once again, the others just let her stew away in her own thoughts for a few minutes.

Finally Nan asked her, "What's the verdict?"

She glared at her. "The verdict is that the whole thing is ridiculous."

Nan laughed at her. "Doesn't mean that something isn't there."

"Sure, probably something is there, but solving this one isn't quite so simple."

"Why not?" Nan asked.

"Because, so far, we don't know that Julie is doing anything wrong. You may like to dance all night long, but just because somebody else doesn't like it, doesn't mean that you have to stop dancing or that it is illegal."

"Of course not." Nan stared at her in astonishment. "Why would anybody not want me dancing?"

"It's not about the dancing. … That's the point," Doreen reminded her. "It's the fact that other people may be offended by it. We don't know for sure that this Julie woman is doing anything wrong—or that she's the one making all the noises and encouraging all the nighttime foot traffic on the creek either. Plus, just because Jethro doesn't like what she's doing or what *whoever* is doing, that isn't enough justification for us to step up and try to stop it."

Jethro looked at her and nodded slowly. "That's fine, and I understand your point, but maybe she could stop all the late-night comings and goings and maybe keep the noise level down a bit."

"That's the interesting part," Doreen murmured. "That's the part I want to know more about."

He looked at her hopefully. "Does that mean you'll take the case?"

She frowned at him. "I'm not really in any legitimate position to be taking on cases anyway," she explained.

He shrugged. "Nan says you can."

"Of course she does," Doreen grumbled with a sigh, looking over at her grandmother with affection. "Nan thinks I can move the stars and the moon sometimes."

"You can," Nan declared. "You're the only person I know who has made as much happen in this town as you have."

Doreen smiled. "That may well be, but that

still doesn't mean that all of this will work out the way you want it to," she reminded her.

Nan had the grace to back off slightly and admitted, "That's true. We don't always get everything we want, do we?"

"No, we sure don't." Doreen faced Jethro. "However, if you haven't seen any of the goings-on, and you can't identify any of the people or the reason for the noise, and you haven't seen the Julie person in question, what is it you expect me to do?"

He looked as if she had just brought up something he hadn't even considered. He let out a slow, heavy breath. "I guess that does make it a little harder, doesn't it?"

"Absolutely it does," she agreed, with a nod. "It doesn't make it impossible, but we do need more information in order to figure out what's really going on." Reaching for her phone, she tapped on it for a moment. "Now, Jethro, do you recognize these people at all? Have you ever seen them nearby?" She held up her phone with a couple of the photos she had gotten of Jed and Tammy. "Have you seen either of these people?" Then she brought up one of Frankie.

Jethro stared at them all and slowly shook his head. "Do you think they're connected?"

he asked evenly.

"I'm not sure about that," she shared, "but it is something that I needed to ask." She stared at the photo of Frankie for a long moment. "I'm particularly wondering about this one."

He looked at it again and shrugged. "I mean, it's possible, and I can't say that I've *never* seen him, but I'm not getting an *Oh yeah, I know that guy* feeling."

"Right, and that is important."

Nan also looked at the photos and shrugged. "They're not the greatest photos either, child."

"Of course not," Doreen conceded. "It's not easy to get clear shots sometimes, especially on the sly." She studied the photos and then put away her phone. "I just wondered if they were connected to Julie somehow."

"Oh, it's quite possible, I'm sure," Jethro noted. "Somebody is coming and going at all hours. She hasn't been there all that long either. Just enough to cause chaos," he muttered.

"This neighbor's house, who actually owns it?"

"That's the Griffins," he replied. "They live in a senior facility not far from where their son is. They're getting on in years now, so I imagine they'll probably sell it soon."

"So, they just rented it out then?"

"I'm not sure that they've got anything to do with it anymore. It's quite possible that the son was taking care of all of that for them."

"So, he would have been working in a property manager role for them then?"

"It's possible, but I don't really know."

"Do you happen to know his name?" She pulled out her phone and tapped in the name, so she wouldn't forget. "Okay, now at least I have a name to start with."

"Oh good," Jethro said in delight. He looked over at Nan, then rubbed his hands together and added, "Maybe we can get this solved after all."

Doreen sighed. "Don't count on it." As she looked for her animals, she found Goliath in his usual place in the flower bed, but she saw no sign of Mugs. She hesitated, looking around. "Nan, did you see where Mugs went?"

Nan pointed underneath her chair. Sure enough, Mugs was sound asleep below her.

Doreen groaned. "These animals," she muttered. "This is like their second home." And of course it was, just like it was hers.

Chapter 26

Saturday Noon ...

A S DOREEN HEADED back home again, she walked very slowly past the house in question, without any new revelations. Well, one maybe. She needed to go clear around the property and get a look at the front, so she could get the lay of the land. That thought led to another, reminding her that she still hadn't made it to the crime scene from the Taser death case. That bothered her. She understood there was really nothing to see, but she always visited the crime scenes, so she really needed to follow through and take a look for herself.

With the animals in tow, she walked through her house, got everybody a quick drink of water, then headed out to the front door and back down the neighborhood again, via the street this time. When she came up the street that led to Jethro's place, she turned there and walked a little farther. She stopped at Jethro's house, then turned and took a look at the house right beside it. Sure enough, it was at the beginning of the inward curve of the cul-de-sac, so he didn't have a direct view.

Still, the home was close by, so any loud noises would have likely bothered Jethro. Given his age and the fact that some things in life would disrupt him and would make him angry, perhaps noise was something that troubled him most readily. Much like Millicent was perturbed by weeds and getting more bothered by the day, it was quite possible that noise had a similar triggering effect on Jethro.

Doreen wandered around the block, taking a good look at the house on her trip back. When she came around again to the front, deciding it was time to head home, the door opened, and a woman stepped out. The woman was dressed normally, wearing jeans and a T-shirt. Doreen studied her carefully, putting her peripheral vision to good use as she wandered slowly along, seemingly letting Mugs have a few minutes sniffing at the weeds and the grass. She noted a fair bit of makeup on the woman, presumably Julie, but not an inordinate amount.

Just then a man stepped out, gave her a kiss, and headed to the car parked in the driveway. The woman gave him a wave, then quickly stepped back inside, slamming the door. The fact that she'd slammed the door was already interesting, and the fact that she had kissed him said something else too. Doreen just didn't know quite how to put it all together, but something seemed off.

She watched as the man got into the car and backed down the driveway. Doreen quickly took a picture of the license plate, an act hopefully disguised as something else entirely, though she still wasn't all that great at that particular subterfuge yet. When he drove off, she gave him a casual wave, and he honked with a pleased grin and kept on going. She smiled to herself.

"So, that was either a happy customer," she muttered, "or somebody who has more of a relationship with this woman than ex-pected." Of course that brought up a whole different set of possibilities. As Doreen stared at the house, still lost in thought, the woman stepped out again, speaking caustically.

"What is your problem?"

Doreen blinked several times, looking a bit abashed and confused. "Sorry, just wool-gathering, I guess."

"Well, go woolgather somewhere else," she snapped. And, with that, the woman stepped back into the house and slammed the door again, harder this time, if that was even possible.

Doreen slowly wandered home, realizing that she had probably looked like a complete idiot standing there, with her gaze glued onto the house, as she tried to figure out what was going on. She shook her head. "Really smooth there, Doreen, very smooth."

Still, it was what it was, and now she was heading home, where she could put some of this down on paper and maybe get it sorted in her head a bit, maybe figure out just what was going on. Right now, it didn't seem all that easy because some of this just didn't make any sense.

Back home, she took the animals straight into the garage, without really giving herself a chance to stop and think, and, with the animals loaded up in her car, she drove straight to City Park. She headed for the back, where she had been a couple times before but had never made it to this little community garden—the scene of the Taser-death crime.

It was a small community garden, and a few people milled around, which meant that at least the crime scene had been released, and the site was now open to the public once again. She got out, wandering closer. One of the women looked over at her suspiciously. Doreen just smiled and kept on walking. Obviously it wasn't her garden, and she didn't really know anything about this. The fact that she was here because of a murder wouldn't make the lady any happier.

As Doreen wandered up and down the gardens, admiring the plants even now ready to harvest, another woman came over and asked, "Do you belong here?"

"I was just admiring the beautiful gardens." The woman looked at her guardedly, though Doreen had no idea why. "Obviously that's a problem for you. Isn't this city property?" she asked.

The other woman hesitated and then shrugged. "We've had some weird happenings lately."

"Right, and I guess community gardens are based on trust, aren't they?"

"Exactly." The other woman nodded. "Then that body was found here."

"Right, I heard something about that," Doreen replied, with a nod. Mugs walked up closer to one of the gardens and lifted a leg on the wooden signpost. The woman didn't seem to care, so Doreen let him. When he was done, he trod closer and sat down and stared up at her. "It's okay, buddy. We just wanted to stop and take a look at the garden," Doreen repeated. "I don't have much of a vegetable garden at home anymore."

"Interesting. There is quite an avid gardening community in town, so I'm sure you could join some clubs and events, if you wanted to do more."

"I guess I could just plant some things and see how it goes," Doreen added, with a shrug. After a few moments of silence, she continued. "That body, was there any news on who it was?"

The other woman shrugged. "No, I don't know anything about it. It wasn't anybody who had a garden here or anything."

"What a strange place to leave it."

"Leave it?" The woman frowned at her.

"My understanding was that it was dumped here."

"Sure, but I don't know why that would be."

"Right, and that's the crux of the matter,

isn't it? Why people do things is always a bit of a mystery."

"Especially when it comes to corpses," the woman noted, with a delicate shudder.

Doreen smiled at her. "Very true. Anyway, I just wanted to come and take a look. So thank you for your patience."

Chapter 27

WITH THAT, DOREEN slowly meandered back to her car, knowing the second woman still watched her. Indeed, the first woman walked over to talk to the second one as well.

Noticing that, Doreen realized again that she really wasn't welcome, quite possibly because they'd experienced theft of the vegetables, which made her sad. There was enough in life to worry about without having people stealing the food that you spent all your time and energy growing.

Back in her car, she sat here for a long moment, contemplating her options, then remembered she hadn't checked in with Mack. She quickly phoned him. When she filled him in, he was not upset but more resigned. "And, of course, you'll look into Jethro's complaint."

"I think it's all connected. I feel it in my gut."

"Fine, yes, go with your gut, Doreen. However, don't forget about evidence too. … So you really think you saw the madam?"

"Yeah, I do," she confirmed. Then she told Mack about Bernard's phone call.

"You and Bernard are awfully close, aren't you?"

She snorted at that. "I wouldn't say *close*, but he did hear about some of the commotion and my involvement with Tammy and Jed, and, well, … he wanted to get an inside line on it."

"Of course he did." Mack's tone revealed that he was bothered by it.

"It's no big deal. I don't care if he contacts me about something like that. Sometimes I reach out and pick his brain about things as well."

"Right, but I will feel much better if you had less to do with these kinds of things."

"Bernard is there because of what I did to help him," she explained, "so getting rid of him wouldn't be that easy, even if I wanted to, which I don't. I have enough trouble finding friends in town, so when I do find somebody who's stable, upright, and not a murderer, I would like to keep them."

Mack chuckled. "I'm not against your keeping him, just keep him at a distance." And, with that, he was gone.

She stared at her phone, smiled, then sent him a text. **You don't need to be jealous of Bernard.**

He sent back a thumbs-up.

They were still not completely solid in their relationship, and Mack wasn't completely sure where he stood. She sighed at that because, of course, there was no need for it.

Mack was in her life and only Mack. Although she hadn't had a chance to really tell him how she felt, she had thought it was obvious. Nan would immediately say that nothing was so obvious as a hidden love and that Doreen needed to do more than just make Mack *think* he was the main person in her life. She needed to make it clear. Making it clear wasn't all that simple, but she was probably making it much more complicated than it really needed to be.

She quickly sent him a photo of the car and the license plate.

When he called her, he asked, "What's this?"

"A visitor at Julie's house," she replied, with a note of irony. "Maybe an okay visitor, I don't know, but at the house in question. So maybe we need to check him out."

"Right. And we care about this why?"

"Because we think it is possibly the madam's house. I was also looking for the son of the property owners, who was potentially looking after the home for his parents, who have supposedly moved into senior housing nearer to him."

"And you want me to run this license plate?"

"It would be nice to know in case the son is the one living there."

"Why would you think that?" he asked curiously.

"I'm just wondering whether he's paying for favors or has a ladylove who he may or may not be aware has been working on the side."

"Ah, that's interesting. I'll call you back in five or so." And, with that, he was gone.

She headed home, then sat down at the kitchen table and wrote out a bunch more notes. She kept writing all these notes, but what she really should be doing was indexing everything. She needed a filing system of everything going on, similar to what Solomon had done. With that thought, she really needed a digital backup too. She groaned at that but was grateful she at least had her notepad, with lots of little bits and pieces of information.

With a shrug, she opened up a Word document and started to set up a file on the Taser killer and the prostitute ring in town. She started with the current case and then worked backward as much as she could. It would be days of work, if not more, since she had to transcribe a lot of her very messy notes. Given her penchant for writing everything down, she had lots of information to put into some sense of order.

When Mack called her back, she was buried in those thoughts.

"What's up?" he asked. "You sound very distracted."

"I figured I should finally set up formal notes on all the stuff I've been doing," she muttered. "I probably should have been doing it all along."

He snorted. "Documentation is huge in my world, and, yes, for you—particularly when so many cases are starting to intertwine—it would likely pay off in the end. The longer you stay here, it helps if you have a good idea of who was mixed up in what. I know that your memory is pretty sharp right now, but that doesn't mean in another three, four, five years, you may forget names and places just based on the sheer accumulation of data, but who knows."

"Right. I guess I should have been keeping typed-up notes from the start."

"Look at it this way," he explained cheerfully, "at least typing and scanning will keep you out of trouble for a little bit."

At that, she laughed. "So, the vehicle?"

He sighed and then continued. "Yes, it appears to be the same person. The son is the owner of the car you saw at his parents' property."

"Wow. So much for having his folks nearby. Based on that very happy smile I saw on his face, he's really liking the way life has turned in his direction."

"I'm sure," Mack noted in a dry tone. "So now the question is, what are you planning on doing?"

"I could have gotten that information by contacting him directly, so I think I'll probably do that anyway and see if he has any idea what she might be doing to earn an income."

"But you don't have anything other than the suspicion that she's into anything else, right?"

"Correct. And I know we need to tie her to Jed and to Tammy. I need to get a picture of her. I had hoped to get one when I saw her earlier, but she was in no mood for a chat. I need something sharp and clear, so I can ask Tammy if this is the other woman, if this is the Julie who lived with them at times. Did you have a chance to interrogate Jed yet?"

"It's been an ongoing progress, but he's not being very cooperative. His fingerprints have come up on several robberies though."

"That's helpful. He repeatedly told me that he didn't kill anybody. Can you keep him in jail based on his having a gun and being involved in prior robberies?"

"It's up to the prosecutor to figure out what he wants to charge Jed with and then to set bail. Afterward we will see if he can make bail or not."

"I guess it depends on how useful he is to Julie, this other woman, as to whether she'll fork out bail money or not, or maybe decide it's a good time to cut ties."

Mack laughed. "I do like the way you think," he said, clearly impressed.

"Yeah, guess I've been around you too long," she teased.

"Maybe, maybe not. Regardless, you have a very unique way of looking at things."

"I've heard you say that a couple times

now, but I'm still not exactly sure what it means."

"I'm not sure either because you really do come up with things that a lot of people don't. It's just the way your brain thinks about things and processes information, as far as I can tell."

"Let me call this guy, the Griffins' son, and see what I can come up with."

"Just remember that you don't have any reason to suspect anything."

"Outside of the fact that Jethro is losing his mind because he's so upset about the extra noise."

"There is that, and you could have talked to Jethro on your own and got that information."

"I *did* talk to Jethro on my own, and I *did* get that information, so it's hardly as if that's anything private."

"I hear you there. Just try to stay out of trouble." And, with that, he was gone.

Chapter 28

Saturday Afternoon ...

DOREEN SMILED, PICKED up the phone, and quickly phoned Callaghan Griffin.

When a man answered the phone, she identified herself, and he said, "Oh, I think I've heard about you." There was curiosity in his tone but nothing problematic.

"Yeah, I'm starting to get a bit of a name," she shared, with a heavy sigh, "and definitely not the kind of name I was hoping to make."

He laughed at that. "What can I do for you?" he asked. "I don't think I've done anything wrong."

"I don't think you have either," she replied. "I'm wondering about a certain house that I understand you own," she began, then went on to provide the address.

"It belongs to my parents, but, yes, how can I help you?"

"Ah, is it for sale?"

"Oh, are you looking to buy a house?"

"Oh no, not so much," she said. "I have one in the same area, just around the corner."

"It's not for sale at the moment, but my parents are getting on, and it's certainly something under discussion on a regular basis," he shared. "It's rented at the moment."

"Oh nice. And that was what, maybe a month ago?"

"Yeah, about that," he said. "Why do you ask?"

"I hate to say it, but some of the neighbors are complaining about an awful lot of nighttime foot traffic and a lot of noise coming from that area, and not coincidentally in the last month."

"Really?" he asked.

Honestly all she heard was sincerity in his tone.

"I don't know why that would be. Alison lives there. She's a friend."

A boyish charm filled his tone. "A friend, *huh*?" she teased.

"Yeah," he said, with a bright laugh. "A friend, and I would hate to have to do anything to change the status quo."

"Right. It's hard enough to find somebody in this world without messing it up when something works."

"Precisely my point," he agreed. "If something is working, I really don't want to chastise her or something."

"And yet people are upset."

"What people?" he asked suspiciously, and then he snorted, "Oh no, don't tell me that you're talking about old Jethro. He complains about almost everything."

"Ah, so has he complained to you about this personally?"

"No, but I lived in that house maybe ten years ago, and he was always getting on my parents about it."

"Were they noisy?"

He hesitated for a moment, then grudgingly admitted, "They did fight a lot. Jethro used to tell them to find ways to get along and to not fight so much."

"I'm sure that went over like a ton of bricks."

He burst out laughing at that. "Not so much, particularly since they'd been arguing for a very long time and had yet to find a way to stop doing it."

"Of course. So, do you think Alison would

be open to my knocking on the door and just asking her to keep some of the traffic and noise down after dark, to not be quite so disruptive to the neighborhood?"

He hesitated.

Doreen added. "That would keep you out of it at least. And then she could complain to you about the nosy neighbors giving her a hard time, instead of you getting after her."

"*Huh*. I am tempted to handle it that way, for that very reason," he noted. "I really, really like her."

She winced at that. "How long have you known her?" she asked.

"Not very long at all," he replied. "It came together really fast, and I fell hard, … head over heels, really."

"Of course, and that's also why you're a little worried about anything changing the status quo, because you don't really have a history yet that you can draw on, when things get tough."

"Exactly. I really don't want things to get tough with her. I would just like to keep things going as nicely as they have been, you know?"

"Well then, let me have a quick chat with her, and maybe she'll be open to some suggestions."

"Maybe," he muttered. "You mentioned noise?"

"Yes, I'm afraid so."

"What kind of noise? And what kind of traffic?"

"People coming and going at odd hours of the night, and the noises are voices, sometimes sounds, like people are carrying heavy things, a lot of it coming from the river way."

"Really? That doesn't sound like Alison at all. Are you sure it isn't one of the other houses?"

"I don't think so. Richard lives in the neighborhood too, and he's heard the extra noise as well. He wasn't sure what to think. This nighttime activity makes everybody a little uneasy, thinking maybe break-ins are happening or prowlers are casing the neighborhood. The concerns are understandable, if you look at it that way."

"Yes, of course," he agreed.

She heard the genuine puzzlement in his tone. She was afraid that this Alison had rendered him completely gullible to what she was doing. "But then again, if you could vouch for Alison and confirm that she doesn't have any criminal activity happening there, that might be enough reassurance to keep the neighbors from calling the police or something. You know how older folks can get when they hear things going *bump* in the night."

"Oh gosh, hopefully we can avoid getting the police involved," he stated in shock. "It does need to be sorted out, and for good hopefully."

"What does she do for a living?" she asked him.

"Oh." There was a moment's hesitation before he went on. "She's in between jobs at the moment."

Doreen slowly nodded. "I know from experience how that is … a rather tough place to be in. I'm sure she was more than grateful when you could help her out with a place to live."

"That's just it, and it's one of the reasons I am helping."

"Yes, yes, of course. And we never really know how bad a situation is until we get close enough, then hear and see some of the problems firsthand."

"As it turns out, she didn't have any place to go. She had a very abusive partner before, and they broke up. She was staying at the same house still, his house, but that didn't work out for very long. She was always afraid of getting beaten."

"Oh no, that's terrible," Doreen cried out. "Where did she used to live?"

"Downtown," he replied. "From the sounds of things, it was a shared or joint house, with several people living there."

"Oh, the poor thing. That's awful," Doreen muttered.

After an awkward hesitation, he whispered, "I think she may be in really big trouble. … She told me how somebody close to her had been killed and that she needed a place to hide."

At that, Doreen's ears picked up. "Oh my, that does sound bad."

"Exactly. So, I'm sure that this problem in the neighborhood has nothing to do with her. She's trying to keep a low profile and rebuild her life, you know? Now, I wouldn't put it past Jethro to be the one responsible for all that traffic, then trying to put the blame on her, you know?"

"I don't know about that. He seems very susceptible to noise and is missing out on sleep, which is making him react badly," she said, "but I'll pop over and talk with her and welcome a new neighbor."

"Oh, that would be lovely, and please let me know how it goes. It's not that I'm trying to get off the phone, but I do have work to do."

"That's fine. I'll let you go." Then she ended the call. With the animals in tow, she got up immediately and walked toward Alison's place. She knocked on the door, but there was no answer. She knocked again and again, with still no answer. Frowning, she stepped back out of the way, and, just as she did, she saw the curtains twitch.

She immediately called out, "Hi, Alison. Callaghan told me that you had moved into the neighborhood." The door opened, and the woman stared at her suspiciously. Doreen tried her best to beam with neighborly sunshine. "I know you don't want any problems with the neighbors, but honestly there have been a few complaints," she began cautiously, "about all kinds of carrying-on overnight."

At that, the woman sneered. "What do you know about carrying on?"

"I didn't mean that kind of carrying-on," she corrected, with a wave of her hand and a chuckle. "Obviously you're entitled to a private life," she murmured, with a gentle smile. "It's more a case of potentially criminal carrying-on."

At that, the woman stared at her, and a hard glint came into her gaze. "Who are you, and what do you know about anything?" she snapped.

"I'm just a neighbor," she murmured, "and I wanted to welcome you to the neighborhood and offer a warning that the neighbors are starting to complain about the visitors at odd hours of the night and the voices and the noise of moving items, particularly from the river pathway."

Alison stared at her and shook her head. "I don't know what you're talking about."

"I'm glad to hear that," Doreen replied. "So it doesn't have anything to do with you, does it?"

"Of course not," she declared, still glaring. "But, even if it did, it certainly has nothing to do with you."

"Maybe not," Doreen conceded, as she nodded with a smile. "That's quite possible, and I'm not trying to upset you."

"Good," she snapped. "Then, in that case, you can leave anytime now."

Doreen took a deep breath. "I can definitely leave, but I really was trying to make things a little easier on you, since some of the neighbors are really quite upset."

"I don't really care about some of the neighbors," she declared, narrowing her gaze. "You have absolutely no reason to be here at all."

Doreen stared at her and then shrugged. "Okay, if that's the way you feel," she replied, then turned to walk away. "Welcome to the neighborhood!"

Alison waited until Doreen was at the end of the driveway, and then the door slammed hard behind her.

Doreen winced and quickly phoned Callaghan back. "Hey, I'm really sorry to tell you, but she didn't take it very well at all."

"Oh dear," he muttered.

"Go ahead and blame me, as she is certain to anyway," Doreen said, with a smile. "It's obvious she's not very happy with anybody intruding in her life."

"I did warn you," he noted.

"Yes, I understand that she's had some tough times, but she certainly didn't seem to be frail, scared of life, or hiding away. She's definitely not a shrinking violet."

"No, no, she isn't like that, but she is very delicate," he added.

Doreen raised an eyebrow at that. "There

was nothing delicate about the way she told me to get lost," Doreen shared. "I don't want to sound like a broken record here, but credible people are definitely upset, and it's only a matter of time before the police get called over it all."

"Oh no, I really don't want my parents to find out about that."

"As the homeowners, the police wouldn't have any choice but to contact them, right?"

"Right," he whispered, but now he sounded worried. "But there can't be anything going on that would interest the police, right? I mean, I trust her."

"Sure you do. … If you've known her for a long time, then obviously you have a good idea of what she would and wouldn't do."

He hesitated but corrected her. "I haven't known her all that long."

"Oh, in that case, maybe you don't really know what she could be doing after all," she asked softly.

"I would hope she wouldn't do anything wrong, but obviously I can't be sure about it."

"I'm not trying to cause you any trouble or strife," she explained. "I'm just trying to warn you that these complaints aren't likely to go away." After a few moments of silence, she spoke again. "When she was living downtown, she wasn't anywhere close to where that guy was murdered, was she?"

"I don't know," he replied. "She did mention something about wanting to get out because things had gotten really violent and ugly."

"Oh dear, that would be enough to send anybody running."

"That's what I mean. She's such a sweetheart that I can't imagine her being mixed up in any trouble."

Doreen took a moment and tried to mentally shift from the rude and cranky woman she'd met at the door to this guy's version of such a sweetheart, and the two just did not compute. "It is quite possible that maybe she knows something too."

"Oh, I don't think so," he argued. "She was just afraid somebody had gotten killed, and she wanted to get out of there before she was next. So, what else could I do?"

"If she had money to pay the rent, that would be one thing, but are you charging her rent?"

"Well, no, not really. I'm just trying to help her out."

"Of course you are, and trying to help people is very important."

"It sure is. Sometimes I don't think we really do enough for our fellow man."

"Exactly, I couldn't agree with you more."

"Oh, good. It's hard to always know just what to do, and I really do like her," he repeated.

"I'm sure you do," she noted gently. "However, that's no guarantee that this will turn out to be good though."

"Oh, I certainly hope it does," he said, and his tone got a little bit belligerent. "After all, I only have your word for it that there is actually a problem."

"That's true enough, and of course you don't want to just listen to anybody."

"Nope, I don't, so I'm not sure if maybe you aren't the one who's trying to cause trouble."

Finding it interesting how quickly the conversation had turned, she added, "In that case, it's probably a really good time to put a stop to this conversation then, isn't it?" And, with that, she disconnected. She stared down at the phone and shook her head. "Good Lord," she muttered. She phoned Mack and filled him in on the call.

"That's interesting," he noted.

"There's a good chance this woman is the same person who was living in the house where Tammy was. I sent her a couple texts, but I haven't heard back yet." Just then, her phone started to buzz. "Actually her response is coming in now." She quickly read it while Mack waited.

"She gave a description of her other roommate that I feel matches the Alison woman I talked to today," Doreen added, and then a grainy photo came through. "Tammy's sending a photo. Wait just a minute. Oh my, that's definitely her."

"This is getting interesting," Mack muttered.

"Tammy said that this woman lived in the house with them and would periodically move out whenever she could get another place to live. However, when things fell through, she would move back in again. When she was there, she ruled the place like a queen bee, and, when she was gone, she ruled with a more distant hand but ruled just the same. Jed was under her thumb the whole time."

"So, we're thinking she's behind all this? We think she's the madam?"

"I don't know. Maybe she had Jed do the killing, although I still don't know why."

"The motive in the Taser death is definitely an unanswered question, but we have identified the body. He's got a lengthy criminal record, and he's been involved in a lot of B&E crimes over the years."

"*Huh*, well that fits then, doesn't it?"

"It fits to your way of thinking," he admitted, with a note of humor, "but not necessarily anybody else's."

"If she's acting as a part-time fence, and the dead guy's out stealing, then he's probably connected to her."

"Yeah, but you're lacking one piece of the puzzle. Remember that little thing called proof?"

"Yeah, you're a bit of a stickler for that, aren't you?" she asked, with a laugh.

"Yeah, I am, so what we need to do is catch her being involved in this mess."

"The most logical way is if you were to talk to her, and, while we don't have the proof needed to solve the case, we have Tammy's confirmation of Julie aka Alison's identity. So you could question her about this Taser death."

"Exactly. I'll go talk with her. Then I'll see you in a little bit." With that, he ended the call.

Chapter 29

Late Afternoon ...

DOREEN WAS STILL typing up her notes within Word, so she could hopefully search and find what she needed later, when Mack phoned her back.

"She's not home," he said in disgust.

"*Great*," Doreen muttered. "She's probably on the run."

"Do you really think so?"

"No, not really. She was too cocky. She might be worried, but I don't think she's really panicked yet. So, no, on the running part."

"I hope not. It's a little hard to capture any of our suspects if you keep sending them running."

"Hey, that wasn't me."

"No? So, who was it then who was talking to Alison about the neighborhood complaints?" he asked, with a bit of an edge to his tone.

She sighed. "Okay, so that was me. And putting Tammy on a bus, that was me, … partly me and Nan of course."

"Don't even get me started on Nan right now," he growled, clearly not impressed that she had posted bail for her armed abductor, Jethro.

"But back to this gal, Alison, if that's really her name," Doreen began. "I didn't mean to make her panic, and I don't think she really has either. She was really very confident. Almost too confident, you know?"

"Which has nothing to do with the situation, as you well know."

"Fine, whatever," she muttered. "Are you coming over here?"

"No, I've just been called back into the office."

"Okay, good enough then. I'll talk to you later." She disconnected, then went back to her notes.

As soon as she figured it was time for her stake-out, she looked at Mugs. "We should probably tell Mack what we're doing, but he won't be very happy, so I don't want to."

Mugs barked at her.

Collecting a backpack full of items that she

thought she might need, she wondered about the level of common sense involved in doing this. But still, she lived here, so any traffic up and down that river concerned her too. She would just watch to see if there was any traffic tonight. Maybe Jethro was just imagining things. She also knew, if Nan had her way, she would have Jethro moved into Rosemoor very quickly. Whether kidnapping charges and carrying a fake gun would be filed against him or not, Doreen didn't know, and neither would Nan at this point in time. So Doreen needed to find out.

Pulling on a black jacket, she quickly dressed for the outdoors on a cooler evening. Since it was midway into fall, once that sun went down, it could get pretty chilly. She slipped out the door with both Mugs and Goliath on foot beside her, not bothering with leashes because they were so close to home. With Thaddeus curled up against her neck, she headed to the creek.

They were more than interested in any kind of adventure right now. She continued down the creek until she was just on the other side of Richard's place. Here she could stay in the shadows and keep an eye out to see for herself if anything was happening or not on the other side of the creek and a few houses farther down. As far as she was concerned, this was just research, this was all just confirming whether Jethro's complaints were on the up-and-up or not. At least that's what she told herself. She knew perfectly well that Mack would have something completely different to say about it. He may have a black-and-white on duty, but what could they really see from the street view? Still, she didn't have a whole lot of options right now, and this was the avenue that had presented itself.

She sent Mack a message, asking if he had found any further connections between the characters, and he replied moments later with a no. When the phone rang, she quickly lowered the volume and answered in a quiet voice, "Hello." Then she changed the ring to Vibrate.

"Where are you?" he asked, his tone sharp.

"Why would you even ask that?" she muttered. "Don't you trust me?"

"Instincts," he barked, "and my instincts are telling me that you're up to no good."

She snorted at that. "Well, sir, your instincts seem to have led you astray this time.

You may apologize later."

"Where are you?" he repeated in a worried tone.

"I'm at the river," she replied.

"Oh, okay." Then he stopped and asked, "Hang on, at your place?"

"Close to my place," she said. "The river corridor is all public property anyway."

"It is, indeed," he agreed slowly, as if thinking his way through this. "Please tell me that you're not sitting in the dark, watching to see what happens at that house."

"If I don't watch, how will I know if Jethro is telling the truth?" she asked in what she hoped was a reasonable tone of voice. But obviously it wasn't reasonable enough because, when Mack blasted her a moment later, she winced and sighed. "So, not a good idea in your opinion, *huh*?"

"If the intent is looking for trouble, it's a great idea," he snapped, with a sigh. After a moment a wry chuckle escaped. "You can't even help yourself, can you? Never mind. Don't answer that. Sit tight. I'll be there in a few minutes."

"Okay. So far nothing's happening anyway."

"Good. That would be a nice change for

once." And, with that, he disconnected.

She smiled and hunkered down into the darkness. It was such a strange feeling to be out here at this time of night. Normally she was at her own place and tucked into bed. However, out here everything was so alive, yet in a way she hadn't recognized before.

She didn't spend much time out in the darkness of night. It wasn't that she was uncomfortable necessarily. It was just something she didn't have any experience with. As she sat here marveling at the birds that would occasionally softly coo around her, Thaddeus would lift his head and look around, then hunker back down again. "It's okay, buddy. I'm not all that comfortable out here either."

Goliath, on the other hand, appeared to be happy as could be, keeping himself busy, hunting in the shrubs and the bushes around her. As long as he didn't catch anything, she would be totally okay. She smiled at that because catching something was a whole different story than killing his prey right in front of her. She had to give him some credit for being a hunter because it was part of his nature, but she also gave him lots of food, so he didn't need to hunt to eat. It was just the personality of a cat that she was up against.

Still, she didn't really want him to kill anything, especially while she was sitting here.

Thaddeus hopped off her shoulder and walked over to a stone and fluffed out his wings in the night air. She wasn't at all sure what he would hunt in his natural environment or whether he would be predator or prey, but this circumstance was one he wasn't accustomed to.

As she sat here, the shadows seemed to grow longer and longer, and the silence grew thicker and heavier. Feeling an instinctive unease, she looked around at the animals to see that their ears were all sharpening in tune with something. She just didn't know what.

"I know," she whispered to them. "Something's going on out there. I just don't know who is moving around." When her phone vibrated, she looked down to see a text from Mack. He was coming through the creek and heading toward her. She smiled with relief, hating to admit that just being out here in the darkness was having an effect on her nerves. She hadn't thought that she would be the nervous type. Still, she'd been through an awful lot lately, and maybe this was normal.

As she waited for Mack to arrive, she heard other sounds. So did Thaddeus, as he returned to the safety of her shoulder. She shifted deeper into the shadows when she heard another male voice, talking to someone, but he was several houses down from her.

"Yeah, I'm just coming up now," he told someone.

He was walking toward her, would have to pass her to reach Alison's house. Doreen stiffened.

"Who cares what some old batty neighborhood watch person says to you," he replied. "I mean, this is working, so let's just keep it up, at least for a while. We need a few months where we can move stuff easily, before we can get into a better situation. If it wasn't for that little mishap, we would have been fine downtown."

Then came silence.

"Yeah, yeah ..." he added. "It's okay. I'm coming in."

And with that, he must have ended a phone conversation and kept on walking.

Mugs was alert, but he was quiet. She placed a hand on his back, as a word of warning, and he calmed down ever-so-slightly, backing up until he sat close to her. There was no sign of Goliath, but Doreen and

Thaddeus sat silently in the dark, staring at the man approaching. Doreen should have been just enough in the shadows that he couldn't see her, but, as he got closer, he stopped, looked around, and asked, "Who's there?"

There was no answer, although she knew Mack should be getting closer too. But where and how far away was he? She didn't know. She waited, and then the stranger snorted.

"Bloody shadows," he muttered, with a half laugh. A sense of relief filled his tone, as if he'd been worried. He kept on walking, going right past her when his phone rang again.

"Yeah, Jed. ... What? ... Oh, you're out of jail? Good." He stopped and looked around. "No, I don't know. She's getting cold feet over this whole thing. You do know we'll have to do something about her soon, right?"

The silence deepened around them, as he listened to his caller.

"I know, man. I don't like working for a woman either, but right now she's the one with the connections to sell all this stuff."

Doreen listened, presumably as Jed spoke on the other end.

"And that is bullshit too. We have so much little stuff here, when we should be dealing with the big stuff with bigger payouts. Big cons, you know? Not all this nickel-and-dime stuff. I blame you for that, by the way."

He snorted, a sound louder than it should have been in the creepy darkness.

"Yeah, yeah, anyway I'm almost there," he replied. "I'll pick up payment and maybe grab us a pizza and bring it back to the house. …I know. I've got your payment too, or at least I hope I will. It depends on if she wants any of this new stuff and thinks she can sell it." At that, he ended the call and headed the last little bit up toward Alison's place.

Doreen waited and watched, when suddenly Mack came down the pathway toward her in the opposite direction. She wondered if Mack and this other guy would meet face-to-face or if he would get to Alison's gate just before Mack arrived. Silently she watched, waiting for the scene to be revealed right before her eyes, as if she had front row seats at the theater. She just didn't know which side would win. She quickly texted Mack that one of the men involved in this mess was walking toward him. She didn't get a response, but suddenly there they both were.

"Hey, who are you?" the stranger asked sharply, and she heard Mack reply.

"I'm the guy who'll take you down to the station to answer a few questions," he replied calmly.

"No way, you ain't got nothing on me at all."

"That depends if you actually own the contents of that duffel bag you're carrying."

"You ain't gonna touch me," he snapped, and, sure enough, a tussle ensued.

She bolted out of the shadows and watched Mack fighting the other guy, as the duffel bag sat on the ground. She snatched it up and backed away with it, but the guy turned and saw her.

"Who are you?" he cried out. When he looked at the bag now at her feet, his face turned ugly.

Just then Mack stepped forward and said, "No, you don't."

"Oh, yeah, I do. I don't know who she is, but she just stole my bag."

"I didn't touch anything in it," Doreen stated. "I'm sure the police will help sort out whose stuff is in this bag."

He looked at the both of them and put his hands out in front of him. "Hey now, I don't know how we got off on the wrong foot here, but things are definitely out of hand. ... We can work this out."

"I'm not so sure about that," Doreen stated, with a smile.

Then from the other side of the gate, a woman asked, "What's going on here?" Then the gate opened in front of them.

She stared from one man to the other and saw the duffel bag. Her gaze slowly raised to look at Doreen, and her face twisted. "You again," she sneered. "What now? Are you out here watching me? Are you a voyeur or something?"

"No, that's not exactly in my wheelhouse," Doreen replied. "But fencing stolen goods is apparently among your many … *talents*, shall we say?"

At that, Alison's face paled and then flushed bright red with anger. She turned and looked at the man standing in front of her. "Steven, did you have anything to do with this?"

"No, of course not," he snapped, as he looked at Alison in anger. "Did you set me up?"

She glared at him. "Choose your words wisely, Steven."

Doreen watched the two of them, her head going back and forth, as if watching a tennis match. Steven and Alison started arguing and yelling at each other. Doreen looked over at Mack and shrugged.

He sighed. "Now that you've both incriminated yourselves, I'll haul the two of you down to the station."

Steven turned to him. "I ain't done nothing wrong. She's the guilty party."

Alison sneered at him. "You're the one bringing me a full duffel bag."

"How did you know it was coming to you?" Doreen asked, with a mocking tone.

At that, Alison turned and took several threatening steps toward her. "You're nothing but an old busybody, always ruining things for everybody else."

"Yeah, that's me," Doreen agreed, with a sigh. "I ruin everything for everybody."

"Exactly," Alison sneered.

"What I really want to know is," Doreen asked, "what you did to that poor guy down at the community gardens?"

Alison turned to face Steven.

Doreen asked him, "That was your buddy, right? I suppose you popped him one, didn't you? Or was it Jed?"

Steven stared at Doreen in shock, then turned to Alison. "You told her that?"

"No, of course I didn't, and shut your mouth." But the cat was out of the bag.

"I didn't pop him one," Steven declared. "That had nothing to do with me."

Doreen replied, "Yet you're the one spouting off to Jed about not wanting to work for a woman and how it was time to take care of her pretty soon too."

At that, Alison turned and stared at Steven in disbelief.

Steven turned to Doreen and growled. "Now would be a good time for you to shut your mouth," he said, with an ugly glare.

"Maybe," she noted cheerfully, "but I figured, by the time you guys are done talking, Mack here should have everything he needs to prove that you're the one who murdered the guy with a Taser because he was trying to double-cross you on some of the stolen goods."

"*He* wasn't double-crossing us. *She* was double-crossing him, and he didn't like it. When he put up a fight, she ordered him to be taken down. Jed did the job, not me," Steven declared, with a headshake. "I ain't into murder."

"You may not be into murder," Mack noted, with an exaggerated heavy sigh, "but if you're

involved in any way, you may still find yourself going down for it."

"And Steven was right in the middle of it,"
Alison added, with a snort in his direction.
"He's the one who dumped the body—and in
a community garden of all places," she complained, raising her hands in frustration. "Who
does that? As far as taking me out, you're the
one who will get popped next."

"I figured as much. Which is why we would
take care of you first."

"*We*?" she asked in a dangerous tone.

"Yeah, do you really think Jed would sit
around while you order a hit on me?" Steven
asked. "Jed and I go way back."

Doreen muttered, "I thought I was a mess,
but you guys are next level." At that, both of
them turned on her. She held up her hands.
"Sorry, just an observation."

"Did you ever find out where Tammy
went?" Alison asked, staring at Steven. "You
couldn't even figure out that much. You are
so lazy and stupid."

"I don't know what happened to her. She
just disappeared."

Mack looked over at Doreen, as she
smiled and nodded at him, adding, "Answers
do come. Just not always in the way we ex-

pect them to. Have you got anybody coming?" Doreen asked Mack.

Just then she heard a shout behind her and turned to see Arnold and Chester. At that moment Steven bolted away from the group in a bid for freedom.

And made it about four feet before Mugs suddenly appeared sideways in the path, his girth solid and stable, sending Steven flying over him to nose plow into the dirt. Immediately Thaddeus flew from Doreen's shoulder to land on Steven's head and crowed loudly, as if he were the winner of some nonexistent fight. Goliath strolled over then in a move only a cat could do, sat down, shot his back leg to the dark sky, and started to clean his butt, right in front of Steven's nose.

Mack sighed. He walked the few steps to hook Steven under his arms and lift him to his feet, Thaddeus still champion-danced on Steven's head. "Not a smart move," Mack noted to his prisoner, as he brought Steven back to Arnold and Chester.

Doreen finally dragged her gaze away from the comedy going on in front of her and turned to watch the newcomers approach. "Hey, Arnold. Back on duty, *huh*?"

He gave her a beaming smile. "Absolutely.

When Frankie came clean about what he'd done and what had happened back then, I was cleared."

"It certainly would have been nice if somebody had told me that," Doreen noted, with an eye roll. "Yet I'm pretty sure these two here will help clear up the rest of it," she added, with a smile.

Arnold looked over at them and snorted. "Well, well, well, look at that, if that isn't our resident madam?"

At that, Alison or Julie or whoever she was glared at him. "Wow, you're still a cop? I thought you would have retired by now."

"I want to be retired now. Looks as if you're headed for jail tonight. How many times have I hauled you in anyway?"

She sneered. "I'll still get out again."

"You might, unless you had anything to do with killing that man."

"You mean the one who was killed with your Taser?" she asked and started to laugh. "I didn't even know it at the time, but that just added to the joy." She turned and looked at Doreen. "This arrogant cop arrested me more times than I can count, just for trying to make a living."

Arnold corrected her. "We call it solicitation

for prostitution. What happened? Did you get tired of our jail? So, you went to Vancouver instead? But you came back." He shook his head. "Just like a bad penny."

"And just like a bad penny," she repeated, glaring at him, "you keep showing up."

And, with that, Arnold snapped his handcuffs on her, looked over at Doreen, and grinned. "See, Doreen? You got this. Doesn't matter what it is, every time I turn around, you've got this."

"Yeah, I don't think Mack would agree," she noted, with a sigh. "Pretty sure he's not too happy with my nighttime activities."

At that, Arnold laughed. "That's because he's looking for *other* nighttime activities."

She flushed, grateful that nobody else was listening at the moment.

Meanwhile, once Chester had taken Steven in cuffs, he looked over at Doreen, Thaddeus now safely back on her shoulder. "There we go, one more case, done and dusted. If you could get good at paperwork, maybe they could hire you to take care of the stuff you are drowning the rest of us in."

"Maybe, but paperwork? I'm not so sure that's my thing."

He laughed at that. "Hey, I'll let you in on

an inside secret. … It's not *my thing* for any cop either."

And, with that, the entire group moved toward Doreen's home. They hadn't gone very far when a shout came from behind.

She turned to see Callaghan rushing up to them.

"What's going on?" he asked.

"Not-so-good news for you, I'm afraid," she replied gently. "However, it will save you a heap of trouble with your parents." As they walked on back, he kept trying to talk to Alison, but she sneered at him.

"God, would you just take this crybaby away from here?" she asked Doreen. "I can't stand all that whining."

"But, Alison, wait. I thought we had something going."

"I just needed a place to live," she declared, with a wave of her hand. "Don't worry. I'll get out of jail soon enough. They can't keep me in."

"We couldn't keep you in before," Arnold admitted, "but times are changing. Your rap sheet has gotten long enough that you won't be getting out quite so fast this time."

Chapter 30

Sunday Morning ...

DOREEN WOKE UP the next morning, then rolled over with a great sense of satisfaction and relief at another case in the bag. This one didn't go quite the way she thought it would, but, when she pondered it some more, they rarely did. She gave Mugs a big hug, and he woofed and snuggled deeper into the covers. "You and me both, buddy," she replied, as she did the same. Her phone rang moments later. "Hey, Nan," she said, with a yawn. "I just woke up."

"Glad to hear it. Jethro really wants to thank you for what you did."

"What did I do?" she asked.

"You got that woman out of there, for starters."

"That's because that woman was connected to a murder I was also investigating," she muttered.

"That's even better," Nan cried out in delight. "I've got more great news. We'll sell Jethro's house and move him down here to Rosemoor. He really shouldn't be all alone, rattling around in that house by himself."

"I certainly agree with you there," Doreen noted. "Does Jethro get any say in the matter?"

Nan laughed in delight. "Of course he does, child. I'm really not that pushy."

"Glad to hear it, Nan. As long as he's happy to move, then that seems to be a good solution and may well prevent future problems."

"And you won't press charges?" she asked in a worried tone.

"Hey, I'm not the one involved in pressing charges against him or anybody else. You'll have to talk to Mack about that."

"I was hoping that you might handle that conversation. I don't think Mack was very happy with me about the whole bail thing."

"You're right about that, but honestly I don't even know that I can talk to him about it," she muttered. "The fact of the matter is that Jethro may have crossed the line with the whole armed kidnapping event and will have to deal with the consequences. It may be out of Mack's hands and left up solely to the district attorney."

"Jethro's also a senior citizen," Nan pointed out, "and that should count for something."

"If it goes to court, you'll have to testify as a character witness then, which will be interesting since you were also the victim."

"Oh, I can definitely do that. What a wonderful idea. I can see how that might prove a bit challenging for the prosecution." Nan said, clapping her hands in delight, yet almost dropping the phone in the process. "So, you'll come? Jethro really wants to thank you in person and may bring extra treats."

"Wait, what? Come where?" she asked, feeling as if she'd missed a part of the conversation. The already amusing image in her mind of a harried prosecutor frantically trying to discredit Nan's testimony on Jethro's behalf—after having just presented her as the frail but sharp elderly victim of a gun-toting madman—was only enhanced as Jethro interrupted the court proceedings, carrying a tray of finger sandwiches and petit fours. Doreen broke into a fit of giggles at the thought, only getting control of herself after Nan sighed heavily.

"You really do need to take a break, dear. It seems all these cases are taking a bit of a toll on you."

On the brink of hysteria, Doreen choked back her laughter. "That very well may be, Nan, but I do recall getting dragged into some of these cases," she muttered.

"Yes, that is quite true, and I am sorry about that."

"It's fine, Nan. I could never say no to you anyway."

"At least you got it solved, and relatively quickly at that. That may have been one of your fastest ones. Oh, now that I'm thinking about it … *huh*," Nan started to chuckle. "You know, child. I think I may have won the big pot."

"What are you talking about now?"

"Of course it's not the *really* big pot yet."

"I don't think I like the sound of this," Doreen muttered. "What are you talking about, Nan? Have you been betting again?"

"Never mind that. You come on down, and we'll have tea," she suggested. And, with that, Nan was gone.

Groaning, Doreen rolled out of bed, deciding that a hot shower was definitely needed. Once she had gotten herself together and was ready for the day, she decided to forego her regular morning coffee and settled on tea first with Nan. Gathering up the animals, she slowly headed down the pathway. If nothing else, this case was another one of those life lessons about people, although she didn't think Tammy would see it that way from Doreen's point of view.

Once she got to Nan's, she noted that both Darren and Mack were here. Mack took one look at her. "Good morning. I didn't expect to see you here."

"Me either, but I got a call, something about Jethro wanting to thank me."

He nodded. "Yeah, I got one too, and I'm certain it's definitely *not* an attempt to bribe us out of pursuing the charges either," he quipped, rolling his eyes.

She laughed out loud. "If your victim wants to testify as to the sterling character of your suspect, do you really have something you need to charge Jethro with?"

He sighed and frowned at her. "It's not that simple."

"It never is," she noted, with a wave of her hand, "and yet it is."

He grinned. "Anyway, don't think you'll get off quite so easily either."

She frowned at him, then stepped over to Nan's patio, but Nan was inside calling out to her and waving her arms.

"You'll have to come through to the living room. It's much bigger."

"Oh, *great*," she muttered. "I don't know that I'm up for a big reception or something. I didn't even get any coffee yet."

"That's okay. We've got coffee on the menu today too."

Doreen gave Mack a surprised look, but he just shrugged and said, "Don't ask me. I don't know anything about it." As they got to the main area, she saw quite a few of the residents sitting here.

Jethro stood up and greeted them. "Thank you all for coming. It seems I owe everyone an apology. But I also owe Doreen my thanks for putting another criminal behind bars," he added, with a big smile, "and making it a whole lot easier to sleep at night." At that, a round of cheering followed.

Doreen looked around at everybody, shaking her head. "I hardly did anything."

"Yes, Nan warned me that you would say that," Jethro replied. Taking a big breath, he added, "I spoke to the Rosemoor management, asking if we could hold a party here for you. I would like to do a *thank you* in a big way. And they've agreed. Now the date that we've all come to think could work would be in four weeks on a Friday, so early enough in December to avoid any other Christmas parties here. Does that work for the two of you? Of course we really need Mack on board as he, of course, has a surprise for you too."

Doreen blinked. It was one thing to spring a party on her, and she was okay with that, but to spring something that Mack might have in surprise? Well, that was something else again. She turned and frowned at him. Plus the whole Christmas season thing was something that she'd shoved to the back of her mind. She'd never had much in the way of a happy Christmas for the previous fourteen years with Mathew and so had no clue what was expected of her in this instance.

Jethro waited for Doreen or Mack to say something. In the silence that followed, he added, "As a celebration, an early Christmas party sounds like a great excuse to honor and thank Doreen. Right, everyone?" Jethro turned and beamed a smile at everyone around them.

Cheers rang up from the crowd gathered here.

"And of course you're welcome to invite anyone you want as well, dear," Nan said, with a benevolent smile.

"Wait, is this just a thank-you party or something else?" Doreen asked suspiciously, her gaze going from Nan to Jethro and then, as if on instinct, she turned to face Mack. "Are we celebrating something else?"

Jethro beamed and said, "I guess that's up to Mack to determine."

Mack frowned at him and shook his head, turning to Doreen. "I haven't a clue."

"Sure you do," Jethro replied, "but Nan did say it would take a bit to get you there."

Doreen pointed her finger at Nan. "Nan, please tell me that you didn't interfere."

"I would never interfere," Nan stated immediately, "but you do know how I worry."

"I understand how you use worry as an excuse for interfering," she declared, staring at her grandmother with raised eyebrows.

"You worry too much." Nan smiled at her smugly. "I guess you'll just have to wait and see." She glanced around at the gathered group. "So, is it a date?"

"Yes!" The room rang with cheers and laughter.

Doreen had her reservations but had to admit that this could be fun.

Epilogue

First Week of December ...

IT WAS EARLY in the evening during the first week of December, and Doreen was curled up in Mack's arms, a blanket wrapped around their shoulders, as they sat by the river, both holding cups of hot chocolate. Goliath and Mugs were lying beside them, and Thaddeus had curled up under the blanket with them.

"It's getting colder but still no snow. That's unusual for here, according to all the locals," she murmured. "I can't believe Christmas is around the corner."

"And getting closer." Mack laughed. "And you're inundated in party preparations, aren't you?"

"I am." She chuckled. "Not sure how I was conned into doing a lot of the preparations for a party that's being given in my honor though." She shook her head. "After more than a decade of no Christmas in any form while I was married, I have to admit that I'm enjoying myself."

"And it's keeping you out of trouble, so it works for me too."

She punched him lightly in the arm. "Amazing to think that peace and goodwill may preside over the holidays. Yet I thought I read somewhere about violent crime rates rising over the main holidays."

"I think that's true. It's stressful for many people. Anytime there is added stress, then eruptions occur."

"True, but, in my mind, a surprise stabbing because someone didn't get a diamond ring, when they live on an instant-noodles income, isn't quite the same."

He nodded. "Maybe not. But what about the young man who wants to buy his girlfriend a diamond ring but can't afford it, so goes on a crime spree to get the money to buy it?"

"If that's what's required to keep her love, then, first, it wasn't love and, second, she isn't worth ruining his life over. But I get your point." She twisted to look up at him. "You don't have a new case, right? You're not just keeping it from me?"

"Nope, no new case." He tucked her closer to him, pulling the blanket around her shoulders. "And that's a good thing, as we have a mess of paperwork to do. Someone keeps solving the cold cases we have backed up, as well as meddling in our current cases. I have to tell you, this person is good, but she's there for the excitement. Yet the puzzling part is, unfortunately she's always there for that dangerous end too. However, when it comes to the cleanup, … she's nowhere to be found."

She turned to him in outrage. "You know I would be if I could be."

His laughter rolled down the stream and then grew louder.

"*Shh*. You're making too much noise."

"We're hardly disturbing anyone."

At that, a loud snort sounded behind them.

She turned at the noises that followed, surmising Richard propping his chair against the back fence and poking his head over the top. "Good evening, Richard. Isn't it a nice evening out?"

His gaze widened. "Are you nuts? It's friggin' cold out here. It's December, in case you don't have a calendar." He cast one more glance at them and then disappeared down on the other side, mumbling something about crazy people.

She burst out laughing. "Have a good night," she called back to him, struggling to stifle her giggles.

When Richard slammed his door, even Mack joined in with her laughter.

His phone rang just then. Shifting the blanket to find his phone, Mack checked the number, then stood and walked a few steps away. "Mack here. What's up?" He listened for a moment, then turned to look at Doreen.

That was a signal she absolutely recognized. She moved Thaddeus to her shoulder and rose, with the blanket wrapped about the two of them.

"Did you say mistletoe?" Mack asked.

She froze at that and turned to face Mack in delight.

His frown deepened as he glared at her. "No, sir. ... Yes, sir. You're correct. I'll be right there."

She beamed at him. "Mistletoe?"

"Yeah, but it doesn't concern you." He walked closer, adding, "Yet it does mean I have to leave. So Merry Christmas and all that stuff."

"Shouldn't it be *Merry Mistletoe* this time?"

He spun to look at her. "What did you say?"

"*Merry Mistletoe*," she repeated. "Makes a great case name."

"Oh no you don't. If I let you anywhere near this one, it would be madness." He shook his head and nudged her toward the house. "Time to go inside, as I have to leave."

"I could stay outside," she protested but more just for fun, as without his incredibly radiating body heat, she was already starting to shiver. Then she stopped and laughed. "That's even better."

"What is?" he asked, as they reached the patio.

"*Merry Mistletoe Madness*," she crowed.

He stopped to glare at her. "Nice try. It's a current case. Nothing cold about this one."

"So maybe it's time I move into current cases," she suggested, her eyebrows lifting and lowering in a Groucho Marx move.

"Heck no." He opened the back door, moved the clan inside, before locking and closing it behind them. He picked up his keys and headed to the front door.

"It has a lovely ring to it," she cried out. When he glared at her, she batted her eyes at him, a big grin on her face.

"Oh no." With a headshake, he gave her a quick kiss and was gone.

She stepped out on the front porch. "*Merry Mistletoe Madness* it is!"

Richard poked his head out the front door. "Anything to do with you and mistletoe would make anyone mad." And, with that, he retreated and slammed his door.

Unperturbed, Doreen walked inside, with joy in her heart. She had no clue what was happening in terms of murder and mistletoe, but it meant one thing. There was a new case. All she had to do was tie a cold case to Mack's current case, and then she was in! With that thought uppermost in her mind, she had to figure out her next move.

This concludes Book 26 of Lovely Lethal Gardens: Zapped in the Zinnias.
Read about Merry Mistletoe Madness: Lovely Lethal Gardens, Christmas Novella

Lovely Lethal Gardens:
Merry Mistletoe Madness
(Christmas Novella)

Can Christmas get any crazier? A new case for Mack and, lucky for Doreen, she finds a cold case connected to it, making her year end on a high note.

All the while she struggles to navigate gift giving and a special party that Nan wants to put on for her at Rosemoor—except Doreen has to solve all kinds of issues, including the missing mistletoe, which Nan insists on having for the party.

And then there are the secrets. Of course it's Christmas, so maybe secrets are to be expected. However, when those secrets involve Nan, maybe Doreen should be worried after all.

Find Merry Mistletoe Madness here!
To find out more visit Dale Mayer's website.
https://geni.us/DMSMistletoe

Author's Note

Thank you for reading Zapped in the Zinnias: Lovely Lethal Gardens, Book 26! If you enjoyed the book, please take a moment and leave a short review.

Dear reader,

I love to hear from readers, and you can contact me at my website: www.dalemayer.com or at my Facebook author page. To be informed of new releases and special offers, sign up for my newsletter or follow me on BookBub. And if you are interested in joining Dale Mayer's Reader Group, here is the Facebook sign up page. http://geni.us/DaleMayerFBGroup

Cheers,
Dale Mayer

About the Author

Dale Mayer is a *USA Today* best-selling author, best known for her SEALs military romances, her Psychic Visions series, and her Lovely Lethal Garden cozy series. Her contemporary romances are raw and full of passion and emotion (Broken But … Mending, Hathaway House series). Her thrillers will keep you guessing (Kate Morgan, By Death series), and her romantic comedies will keep you giggling (*It's a Dog's Life*, a stand-alone novella; and the Broken Protocols series, starring Charming Marvin, the cat).

Dale honors the stories that come to her—and some of them are crazy, break all the rules and cross multiple genres!

To go with her fiction, she also writes non-fiction in many different fields, with books available on résumé writing, companion gardening, and the US mortgage system. All her books are available in print and ebook format.

Connect with Dale Mayer Online

Dale's Website – www.dalemayer.com
Twitter – @DaleMayer
Facebook Page –
geni.us/DaleMayerFBFanPage
Facebook Group –
geni.us/DaleMayerFBGroup
BookBub – geni.us/DaleMayerBookbub
Instagram – geni.us/DaleMayerInstagram
Goodreads – geni.us/DaleMayerGoodreads
Newsletter – geni.us/DaleNews

Milton Keynes UK
Ingram Content Group UK Ltd.
UKHW020139270824
447474UK00005B/92

9 781778 865138